ROCKING THE POND

ROCKING THE POND

THE FIRST SEASON OF THE MIGHTY DUCKS OF ANAHEIM

DEAN CHADWIN

POLESTAR

BOOK PUBLISHERS

Rocking The Pond

Published by
Polestar Press Ltd.
1011 Commercial Drive, Second Floor
Vancouver, BC
Canada   V5L 3X1

Cover design by Jim Brennan and Sandra Robinson
Editing by Julian Ross
Cover and author photographs by Chris Relke
Printed in Canada by Best Book Manufacturers

Canadian Cataloguing in Publication Data

Chadwin, Dean, 1965-
    Rocking the pond

ISBN 0-919591-03-5
        1. Mighty Ducks of Anaheim (Hockey Team)—History. I. Title.
GV848.M53C5 1994   796.932′64′0979496   C94-910611-9

Acknowledgements

The cover of this book with my name standing alone reinforces a great man theory of history, as if I am solely responsible for the work contained herein. This would be as ridiculous as Mike Keenan claiming full credit for the Rangers' Stanley Cup victory. If not for the efforts of a number of people, this book simply would not have been possible. I am especially grateful to Dave Davis, sports editor of *Los Angeles Weekly*, for publishing my first articles and for providing the original idea for this book. During the course of covering the Mighty Ducks, I was given tremendous help by an unsurpassed public relations staff: Bill Robertson, Rob Scichili, and Matt Stys. Players and front office personnel alike were generous with their time, but Tim Army, Bobby Dollas, Jack Ferreira, Stu Grimson, David McNab, Don McSween, and Tony Tavares must be noted individually for their extra consideration. A boatload of friends and relatives supported my efforts while I was on the road or working on the manuscript. My thanks go out to Ben and Vera Deutsch, Ethel Chadwin, Rebecca Chadwin, Dimitri Racklin and Mary Beth Cavanaugh, Rob Krevolin, Rich Krevolin, Gary Levene, Marian Treger, Steve Tucker and Noel Riley Fitch. David Warren, Jonathan Weiss, Paul Feinberg, and Don Laner went far beyond the call of duty by looking at parts of the unfinished manuscript and offering serious advice. Whether they realize it or not, they are owed. That this book resembles the work I originally envisioned is a credit to Julian Ross, my editor at Polestar Press. Julian helped to guide a rookie author through the bewildering, exhilarating process of getting it all on the page. Once again, thanks to all.

*For Mark and Adrienne, my parents,
who have been incomparable in their
devotion and intelligence.*

Rocking The Pond

Cast of Characters

The Bosses

Michael Eisner	Disney CEO
Gary Bettman	NHL Commissioner
Bruce McNall	Owner, LA Kings
Tony Tavares	President, Disney Sports Enterprises
Ron Wilson	Head Coach
Al Sims	Assistant Coach
Tim Army	Assistant Coach

The Talent Seekers

Jack Ferreira	General Manager
Pierre Gauthier	Assistant General Manager
David McNab	Director of Player Personnel
Paul Fenton	Pro Scout
Al Godfrey	Midwest Scout
Richard Green	Northeast Scout
Thommie Bergman	European Scout
Alain Chainey	Canadian Scout

Players: The Present

Patrik Carnback	Center
Bob Corkum	Center
Stephan Lebeau	Center
Anatoli Semenov	Center
Jarrod Skalde	Center
Shaun Van Allen	Center
Peter Douris	Right Wing
Todd Ewen	Right Wing
Steven King	Right Wing
John Lilley	Right Wing
Joe Sacco	Right Wing
Terry Yake	Right Wing

Stu Grimson	Left Wing
Troy Loney	Left Wing
Tim Sweeney	Left Wing
Garry Valk	Left Wing
Bobby Dollas	Defenseman
Mark Ferner	Defenseman
Sean Hill	Defenseman
Bill Houlder	Defenseman
Alexei Kasatonov	Defenseman
Randy Ladouceur	Defenseman
Don McSween	Defenseman
Myles O'Connor	Defenseman
David Williams	Defenseman
Guy Hebert	Goalie
Mikhail Shtalenkov	Goalie
Ron Tugnutt	Goalie

Players: The Future

Paul Kariya	Center
Steve Rucchin	Center
Johan Davidsson	Right Wing
Valeri Karpov	Right Wing
Mike Maneluk	Left Wing
Scott Chartier	Defenseman
Nikolai Tsulygin	Defenseman
Oleg Tverdovsky	Defenseman
John Tanner	Goalie

Preface

Opening Night

My dad's gonna be up there watching me tonight.
—Ron Wilson

Friday, October 8th, 1993. Mickey Mouse was about to put on skates. The creators of the Magic Kingdom had ventured outside the world of fantasy and imagination to enter an arena where their success would be judged not simply aesthetically or financially, but also in wins and losses. Tony Tavares, Jack Ferreira, Ron Wilson and a bucketful of other new Disney employees had put together the company's biggest opening night in nearly four decades.

Two famous senior citizens anxiously awaited their first date: the sixty-five-year-old Walt Disney Company had joined the sixty-six-year-old National Hockey League. Disney boss Michael Eisner and recently installed NHL chief Gary Bettman enjoyed each other's company as they watched the initial flight of the Mighty Ducks of Anaheim, both hoping for a smooth takeoff. Eisner especially wanted to see his latest venture get off to a good start.

Of course, Eisner had attended big opening nights before.

Disney invested millions in movies, and each film's debut was seen as a significant moment for the whole company. Occasionally, a "Pretty Woman" or an "Aladdin" would be a huge success from a box-office and perhaps even a critical standpoint. However, the way Disney cranked out films, no one opening was that important. A dozen bad openings could be saved by a smash hit later the same year. With foreign distribution and video a big chunk of the financial mix, a movie with a mediocre opening often proved to be a success. But the new hockey team would have no such luxury. If the Ducks failed to compete on the ice, they couldn't make up the difference in secondary markets.

The grand opening of Disneyland represented the only greater risk in the company's history. Some thirty-eight years earlier, before Wilson, the Ducks' head coach, was even born, Walt Disney had struggled to get financing for his dream, putting his own personal fortune at risk. The park opened on July 17, 1955, a day which became known in-house as "Black Sunday" because nothing went according to Walt's blueprints. Walt expected to host 15,000 guests. More than double that number crammed the park, many entering with fake tickets or by climbing over the back fence. The park itself was far from finished. Rides and drinking water were scarce and lines were outrageously long. Despite the real problems, the favorable publicity created by Walt's TV programming and his friends in the press attracted huge numbers of tourists from the very beginning.

The theme parks became a large part of the entertainment empire's success, but tonight Disney would enter a whole new world. Professional sports was a world where their product was inexorably tied with that of a number of other owners, both individual and corporate, where they would be represented by tough young men who occassionally pounded each other out, and where, like it or not, image was not everything. What the scoreboard said at the end of the night was all that mattered.

Tonight, over two hundred media, seventeen thousand fans and a cable TV audience across North America would be watching the unveiling of the Mighty Ducks of Anaheim, an expansion franchise in the National Hockey League. Team President Tony Tavares had had to go from no players, no coaching staff and no office to home opener in seven months, a Herculean task. Tavares' first recruits included General Manager Jack Ferreira and Assistant General Manager Pierre Gauthier, who were responsible for assembling the Ducks' roster in an expansion draft from those players left unprotected by the existing teams. While the new team worked to assemble an on-ice product, the front office could rely on Disney's pre-existing merchandising strength: the team's logo was well-designed and the name "Mighty Ducks" well-known, thanks to its connection to an Disney movie about a youth hockey team with the same name.

If Disney had a certain identifiable product line, then so did the NHL, and the intersection between family-oriented entertainment and violence on ice seemed strained. A nation of hockey-loving Canadians worried. Of course, other large U.S. multi-national corporations owned NHL teams, but this was different. Many Canadians felt helpless, believing that hockey, their national game, was changing in ways that were beyond their control. Disney was an easy target for that frustration. No Canadian cities were even considered during the invitation-only expansion that put Disney and Blockbuster in the league. And when Eisner named the team after a fictional kids' team, that only reinforced the impression that the game had sunk further into greed and commercialism. The name "Mighty Ducks" seemed to be a direct challenge to those who saw the sport as religion, a trust to be preserved and cherished. Disney didn't seem to have any respect for what had gone before them. Eisner had already voiced his desire to look into the shootout to settle ties during the regular season and to find a way to reduce fighting.

If Disney's influence disturbed Canadians, Bettman's ascendance mystified them. What did an NBA executive, an outsider, know about hockey? Bettman had come by his interest in the game honestly as an undergraduate at Cornell in the early '70s when the school was an NCAA powerhouse. Yet defenders of the status quo worried when Bettman made it clear that he saw the NHL as the last major sports league in need of growth. To those north of the border, "growth" was a code word for expanded American influence as the drive for a network TV contract became central. Eisner and Bettman were viewed as powerful allies who would think nothing of hockey's traditions. Not just the location of franchises, but the essence of hockey itself was up for grabs. The purists wondered, what would Disney and Bettman try to do to *their* game?

The crowd in Anaheim had other, more concrete concerns. Tickets were scarce, and supporters arrived early. The Ducks' home rink, the Anaheim Arena, sparkled like a beautiful new mall with its arched glass windows, wide concourses, and marble floors. Traffic was heavy, especially for fans new to this venue who didn't know that the arena lot could not handle everyone's parking needs. In a place where the car culture dominates, tough parking can become an easy excuse to do something else.

Those fans who'd found the adjacent lots and were inside the Arena by 7:40 p.m. were treated to a half-hour pre-game ceremony. By now, the Arena had been rechristened the Arrowhead Pond of Anaheim. Arrowhead, a local bottled water company, paid a million dollars for the right to be tied to the Ducks during their first season. Their logo was visible outside and inside the arena, and their name would be repeated *ad infinitum* on TV and radio broadcasts.

Perhaps that money would produce more showmanship than substance. During the festivities, Disney spent a reported $450,000, a larger amount to entertain their fans than they would dish out on many of their player salaries for the 1993-94 season. The extravaganza had required two weeks of practice and featured ice dancers, fireworks, the descent of the Duck mascot from the rafters and loud music that included a song from "Beauty and the Beast" inviting the crowd to "Be our guest." While some curmudgeons in the press box wondered what any of this had to do with hockey, the fans below, especially the younger ones, enjoyed the show tremendously. The spectacle, unlike anything anyone connected to the league had seen before, ensured that a crowd full of hockey novices would at least enjoy part of their evening at the Pond.

As the show dragged on, the Duck players waited anxiously in the locker room, unaccustomed to the long break between the pre-game skate and the game itself. Meanwhile, Ron Wilson filled out his lineup sheet with the 20 names—18 skaters and two goalies—that would play tonight. The sheet, which must be filed with the game referees before the face-off, includes a place for team name. Wilson, who'd assisted Pat Quinn with the Canucks during the previous three years, had initially penciled in Vancouver as his team name during the first two exhibition games before realizing his error. Tonight, he stopped to make sure he got it right. After a week of parades, luncheons, and press conferences, even the coach was nervous, worried that his team would not perform as well as it had in a very competitive pre-season.

For Wilson, his first regular-season game as an NHL coach held added meaning. Anaheim's opponent, the Detroit Red Wings, owners of the best offense in the league, were seen by most analysts as a Stanley Cup contender. The Ducks would immediately face a severe test immediately. More than that, the Wings represented a homecoming of sorts for Wilson. His father Larry and his uncle John had both played for Detroit in the 1950s. Larry Wilson, who died in 1979, had coached the Red Wings for a few games in 1977. Ron felt his father had been mistreated by Detroit both as a player and as a coach. He wasn't bitter with the Red Wings, but there was no question that a victory tonight would be special.

John, who had also coached the Red Wings in the early 1970s, was on hand to watch Ron's debut. He had already told Wilson how proud his father would have been to see him behind the bench. Yet Wilson, confident yet still curious if he really belonged in the NHL as a head coach, wondered if tonight he would somehow be exposed as a fraud.

With the pre-game celebration almost over, it was finally time for the new team to be introduced. All players have their pre-game rituals: touching a goalie's pads or tapping a teammate's stick in the entrance tunnel. The order that players skate on the ice holds special importance. The first man on ice was goalie Guy Hebert, chosen to start the opener because he'd shut out Detroit once last season, with enforcer Stu Grimson skating right behind him to the roar of a juiced-up crowd.

At most Southern California pro sporting events, concession lines remain long from start to finish. Tonight, ten minutes before the puck was to drop, nary a soul could be found in the concourses of the Pond. The crowd was on its feet, cheering wildly for their newest heroes. The loudest cheers came for veteran forwards Anatoli Semenov, the Russian playmaker who'd scored a game-winning overtime goal to close out the pre-season, Grimson and Wilson. As the intros dragged on, the players already on the ice shifted back and forth on their skates, anxious to get into the flow of the game.

If the Ducks were a little nervous, they had good reason to be. Among the 20 men who dressed for the game, their international roster—ten Canadians, seven Americans, two Russians, and one Swede—included 12 players with less than two full years of experience. But this was not a talented yet inexperienced young team, like the Edmonton Oilers of the late '70s. The average age of the Duck starters was 25. Most of these players had failed to reach a high enough level to contribute in the NHL in the eyes of their former teams. If not for the Ducks, most of them would still be moving back and forth between the minors and fourth-line status in the majors. This night was a first, not only for Disney, but also for many of the players who had never been secure in their status as NHL players.

More than anything else, these guys lacked goal-scoring punch. The eighteen starters had combined for only 297 career goals. The Red Wing lineup, coached by Hall-of-Famer and six-time Stanley Cup champ Scotty Bowman, featured Paul Coffey, Steve Yzerman, and Dino Ciccarelli, each of whom had netted more goals than all the Ducks together. To make things worse, Goliath was angry, the Red Wings having lost their season opener in Dallas against the Stars. Despite the loss, Bowman started third-string netminder Peter Ing against the Ducks, an implicit message to his players to score early and often because they wouldn't want to leave the outcome of the game in the hands of their inexperienced goalie.

Of course, Wilson had installed a conservative, defense-oriented system designed to keep scoring down and to keep Anaheim in games against more talented opponents. During the pre-season, the Ducks had held their opponents to under three goals a night. The strategy had worked—four of the five games had been close as the Ducks struggled to put the puck in the net. The Ducks also found hope in the knowledge that two recent expansion teams had won their openers against strong teams, Tampa Bay beating Chicago and Ottawa upsetting the hallowed Canadiens.

Anything was possible. Wilson sent Semenov out to take the draw, with linemates left wing and team captain Troy Loney and right wing Terry Yake, along with two veteran defensemen, nine-time Soviet all-star Alexei Kasatonov and mustachioed Randy Ladouceur in front of goalie Guy Hebert. Detroit's brilliant young center Sergei Fedorov won the opening face-off from Semenov, and Hebert was immediately under attack.

The Ducks watched helplessly as the Wings weaved through their zone uncontested, firing open shots from the point and crashing the net. Guy withstood the first few rushes, but Bowman rotated his lines quickly to maintain the pressure. During Fedorov's second shift, he made a nice pass to right wing Ray Sheppard who found rookie defenseman Aaron Ward open at the point. Ward fired through a crowd of players and the puck squirted by Hebert. Perhaps it had deflected off the skate of Duck forward Steven King, but Ward had his first NHL goal.

It would prove to be his only NHL goal of the season as Ward spent most of the remaining season in the minors. Ironically, on a team with more than a half-dozen stars, one of Detroit's nobodies had scored the first goal ever on Anaheim's team full of unknowns. Just two minutes and thirty-four seconds into their debut, the Ducks were reeling, down a goal and unable to keep the Red Wing attack out of their zone.

Things only got worse. Shift after shift, the Red Wings toyed with the Ducks and looked as if they had a man advantage when the two teams were skating even. Detroit pelted Hebert with shots as Anaheim struggled to enter the offensive zone. Instead of dumping the puck and chasing it into the corners, the Ducks were trying to carry the puck across the Detroit blue line with almost no success. Seven minutes into the game, the Ducks still had not gotten a shot on goal. Finally, defensemen Billy Houlder and Sean Hill put some strong shots on net from the point as both teams' stickwork became a little nastier.

The apparent light at the end of the tunnel turned out to be an on-coming train. A minute later, Red Wing strongman Bob Probert made a nifty pass through traffic at center ice to a slashing Fedorov who immediately got the puck to Sheppard flying in on the right wing. Sheppard went by Anaheim defenseman Mark Ferner and then flipped a quick shot over Hebert's right shoulder.

Up two goals, Detroit continued to pound away. Keith Primeau and Yzerman camped in front of the Duck net looking for rebounds until Sean Hill took down Yzerman, drawing the team's first penalty, a two-minute minor for hooking at 11:31. The Red Wing pressure continued during the power play as the Ducks failed to clear the puck even once but Hebert made three brilliant saves to keep the game close.

Just a minute after the Ducks killed off their first penalty, referee Ron Hoggarth, who'd arrived at the rink wearing a Mighty Duck tie, proved his impartiality by whistling Duck Steven King for a holding penalty in front of the net. As play stopped, Stu Grimson and Bob Probert started jawing. The two brawlers, who had had many memorable duels when Grimson was a Blackhawk, had barely started to fight when the officials pulled them apart, much to the disappointment of Anaheim fans seeking any sign of life in their team. Grimson received a double-minor penalty while Probert only got tagged with one minor.

Suddenly, with five minutes left in the period, the Ducks were faced with having to kill a two-minute five-on-three Detroit power play. The Wings' stars put Hebert out of his misery quickly. Fedorov scored into an open net just 23 seconds into the power play after Yzerman made a beautiful cross-ice pass to an unmolested Fedorov. The Ducks recorded a moral victory when they killed the remainder of the one-man advantage. Late in the period, Duck center Bob Corkum even got off a tough backhand shot from in close that Ing had to glove. As the clock wound down to end the first twenty minutes of Mighty Duck hockey, the scoreboard read: DETROIT 3–MIGHTY DUCKS 0, the Ducks had been outshot 20-7, and the home crowd rewarded the abysmal effort with a mere smattering of applause.

The Ducks' main triumph once the puck dropped occurred off the ice in the Team Store on the east side of the Pond's Plaza Concourse level. The store, with TVs which allowed fans to follow the action while buying shirts, pucks, jackets, and other souvenirs, was crammed all game long with collectors who bought up more than $300,000 in opening night memorabilia.

Ogden, the arena manager, sold $207,500 in concessions. The Ducks would receive roughly $45,000 from that pool. In total, the 17,000-plus fans had spent an average of $30 per person inside the arena, a phenomenal number, double or triple that of an average night. The gate, after taking off 6% for rent, gave Disney another $350,000 in ticket revenue. The parking produced another $10,000. Other revenue sources like signage or luxury boxes were more difficult to allocate accurately on a per-game basis, but it's been estimated that, on Opening Night, the Ducks received about a million dollars in gross revenue.

Against that, you had to balance a variety of costs, including the costs of the merchandise itself. With one of the lowest team salaries in the league, roughly $100,000 per night, the Ducks probably turned a profit on opening night, even after the pre-game festivities were accounted for. When you realize that playoffs are where the real money rolls in to teams, the numbers had to be reassuring for both Bettman and Eisner. Hockey in Orange County would fly. The franchise was already worth more than the $37.5 million it had cost Disney, assuming it could lift its on-ice performance to a respectable level.

Unfortunately, back on the ice, the second period began as the first had ended. Two minutes in, Fedorov found Sheppard on a breakaway but Hebert came out to cut down Sheppard's angle and stopped the puck. Frustrated, Fedorov took a silly tripping penalty as he was going off the ice half-a-minute later. Twenty-two minutes into the season, the Ducks had their first power play. The first unit—Semenov, Yake, Loney, Kasatonov, and Ferner—failed to even get a shot on the net during the first minute of the penalty, but late in the power play, Steve Chiasson whacked at a Duck standing in the slot and got whistled for slashing.

A two-man advantage for twenty seconds. The Ducks worked to win the face-off. Terry Yake controlled the puck along the boards and got it back to the left point where Billy Houlder immediately fired a bomb on net. The puck flew off Ing diagonally across the ice to the other point where Sean Hill caught the puck, skated in and fired a shot up high past Ing. The red goal light came on. Hill, at 23 the youngest Duck in uniform, leapt for joy. A Duck mask that hung above the Detroit net flashed its red eyes in approval and fireworks exploded from the rafters. At 4:13 of the second period, Sean Hill, a kid from Duluth, Minnesota who had already represented the United States in the 1992 Olympics and played for Montreal during their 1993 run for the Stanley Cup, had just added another memorable moment to his career, scoring the first goal in the history of the Mighty Ducks of Anaheim.

The celebration seemed to energize the Ducks as they actually outshot Detroit 6-1 during the early minutes of the second period. Hill got another chance and Loney tried to stuff the puck home. The momentum had shifted until Primeau set up Yzerman in front of the net and Garry Valk flattened Yzer with a wicked cross-check. Although unable to score during the advantage, the Red Wings reasserted their dominance. Just after the power play ended, Detroit's Slava Kozlov threaded the needle with a beautiful pass that Keith Primeau, alone in the slot, flipped over Hebert easily. Just three minutes later, Primeau set up Chiasson who jammed the puck home. Detroit was up 5-1 and the rout was on.

Before the game, Hebert had been confident. "We plan to be within a goal or two entering the third period most nights," he had said. "We'll give our fans a lot of good games. We'll be competitive." Not tonight. The third period began with Anaheim down four goals and the home crowd restless. Boos rained down from the far reaches of the arena. Not for the players, at least not yet, but one of the "great ideas" for entertaining the fans had nose-dived. A singer had been made up in white to look like a rock star from the north pole. The Iceman carried a guitar and wireless mike through the crowd and sang rock songs during breaks in the action. Unfortunately, the sound system was overamplified and no one seemed to have told him when not to sing—for example, after opposition goals. Even more unforgivably, his appearance seemed to annoy and even frighten young children, the very audience he'd been designed to please.

While the Iceman's performance represented the primary opening night off-ice failure, back on the frozen white surface, mistakes continued to pile up. Early in the third period, Yzerman swooped behind the Anaheim defense, skated behind the net and fed Primeau out in front of the net for another easy goal. Three minutes later, Detroit closed out their scoring as Micah Aivazoff joined Ward in recording his first NHL goal.

With their team down 7-1, the sellout crowd of 17,174 started to bail out of the Pond though most of them had no reason to be up early on a Saturday morning. They had lost all hope and, with no post-game ceremony in store, they'd lost interest as well. In the middle of the period, the Ducks got another two-man advantage. Team captain Troy Loney stuffed home a sweet pass from Semenov to give the Ducks their second and final goal of the night. All that was left was the Probert-Grimson rematch after the game got chippy. With five minutes left, what was left of the crowd chanted "Stu, Stu, Stu" as Grimson won the battle against a half-hearted Probert. Both players were ejected and the Red Wings won the war a little while later as the clock ran out. The scoreboard read: DETROIT 7–MIGHTY DUCKS 2.

The score demonstrated that the Ducks had been outclassed, which everyone had expected. What was more surprising was that they had been outworked. After this opening night, Wilson had no way to know if his team would be able to regain their balance. They'd been shelled. Maybe they weren't as good as they'd showed in the pre-season. It could be a very long year.

"I think our players were overwhelmed," said Wilson right after the game. "We stood around most of the game and never got a rhythm. That's the worst we've played. Unfortunately, we just didn't compete tonight."

Wilson searched for some explanation for the disappointing effort and wondered if all the pre-game excitement had been a distraction. "We might have been emotionally drained after all the hoopla with the parades. These guys are mostly third-and-fourth-line players and they were being treated like celebrities, and maybe we let that affect us," Wilson theorized. "We were hoping it wouldn't happen but it did and that's reality. We appeared very tight. I could see the first period being like that, but we just didn't settle down. It's just one game. It's not the whole season. We've got 83 to go."

Wilson's rationale seemed plausible, but maybe there just wasn't enough talent on the roster. Unfortunately, the first night's efforts did nothing to soothe Wilson's fears that his team would not be able to compete. Would he have to coach a nightmare season like Ottawa's last year? If the team didn't rebound quickly, they could get buried. There were no easy games during the homestand and the Ducks couldn't afford to go on a difficult Eastern road swing winless. The pressure would become unbearable. Wilson only hoped that his players would ease his fears against the Islanders two nights later.

1

Mike's Mighty Dream

This land couldn't support a goat.
—Jose Ontiveros in 1857, after selling the area that is now Anaheim.

In the summer of 1992, a tremendous structure began to grow in a large lot alongside the Santa Ana river in Anaheim. The $103 million Anaheim Arena was nearing completion without a major tenant in sight. After noticing the building during one of his frequent trips to the home of Disneyland and his son's youth hockey league, Disney chief Michael Eisner became curious. A year later, Disney-owned KCAL TV, which was to carry the Ducks' games, ran an hour-long special entitled "The Making of the Mighty Ducks" just before the start of the inaugural season. More than a chance to promote the team, it was also an opportunity to create the always essential creation myth, including Eisner's memory of the deal.

"There was this beautiful arena being built. I thought it was an office building," Eisner recalled. "My son's hockey rink is just down the street and I saw this giant thing. I called up the city and asked them what are you building there and they said an arena. I said, 'Who's playing there?' And they said, 'Nobody yet.' I said, 'Does somebody have a hockey franchise?' They said, 'No,' and I forgot about it. Then about two weeks later I ran into Bruce McNall and I said, 'Have you seen that arena?' And he said, 'Do you want a hockey team?' I said 'No, I just want to know what's going on there.' About two weeks later, he asked me again, and I don't know, I saw *Field of Dreams*, there was an arena and no team and I added two and two together, it came out to about 11 and I went and got the franchise."

That version of the creation story is warm and fuzzy, pre-sanitized for easy digestion. It wasn't that simple.The deal included hardball backroom financial negotiations and reflected a city's self-image and the NHL's new direction. One thing is certain: the team would never have arrived without a building in place. And the city of Anaheim would never have constructed an arena if they hadn't had a long-seated ambition to be the leading city in Orange County. The Ducks' roots could be traced all the way back to the 19th century, a hundred and thirty-five years before Eisner laid eyes on a nascent arena.

In 1857, fifty German families unhappy with urban life in San Francisco raised $37,500 and sent an Austrian named George Hansen south to purchase a tract of land in the country that would support them. Hansen discovered an 1165-acre parcel bordering the Santa Ana River that had been inhabited by Gabrielinho Indians and purchased the territory for about $2 an acre, along with water rights. The German colony was organized so that eight of every ten acres was planted with grapevines, one acre with fruit trees, and one acre reserved for houses and farm buildings.

Anaheim, the German word for Ana's home, was the name given to the community that grew along the Santa Ana. It was a land rife with mustard seed plants, wild grasses, cactus, sage and sagebrush. Sycamore grew on the flats, while willows grew in the stream bottoms. Thousands and thousands of cattle roamed the plains. Cottontail and jack rabbits, coyotes, grizzly bears, mountain lions, gray wolves, wildcats, and a wide variety of fowl populated the region. Even ducks could be found in the river that today is little more than a flood control channel. Despite all this abundance, prior attempts at farming the land had proven difficult because of the low rainfall.

Anaheim was the first planned community in the state and the school curriculum was conducted in German. Throughout the early settlement period, the colony's population was almost entirely immigrant, as Poles, Spaniards and Chinese joined the Germans. Natural disasters haunted the early settlers, who proved to be extraordinarily resilient in finding new means of survival. Their ingenuity and determination ensured that Anaheim would become the longest-lived community in the area.

A severe flood in 1862 caused outbreaks of disease, and the great drought of 1863-64 killed off thousands of cattle. Starving to death, the cattle ransacked Anaheim's vineyards. Nevertheless, by 1885, Anaheim's forty-seven wineries made it the wine capital of California. Anaheim proclaimed itself the "garden spot of Southern California," a first attempt at tourism which included a sanitarium for those suffering from respiratory ailments. Later in the same decade, a series of viruses destroyed almost every vineyard in the Santa Ana Valley. The locals rebuilt the economy, turning their vineyards into orange groves. For sixty years, the citrus industry remained supreme, eventually leading to the naming of Orange County after the area's primary cash crop.

After World War II, the manufacturing and tourism sectors exploded and gobbled up most of the area's farms. On the manufacturing side, two defense contractors, Rockwell and Northrop, along with fast-food giant Carl Karcher Enterprises, established a toehold. In the tourism sector, the construction of Disneyland triggered an explosion and to this day Disney remains the key employer. Dozens of nearby hotels and restaurants depend on Disney's customers. The convention center a few blocks away, along with the Anaheim Stadium two miles to the east, further cater to the interests of visitors. As the economy boomed, the population skyrocketed, swelling to over a quarter-million residents by 1990.

At the beginning of the decade, the city council, anxious to spur new growth in an economy stalled by cutbacks in the defense industry, considered construction of a new city-owned arena that would bolster the sagging tourism sector. They were ready to reshape the city economy again to ensure survival. The city council in Santa Ana, the county seat a few miles down the road, had begun plans to develop an arena. Santa Ana's plans were dependent upon securing a major tenant before any construction. They did not want to be left holding the bill for an empty building.

When Anaheim heard about Santa Ana's plans, it stoked their competitive juices. Anaheim, as the oldest city in Orange County, has always seen itself as the cultural center of the region. Believing that they needed to secure their status as the only destination in Orange County for extended vacations, the council members authorized the building of a huge arena just down the block from the thirty-year-old Anaheim Stadium where the Los Angeles Rams and California Angels play. To build the new arena, the city had to insert an escape clause in the Rams' Anaheim Stadium lease. Frustrated by perceived favoritism towards the Angels, Anaheim's original tenant at the Stadium, the Rams wanted the freedom to explore other possibilities within a few years.

The council knew that the new arena would host concerts, ice capades, tennis exhibitions, and rodeos, but they needed to attract NBA and NHL franchises. The city reached an agreement with Ogden Services, a stadium operator, to share some of the cost of building the arena. Ogden would service the debt once the stadium became operational, but Anaheim would own the property. If the city failed to secure either an NBA or NHL franchise, it would have to pay off $2.5 million worth of debt for each of the first eight years of operation. If there was one tenant, the city would be out $1.5 million per year according to the complicated agreement. When a projected two years of construction commenced on the $103-million facility in June 1991, no tenants had been secured. Some council members apparently believed that they could attract a team easily.

Their confidence would have been muted had they talked to the city council in St. Petersburg, Florida. St. Pete had built a state-of-the-art baseball stadium with assurances that they would either be awarded an expansion team or that an existing franchise would move there. A number of potential suitors—the Pittsburgh Pirates, Milwaukee Brewers, and Chicago White Sox—all came calling, only to use St. Pete's limitless interest as leverage to secure a better deal from the folks back home. When the baseball owners selected Denver and Miami as the sites for expansion, St. Pete felt angry and jilted.

When Anaheim looked at the NBA, they thought that they might be able to get either the Lakers or the Clippers to move from L.A. County down the road to Orange County. Not only would the new arena have the luxury boxes that the old arenas were lacking, the area around the site was safer and the local demographic was more up-scale.However, what seemed important wasn't.

Lakers' owner Jerry Buss also owned the Forum and had made his money in real estate. He wasn't about to move his team and destroy the value of his property. Clipper owner Donald Sterling could have looked at the mediocre crowds at his games in downtown L.A. or his poor lease at the Sports Arena with a critical eye and considered moving. Sterling, however, had homes in both Malibu and Beverly Hills, an impossible distance, physically and psychologically, from Anaheim. Owning a Los Angeles-based team fed Sterling's ego. By keeping the Clippers downtown, he could mingle with Billy Crystal, Tommy Lasorda,

Al Davis, and Pia Zadora. Celebrities didn't live in Anaheim.

If getting a local team to move south down the Santa Ana freeway would be impossible, the chance of getting an expansion team was remote. The poor crowds at Clipper games ensured Sterling would oppose any expansion of the NBA to Anaheim. Sterling had paid Buss $13 million to move the San Diego franchise to Los Angeles in 1984 and had foregone the right to share in the money paid by new expansion teams a few years later. While few fans drove in from Orange County to see Clipper games downtown, those fans constituted a part of his potential TV and radio audience if the team improved.

Even if a new basketball franchise could be approved, it would cost between $100 million and $150 million after indemnification fees were paid to Buss and Sterling. Who in Anaheim could afford that? Meanwhile, the NBA commissioner's office had been making noise about international expansion to expand the markets for the league's merchandising. The NBA picture for Anaheim looked bleak.

With an NBA entry unlikely, the Anaheim council turned to the NHL. In 1990, Anaheim had been one of the ten final bidders during the search for two new teams. Hungry for a cash infusion, the NHL owners chose Tampa Bay and Ottawa, the two bidders that promised $50 million in cash in two quick installments.

That expansion proved to be a compromise among two competing ownership cliques. The Canadians, who were worried they were losing all their power, had never dominated the league's markets, but with the increased emphasis on TV, they were afraid of being wiped out. Ottawa's entry meant eight Canadian teams in a twenty-four team league, reestablishing the 1 in 3 ratio in the NHL that existed during the "Original Six" era when Toronto and Montreal represented Canada. For the American owners, a franchise in Tampa Bay reawakened development of the Sunbelt and opened up a large TV market.

Compromise or no, Anaheim's hands were empty and the next expansion left the city in the cold as well. The Gunds, who had sold the Minnesota North Stars to Norm Green, were awarded a franchise in San Jose, another Sunbelt city with a huge TV market. The new team in San Jose drew well, but after a few years in Minnesota, Norm Green was unhappy with his profit margins and began to seek out a new market to play in.

During the summer of 1992, Green quietly looked at a number of locations, including Anaheim. Bruce McNall, the owner of the Los Angeles Kings and newly-installed chairman of the board of NHL Governors, stepped in to tell Green that Anaheim was not available. Green was directed to look somewhere else and eventually settled on Dallas.

Unlike previous league expansions which involved a public bidding process, this time the NHL was acting behind closed doors. McNall had brought the greatest hockey player ever, Wayne Gretzky, to Los Angeles five years earlier in an effort to broaden the sport's appeal. The game had become more popular in the American Sunbelt, but it hadn't exploded. Network TV remained uninterested. Following his appointment to chair the NHL Board of Governors, McNall wanted to create a legacy as the builder who moved the game into the 21st century while expanding its audience.

He saw Disney as a possible catalyst for all his goals. McNall had developed a friendship with Eisner and had invited Michael and his family to attend a number of Kings' games as McNall's guest. At the same time, McNall knew if he could entice Eisner to start a team in Anaheim, he could use the territorial infringement fees when the Kings decided to build their own arena.

Unlike many corporate executives that spout pleasantries about balancing business and family responsibilities but don't carry them out, Eisner has been a devoted father throughout his career. In fact, his committment to both his parental role and his children's interests grounded his tastes in family entertainment.

Eisner also relaizes that to judge his own creative sparks, he needs a filter that reflects other people's tastes. That filter has often been his wife Jane, who Eisner credits with shooting down so many of his bad ideas.

Eisner had become engrossed in hockey through his sons' involvement in the game. Around the world of youth hockey, Eisner was amazed by the devotion of the players and the parents. Jane pressed him to do a movie about a kids' team, but Michael resisted until he heard about an idea pitched by a struggling actor and screenwriter named Steven Brill.

Brill's story centered around the redemption of an attorney whose greed gets him into trouble before he rediscovers life lessons through coaching a team from Minneapolis to the national title. Brill called the team "the Mighty Ducks" because he'd always admired the flying patterns of ducks. It was a formula picture, but so were most of Disney's youth-oriented films. The idea clicked for Eisner and the studio went ahead with the low-budget picture.

About the time Eisner became aware of the possibility of getting an NHL team in Anaheim, the movie hit screens across America. Kids just could not get enough of it, seeing it over and over again as the multiculturally diverse youth hockey team became the 1990's Bad News Bears. The film grossed over $50 million in North America. Eisner could recognize a clear demand for product, but would it translate into box-office sales for the real game? To analyze that question, Eisner brought in an expert.

Tony Tavares, who had been involved in running arenas across America as CEO of Spectacor Management Group, was consulting McNall in late 1992 about the possible construction of a new arena along with advising him about his problems with the CFL's Toronto Argonauts. As negotiations started to heat up between Disney and McNall, McNall asked Tavares to meet with Disney.

The Disney people thought Tavares could help them in negotiating their lease with Ogden, who was the arena manager in Anaheim. Disney asked McNall's permission to use Tavares as a consultant and Bruce granted that permission, albeit grudgingly, according to Tavares, "because he was trying to sell off his territory, and Michael was trying to buy a piece of his territory. Both parties agreed not to put me in the middle on anything being negotiated back and forth. When it came to other analyses, Bruce let me be involved."

"I worked with the strategic-planning group at Disney. We basically came up with all the numbers about whether this would be a profitable venture, what kind of lease would we have to get, and so on," explains Tavares. "I had been in and around sports teams for most of my business career. SMG basically ran buildings for St. Louis, the Islanders, Pittsburgh, and others. I knew a lot of the owners and players in the NHL. What I clearly brought to the table on the business side was experience in negotiating leases, which is a major component part of the business today."

With his experience in the NHL, Tavares could reassure Eisner that the downside risk in entering the league was minimal. A few years earlier, Disney had considered purchasing an expansion NBA team for Orlando, but the numbers hadn't worked out. The NHL was different because of its lower entry fee and its lower salaries. "Until a few years ago, the NHLPA has been the weakest players' union among the major sports," says Tavares. "There was more sanity in the NHL in the past than in other sports."

Despite the lack of revenues from a major national television contract in the United States (teams received less than $1 million each from a deal with ESPN), many teams were clearly earning a healthy profit. Thanks to favorable lease arrangements, franchises in Boston and Detroit were making well over the 20% profit from gross revenues that was a Disney target. The company could enter the league for the effective cost of one big-budget film. Eisner didn't even have to take the decision before Disney's board of directors.

Disney saw unrealized opportunities for merchandising in the NHL. The wild success of the marketing of the San Jose Sharks led Disney to believe that the financial opportunities there were tremendous. The league's members shared merchandising revenues except in team stores or at the home arena. Eisner wanted more and Disney negotiated an agreement with McNall to expand their exclusive arrangement to their theme parks and at Disney stores across America.

Anaheim needed a team, and so did Ogden, the arena manager. No matter what penalties the lease contained for the lack of a major-league tenant, Ogden would be better served by having a tenant. Lease negotiations got underway in November, but Disney didn't feel it had to have the lease signed before agreeing to enter the league.

McNall wanted Disney in the NHL, but he also wanted a $25 million encroachment fee. Ottawa and Tampa Bay had paid $50 million to join the league. Eisner refused to pay a $50 million franchise fee plus $25 million for encroachment. After all, the Hartford franchise had been sold for only $38 million just four years earlier. What to do?

When McNall and Eisner seemed to be stuck on this part of the deal, the Anaheim council approached the International Hockey League about acquiring a top minor-league team. If Disney backed away, the city needed to have a team, any team, in place for the '93-'94 season. Later that month, McNall decided that Wayne Huizenga and Blockbuster could pay the $50 million fee for the Miami team with no compensation to the team upstate in Tampa Bay and that he would call the Ducks' costs a $50 million expansion fee. In fact, half of that money would go straight into McNall's pocket instead of being shared with the other owners.

These deals were negotiated without the knowledge of most other owners in the anticipation that they would approve the deal because they would each receive over $3 million and they wanted Disney in the league. McNall brought in acting NHL president Gil Stein to help with the expansion process. Months later, McNall tried to pay Stein back by sponsoring him for election to the Hockey Hall of Fame, but this sham vote was uncovered and thoroughly denounced.

The expansion deal had to be done behind closed doors because Disney felt it was bringing at least as much to the table as the NHL. "The closed-bidding process was critical because Disney wasn't going to get involved in a sweepstakes for a team. It's the nature of the beast," recalled Tavares later. "The company is held in high esteem by outsiders and holds itself in high esteem and believed it was bringing value to the NHL. It's like the guy who doesn't want to apply for a job, but would accept it if it were offered to him. Being involved in a process like the earlier one would not have been attractive to Disney at all. They would have passed."

At the winter meetings of the NHL Board of Governors in early December 1993, the league's owners voted to approve the awarding of expansion franchises to Disney in Anaheim and Blockbuster in Miami. The statement was clear. They wanted a bigger U.S. audience and they wanted it now. The NHL had fully committed to bringing the game into the Sunbelt, and the new owners believed that the two entertainment giants could create new ways to promote and present the game. "We think there's great growth in hockey," Eisner told the assembled media. "In the way hockey is shot, I think we can be creative in creating stars. We do it in the movie business."

McNall, of course, was ecstatic, telling everyone he encountered that the expansion was "huge." The network TV breakthrough might be just around the corner, his Kings would have their travel schedule reduced significantly and he would pocket

$25 million. Huge, indeed.

For Gil Stein, the meetings did not go as well. He had managed to offend almost every owner in the league in a short time as league president. As the NHL moved to centralize power in a new commissioner's office, it soon became clear that Stein would not be that man. The owners decided to raid David Stern's NBA offices for Gary Bettman, who was perceived to have the energy, training and contacts to put the NHL on the map. Stein did not leave empty-handed. In reward for walking away silently, Stein received a golden handshake worth almost $3 million.

When the expansion deal was announced, the Los Angeles media responded with undiluted enthusiasm, showing an almost proprietary interest in having another local pro franchise. From a greater distance, some critics, including the *New York Times*, speculated that Disney had stepped in to save Anaheim in its lease with Ogden in exchange for favors down the line, specifically with respect to the planned $3 billion expansion of Disneyland called Westcot, along the lines of Epcot in Florida.

The two transactions were entirely separate, according to insiders. "Each part of Disney negotiates hard and one deal had nothing to do with the other. That was speculation by the *Times*, but it clearly is not true. What special favor was extracted? There are none," said Tavares several months later after completing the lease agreement. "There's no promises that have been made behind closed doors or anything like that. I have never heard of an occasion where Disney said anything to the city of Anaheim or Orlando like 'if you do this, this, and this, then we'll do this, this, and this. And if you don't, we won't.' I've never heard of anything like that. Disney's decision to join the NHL was strictly made on a business decision. Now, bottom line, if this was in Sarasota or Des Moines, Iowa, would Disney be interested in it? Probably much less so than having it in Anaheim or Orlando because we had synergistic rationale at work. It doesn't hurt

Disney to have a team in Anaheim."

The announcement of the NHL expansion confirmed that Anaheim had secured its status as the major Orange County tourist destination. December 1992 was the first month of a new era in NHL history, the first real attempt to compete with pro sports' other major leagues. The Bettman era promised the end of hockey's sideshow status in the United States. In Anaheim, nobody could produce players, uniforms, coaches, or even that essential legal document, a signed lease, but the land that once couldn't support even a goat now had itself a hockey team.

2

You're A Duck!

It must be beautiful here in the summertime.
    —Jack Ferreira, after a scouting trip to northern Saskatchewan

On March 1, 1993, the scene outside the almost-completed Anaheim Arena looked like something out of a Fellini movie. At a press conference announcing that the Mighty Ducks of Anaheim would begin play during the '93-'94 season, Eisner, wearing a uniform jersey from the kids' movie, and the more conservatively attired McNall and Bettman tooted duck calls in unison to herald the new franchise. The smiles all around appeared genuine, not even the slightest hint of sheepishness creeping around the edges. After all, the league had Penguins in Pittsburgh, why not Ducks in Anaheim?

When Eisner had proposed the name to the league office, a number of NHL insiders had tried to talk him out of it because they feared becoming a laughing-stock. Eisner, inured to jokes about running a Mickey Mouse operation and secure in his marketing expertise, remained firm. If he named the new team after the movie, his team would have immediate name recognition. After the jokes ran out, the identification would linger. Then when the Mighty Ducks sequel was released the following spring, the goodwill generated by the team would reflect favorably on the movie. The league's "dignity" meant little; synergy was everything.

At the same time, Eisner was careful to stress the importance of Anaheim in the team's name. Unlike his neighbors, the Los Angeles Rams and California Angels across the street, Eisner embraced his Orange County location, directly appealing to local pride. During the press conference, Eisner also announced that Tavares, who'd been the key consultant during the decision-making process, would become the President of Disney Sports Enterprises, Inc., a subsidiary of the parent company that would run the hockey franchise, along with exploring other ventures into the world of professional sports.

March, April, May, June, July, August, September. Seven months to get up to speed for competition in the National Hockey League. Other teams had taken years to get going. The pressure would be enormous. Tavares had the go-ahead to put together an organization. He set up shop in a hotel a few miles away in Garden Grove. His office in the building Eisner had christened the "Pond of Anaheim" wouldn't be ready for months.

The first priority had to be finding a general manager. Eisner wanted Tavares to narrow the candidates down to a few before involving him. "I wasn't looking for a good-old boy, someone that fit into that category in the NHL," Tavares said later. "A plus would have been someone that had expansion experience. Since I did not personally possess a great deal of experience in the inner workings of the NHL, it had to be someone with some NHL experience as a GM or as an assistant GM. I was looking for somebody that had drafted well because I had done enough leg work to know that very few teams had done a great job over the year at drafting players."

Tavares' search uncovered two top candidates: Jack Ferreira, director of Pro Scouting with the Canadiens who'd been GM in Minnesota and San Jose, and Pierre Gauthier, the Scouting

Director for Quebec. Both men had spent many years on the road searching for talent. Ferreira, who'd minded the nets at Boston University in the 1960s, could pick apart the strengths and weaknesses of a skater. Ferreira had coached in the Ivy League and WHA before moving into scouting for NHL teams.

Ferreira's sharp reflexes revealed his past life in the nets. He was about the same age as Tavares and had similarly spent his formative years under the spell of the Boston Bruins. They spoke the same language. Gauthier, a native of Montreal, had a good eye and a sharp mind. In the end, Ferreira's prior work proved critical. He'd been a key in selecting the roster that made Calgary the only serious challenge to the Oiler dynasty in the mid-80s.

"Jack's experiences in Calgary and that he'd been through an expansion in San Jose were important," says Tavares. "What ended up happening was we hired Jack because of the scouting experience in combination with the start-up experience and the fact that he knew his way around the NHL, but Pierre was our second choice."

The team needed an Assistant GM to handle the amateur and pro scouting. Tavares interceded on behalf of Gauthier. "I suggested to Jack that we had to organize things fast. I asked him if he knew Pierre. He said he liked Pierre a lot. I was candid with him and told him that Pierre finished second to him in the sweepstakes to be GM. Jack graciously agreed to interview him. When he finished, he came back and said 'this is easy. I don't even have to talk to anybody else,' and he ended up hiring him."

The hirings of Ferreira and Gauthier were announced concurrently in late March. The two old friends were a perfect fit because of the needs of a fledgling organization. Each man had expertise in one of the two key talent pools for a club that would first secure talent from pre-existing teams and then have to go into the amateur pool. "Jack had for the past year been scouting the pros, and Pierre had been concentrating on the Juniors," says

Tavares. "We had a combination of people that made us feel very comfortable that we were going into the draft prepared. We had to fit our needs because of the emergency nature of the situation."

While Tavares assembled a marketing and public relations staff, Ferreira put together a scouting staff. He hired one of his former players, Paul Fenton, who had been out of the league only a year, to scout the NHL teams for the rest of the season. He picked up Al Godfrey, an old friend and veteran scout, from the Central Scouting Bureau with an expertise in amateur talent. He hired Richard Green, an old buddy from college, away from the Islanders. Ferreira would later hire Thommie Bergman and Alain Chainey to fill out the scouting staff. Prior to being hired by the Ducks, Ferreira, Gauthier and Godfrey had already criss-crossed Canada, the U.S. Northeast and Europe in search of young talent.

Ferreira looked at six factors when judging hockey players: size, strength, skating speed, strength and release of shot, competitive drive, and hockey sense. You could make a player a better skater or a little stronger or even teach him how to shoot faster. But there were limits on how much you could do with weaknesses in the other areas.

If a prospect was small, that wasn't going to change. It wouldn't eliminate someone, but the player would clearly have to be NHL quality in other areas. In San Jose, one of the key lessons Ferreira had learned was to not put together a team of small players or you'd get blown off the ice a lot of nights. Hockey sense seemed to be a gift, not something you could instill in someone once they became an adult. All players could be taught simple systems, but the vision to create at high speed in traffic or to sense where to be defensively, well, that was rare.

Jack had a trick for determining how good a competitor a player was. Of course, he'd watch to see if the player was on the ice during key situations and how he performed there, but then

Jack would ask teammates who they would pick first if they were choosing sides for a game. Teammates knew who the leaders were.

The rule was simple. You couldn't project someone into becoming a quality NHL player unless he was NHL level along one of these six dimensions. As the newly assembled front office put together the players they wanted to take in the expansion and entry drafts, that criterion would be kept in mind. Jack wanted to seek players with an upside, the potential to grow into better performers, and he didn't want any with off-ice problems. In both Minnesota and San Jose, Ferreira had acquired a few talented but troubled players, hoping they would turn the corner. "I've had enough of that," Ferreira told his staff. "We will not inherit anybody with those kinds of problems."

In mid-June, the Duck team descended on Quebec City to put together a roster for the upcoming season. As the scouts, front office personnel and even Eisner himself arrived in the heat of a Canadian summer, the team still lacked a scouting director and a coach, although top candidates had emerged. The empty positions left the expansion draft in the hands of Jack Ferreira, who had performed the same task for San Jose two years earlier. In San Jose, the initial dispersal draft gave the Sharks a very young look as they pulled a lot of kids they'd developed out of the North Star system. That San Jose team struggled to compete, and Ferreira had learned two valuable lessons. He wanted a team that was a little older, and a lot bigger. The Sharks had been manhandled during their first year. "When you're a new team, nobody respects you—not your opponents, not the refs," asserts Ferreira. "We wanted to minimize that problem with big, veteran players."

Sensitive to the problems created by weak expansion teams, the owners gave the Ducks and the Panthers a much better chance to be competitive than they'd allowed Ottawa and Tampa Bay. Each pre-existing team would lose two players, but unlike previous drafts, the established teams were only allowed to protect one goaltender. The Ducks and Panthers would each take three goalies, eight defensemen, and thirteen forwards. Ferreira figured to capitalize on the advantage in goaltending by making that area a team strength. The day after the expansion draft, in Phase II of the draft, Ottawa and Tampa Bay were allowed to take one goalie left unprotected by the Panthers and Ducks. The Ducks would end up with at least two solid goalies, and Ferreira had his eye on a top minor-league goalie he believed they could get in the entry draft.

When the Ducks got the protected list the day before the expansion draft, they found few surprises, although Hartford's decison not to protect 24-year-old Terry Yake, the team's third highest goal scorer, caught everyone's attention. Instead of worrying about what Florida was going to do with the first pick, Ferreira focused on his own wish list. After the Panthers grabbed John Vanbiesbrouck, Pierre Gauthier stepped up to the microphone and announced, "The Mighty Ducks of Anaheim select Guy Hebert of the St. Louis Blues."

Jack had liked Hebert for years now, having seen him blossom in the Goodwill Games a few years earlier. Fortunately for Ferreira, he'd followed the Blues for a few games while with Montreal and when CuJo, Curtis Joseph, had been ailing. Filling in, Hebert had played well. With their next two picks, the Ducks took Glenn Healy and Ron Tugnutt. Gauthier knew Tugnutt from the Quebec organization and was impressed with his skills and his character during poor seasons. The Ducks expected to lose Healy in Phase II of the expansion draft. A day later, Tampa Bay snatched him up and immediately dealt the veteran goalie to the Rangers for a third round pick in the amateur draft.

When he went for skaters, Jack knew the hard thing to find would be goal scorers and offensive defensemen. What Ferreira decided to do was go after players that he felt had been lost in their organizations; kept in the minors or in a reduced role at the

NHL level because of conflict with coaches or depth at their position.

Some of the picks on defense were easy. The Devils chose not to protect longtime Soviet All-Star Alexei Kasatonov because of his age and contract status. Kasa was slowing down and had never been the player he was for the Central Red Army team, but Ferreira believed he could be the top all-around defenseman available to the expansion teams. Sean Hill's big shot and competitive fire were lost in the shuffle behind Montreal's solid young corps of defensemen. Billy Houlder was buried in the Buffalo organization but had been one of the top minor-league defensemen. The Ducks needed someone to run their power play unit and Houlder was seen to have as good a chance as any with his big shot from the point. Randy Ladouceur, a veteran stay-at-home defenseman from Hartford, had been someone Ferreira had wanted Montreal to acquire. He would be a solid anchor.

Perhaps the biggest surprise among the defensemen taken was Detroit's Bobby Dollas. From an organization with so many gifted young scorers, the Ducks had expected to take a potential goal-scorer off the Red Wings farm team in Adirondack."We went to watch Adirondack to see Chris Tancill and we were in to watch him maybe five times. Pierre went a couple of times, I went a couple of times and Paul Fenton went in," explained Ferreira later. "We'd come back and we'd talk about him—because we knew we needed scoring and he's a scorer—and it always seemed that somebody would say, 'But you know who else played well was Bobby Dollas.' Finally we looked at each other and we said, 'Hey, Bobby Dollas is the guy we're going to take.' That's how we got Bobby Dollas. That guy just kept coming to us. Detroit probably did the best job of limiting what was available. So we took Bobby."

Dollas' true ability was unknown. He'd become a dominant minor-league player and had been a first-round pick for Winnipeg back in 1983. Maybe he had finally reached his potential or perhaps he was just dominating raw kids seven or eight years younger than he was.

They had to take someone off the Ottawa roster, which was a bad joke, and Jack liked Mark Ferner—who had the potential to add depth to the defensive corps—better than any of Ottawa's forwards. David Williams was another conservative defenseman that Jack knew from San Jose. The hope was that Kasa and Laddie would be the glue that held this group together while Hill and Houlder developed their talents into productivity. Ferner and Williams were seen as fill-ins. Unless a player was acquired by training camp, the Ducks were going to have to play one of their defensemen out of place. Only Hill and Williams had natural right-handed shots.

Up front, the Ducks started by taking two gifted young wings, Steven King of the Rangers and Tim Sweeney of the Bruins. These guys had been among the top scorers in the American Hockey League. Ferreira had drafted Sweeney out of Boston College when he was at Calgary, hoping that he might develop along the lines of fellow B.C. alum Joey Mullen. If King and Sweeney were expected to carry a big part of the scoring burden, the next two picks, Stu Grimson of Chicago and Troy Loney of Pittsburgh were picked for their size and veteran leadership. Both men had played for the Stanley Cup and were willing to mix it up for the sake of the team. For those who expected Disney to assemble a team better suited for the Ice Capades than battles along the boards, these two picks signaled a call to arms.

The next five picks, Terry Yake, Jarrod Skalde, Bob Corkum, Anatoli Semenov and Joe Sacco, represented offensive hope. Yake had proven that he could put the puck in the net in the NHL. Skalde and Sacco were young, fast skaters who had decent minor-league numbers. Semenov, the oldest forward picked, would distribute the puck, setting up his teammates the way he'd fed Pavel Bure through much of the prior season in Vancouver.

Corkum had just played his first full season in Buffalo as a fourth-line center, almost exclusively backchecking as he tallied just ten points, though Fenton knew he was also strong going to the net. Ferreira saw Corkum as more than a one-way player. He remembered an AHL playoff game between Rochester and Binghamton two years earlier when Corkum was the dominant player on the ice. As well, he recalled that as a college athlete at the University of Maine, Corkum had also played varsity football and baseball.

The remaining four picks testified to the thin talent even in a year when the draft was more equitable for the new teams: Ferreira hoped for but did not expect significant contributions from Loach, Thomson, Halverson and Bawa. He needed more depth and skill up front, and he would have all summer to search for it. "We're really pleased. I think we've got some NHL goaltending," said Ferreira immediately after the draft. "We've got an experienced defense. We'll try to supplement that with a couple of young guys either through the draft or free agency. Up front, we've got some good size and good speed and guys that can check. Scoring's going to be tough some nights."

When Ferreira called Bobby Dollas to tell him the news, Dollas was ecstatic. Freed from a Detroit organization that no longer believed in him, Dollas kept Jack on the line as he and his wife tried to decide what uniform number he should select. The question confirmed his new-found significance. A low number meant a place on the team was all but his. After a few minutes of discussion, Dollas asked Jack for the number two.

When Troy Loney returned home from a fishing trip with some buddies, his younger brother shouted at him derisively, "You're a Duck!." The news shocked the veteran forward from Alberta. He was comfortable with the Penguins, a Cup contender every year. He'd have to start over again. Increased ice time would be good, but was it worth a decreased chance at another title after he'd just turned thirty?

The initial uncertainties of new Ducks would have to be addressed later by an as-yet-unnamed coach. While Ferreira, Gauthier and Tavares were satisfied with what they accomplished in the expansion draft, none of the players they'd just taken had the potential future of the amateurs that they were about to select. With the entry draft less than forty-eight hours away, the focus shifted quickly to a different set of concerns.

It was common knowledge Ottawa would take Alexander Daigle with the first pick. After that, things were up in the air. Would San Jose, owners of the second pick, keep it or trade it? What did Tampa Bay, picking third, want? If those uncertainties were not enough, the Ducks had to worry about Florida's plans. By virtue of a victory in a coin toss, the Panthers had the right to choose one of two options. They could select before Anaheim either in 1993 or 1994. This season, the decision would mean the fourth instead of the fifth pick. After Tampa Bay picked, Florida would annouce their decision. If they went fourth in 1993, they would choose second in 1994. By dropping down to fifth in 1993, the Panthers would secure the top pick in 1994. The class of 1994 had not really come into shape, but no Gretzky or Lemieux stood out as the next generation's superstar. With no clear-cut number one in '94, the Panthers would wait through the first three picks before making their decision.

What the Ducks knew for sure was that they wanted the Next One. Paul Kariya, a little left wing from Vancouver, had just become the first freshman to win the Hobey Baker Award signifying the best college hockey player in the United States. Kariya had scored 25 goals and 75 assists in leading the University of Maine to 42-1-2 record. The team became state heroes when they won the NCAA title by coming back from being down 4-2 in the third period of the final, behind three assists by Kariya.

Kariya wore the number nine in honor of his idol Gretzky. And he had blue blades on his skates and wore his shirt half tucked in like the Great One. "Gretz has been my idol ever since I can remember," Kariya says. "I really studied the way he played." While any comparison to Gretzky is a daunting burden for Paul, the similarities are unmistakable. Kariya's vision and passing set him apart from his peers. His small stature and boyish good looks make him appear almost vulnerable on the ice.

Even Eisner was concerned about Kariya's lack of size. The morning of the entry draft, Eisner wanted to know how short Kariya really was. "Is he only five-three?" Eisner wondered. Eisner's son Eric, who had come along to Quebec to get an inside look at his favorite game, reassured his farther that Kariya was five-ten. Well, maybe on skates.

The funny thing about Anaheim's interest was the way they hid it. Even if Ferreira believed Kariya would develop into an NHL superstar, he didn't want to tip his hand to the other teams around the league. The Ducks invited a number of players in for interviews, but Kariya was not among them. Paul liked the idea of playing for a new team, but he assumed Anaheim had lost interest because they had not maintained contact. Unlike a college recruiter, pro teams don't have to court their intendeds and, with nothing to lose, Anaheim was playing it close to the vest.

In the middle of a brutal summer, on the day of the amateur draft, the heat inside Quebec City's Le Colisée was suffocating. Ferreira, Gauthier, Tavares and Eisner sweated out the wait to see if they would get their man. After Ottawa followed their plan and picked Daigle, San Jose traded the number-two pick to Hartford to get extra picks later in the draft. Hartford snatched up a huge defenseman named Chris Pronger. With the third pick, Tampa Bay passed on Kariya to take Chris Gratton.

Now the ball was in Florida's court. They could either make

the next pick now and accept the number-two in 1994 or wait a pick and claim the number-one in 1994. In the end, Panther GM Bobby Clarke wanted size and preferred Rob Niedermayer to Paul Kariya, and he knew the Ducks would not take Niedermayer. The Panthers passed the pick to the Mighty Ducks, pushing Florida's advantage a year away into the murky 1994 draft picture.

Everyone at the Ducks table breathed a huge sigh of relief. "We got him, we got him," exulted Tavares. Ferreira ceded the limelight to Gauthier again, who announced Paul Kariya's name to the cheers of the gathered crowd. The Ducks had drafted what they felt was the most skilled player in the draft and the nicest kid in the world. Kariya had pledged to play for Canada in the '94 Olympics and the Ducks didn't expect him to join them until March at the earliest, but Gauthier, for one, thought it was for the best. He wanted Kariya to face tougher international competition and spend more time working on his game.

Picking Kariya began a long period of talent acquisition. Among their remaining ten picks, the Ducks snatched up five Russians, including two gifted kids named Nikolai Tsulygin and Valeri Karpov. In the fifth round, Ferreira got his third goalie. Mikhail Shtalenkov, at twenty-seven the second oldest player drafted, was the tenth goalie taken in the draft. The nine goalies grabbed before him were still teenagers. Most teams remained too conservative to draft older players, but Ferreira thought Shtalenkov had been the top goalie in the IHL during the prior season, his first in the United States. After playing six years as the number-one goaltender for Moscow Dynamo, Shtalenkov was reaching the peak of his career and had the top-level experience to be ready to play in the NHL right away.

By the time everyone bailed out of the sweltering heat of Le Colisée, Ferreira was thrilled with what had been accomplished. The roster still had holes, but the goaltending was deep and, in

Kariya, Ferreira had his superstar-in-waiting, a player whose skill level was beyond any he'd acquired in his prior GM jobs. Before anyone had put a skate to ice, the long-term Duck future looked bright.

3

The Disney Rules

As Mickey's personality softened, his appearance changed...I am not sure that the Disney artists themselves explicitly realized what they were doing, since the changes appeared in such a halting and piecemeal fashion. In short, the blander and inoffensive Mickey became progressively more juvenile in appearance.
—Stephen Jay Gould, from "A Biological Homage to Mickey Mouse" in *The Panda's Thumb*

When Disney held a press conference on June 7, 1993 to unveil the new logo before drafting any players or even acquiring a coach, one could not help but reflect on Gould's analysis of the changes in Mickey Mouse. According to Gould, Mickey had evolved into a more youthful character because his physical qualities, like those of an infant, would provoke human tenderness. That evolution appeared haphazard, but the new hockey logo would be anything but. Everything Disney did now was subject to intense internal scrutiny.

Eisner presented the Mighty Duck, its appearance reflecting a new, more adult Disney. "The official logo, as you can see, is a mean goalie mask," Eisner announced. "We wanted something that was between Disneyesque and hockey mean. We're one step closer to skating. Now all we need is a coach and players and we'll be in great shape."

Even the color scheme was deliberate, according to Tavares. "There's a lot of foresight put into everything. You have purple in that uniform, you have green, you have silver. If purple falls out of favor, you could see a predominantly green uniform. If green falls out of favor, you could see a predominantly silver uniform. It was funny when we submitted our color scheme to the league," explained Tavares. "They said 'what is your dominant color?' We said, 'we don't have one.' They said, 'you've got to have a dominant color.' We said 'that's the uniform, approve it or reject it, those are our colors.' They approved it. So we've kept the door open for a variety of changes for ourselves that could prove positive."

The character in the logo belonged in a horror movie. Many people who had a fixed view of Disney could not have been more surprised if Eisner had announced the team would play naked. A duck would appeal to children in almost any form, but to sell to adults, it required a certain aura of toughness. Mighty Duck-wear might not become gang colors like Kings' or Raiders' shirts and hats, but it wasn't syrupy sweet, either.

After Eisner took command, Disney no longer ran from the darker side of human nature, as long as there was profit to be made. The corporate aura had shifted significantly over the past ten years. The studio's most commercially successful films during Eisner's first decade included *Pretty Woman*, a comedy, however light, about a romance between a greedy businessman and a prostitute and *Who Framed Roger Rabbit?*, a combination of live action and animation that was rife with violence and sexual innuendo.

While the theme parks remained frozen in a peculiarly American brand of innocence that appealed to visitors from around the world, even in that sector of the company Eisner pursued aggressive expansion. Furthermore, what had been seen as the sleepiest of the studios in Hollywood, with shorter work days and a country club atmosphere, was converted to an incredibly productive environment.

What Eisner understood perfectly was the adrenaline rush that work creates for people in the entertainment business. The sporadic nature of the business fosters a widespread sense of manic-depression. When a film's being made, the energy is electric, a group of workaholics run wild. Between jobs, however, many of those same employees struggle to find joy in waiting. Eisner just decided to tap into that willing labor force by offering a promise of more films—steadier work in exchange for lower wages, relative to industry-wide standards, and longer hours. The unspoken in-house message was clear—the seven day work week had become the rule, not the exception.

Another way to keep costs down during a period of growth was to use talent that had fallen out of favor or was yet to be discovered. Instead of rushing to develop Bruce Willis, Eddie Murphy or Harrison Ford projects, Disney used Bette Midler and Richard Dreyfuss at a time when their film careers were on the downside, as well as a relatively unknown Julia Roberts to star in their key films. Once seen as outsiders in the motion picture business, the expansion under Eisner, which included development of adult product lines and hardball negotiating tactics, signaled a new attitude.

Could the same strategy work for the ownership of a hockey team? An employer could certainly expect and demand long, hard hours from the players and the staff surrounding them. Disney could even negotiate hard to keep salaries down. But to win without recognized stars at the peak of their game and market value did not seem nearly as possible as pulling off a surprise hit in the movies. Would Disney even try that route?

While Disney was growing and mutating into a competitive supplier of adult entertainment, Eisner also exploited Disney's pre-existing strengths. The most important of these was its size and interconnectivity. The word "synergy" seems to be on the tip off every Disney executive's tongue. The Mighty Ducks were just a small part of a monstrous empire. The total start-up costs of twenty-six NHL teams, a league's worth, would only cost about half as much as EuroDisney, whose financial struggles were already starting to burden the otherwise-healthy corporation.

With so many different things going on in this multi-billion dollar corporation, Eisner had to hire the right people and then delegate responsibility. Tavares, the point man for the Ducks, created a corporate atmosphere that was entirely different from the rest of the corporation. For a motion picture development executive, saying yes is prohibitively expensive. Green lighting a project commits millions of dollars. Decision-makers in the film industry become masters at the art of maybe, optioning projects to keep them away from competitors and then freezing them in development. Hollywood deal-making is a world of shadows and lawyers where people can survive for years between actual projects being made.

Tavares would have found such an atmosphere stifling. A can-do personality, he always wanted more, whether it was scouting or promotional work or analysis of the roster. His restless, energetic spirit set the tone for the entire franchise. His relationship with Ferreira has been central. "Jack's in my office a lot. One of the things that Jack seeks out is my analytical abilities," says Tavares. "What he uses me for is a sounding board; I force him into the analysis process."

Ferreira's relationship with Tavares differs from his prior jobs in Minnesota and San Jose. "The thing I like about working with Tony is Tony is very analytical. I call it mental gymnastics," explains Ferreira. "We talk a lot and he throws a lot of situations at me. If this were to happen and that were to happen, how would you react? Is this the type of player you would be looking for? Also, he is well-briefed about what our philosophy is, what we're gonna do in the entry draft, what we're gonna do on trades. He has never come to me nor do I expect him to come to me and say 'get rid of this guy or get rid of that guy or whatever.' He never comes and tries to force anything on me."

From the outset, the hockey people were set free to do what they needed to do with little outside interference. "What I do is I keep people out of the hockey business. I do indeed run Disney Sports Enterprises. There is precious little in the way of interference from Disney corporate here. There will never be any pressure put on the hockey side, decisions on trades, as long as I'm here," says Tavares. "I welcome input on the business side and the marketing side and things of that nature, but there is nobody, in my view, in the Disney organization that has the expertise about hockey that Jack and Pierre do. I have seen an abundance of mistakes made at other franchises where owners get too involved in their own business."

If the Ducks were not going to be a source of free publicity to boost Eisner's ego, then were they simply another investment for the corporate bosses to be judged by its profit-and-loss statement? Not according to Tavares. "Is Disney Sports all about return on investment? Not really, though that's a part of it. You want to do well, and we will always strive to be a profitable organization, but I think what we provide is some synergies. If we can get out there and be one of the teams that's always competitive for the Stanley Cup, I think we can provide a source of pride to the Disney organization. That's a goal that we have. That's an intangible that's very difficult to analyze on a financial statement."

Ferreira confirmed the lack of interference. "Working for Disney hasn't been much different than working for any other company. I report to Tony Tavares. Reporting directly to Disney doesn't happen for me. Michael's comments about the game reflect more upon the entertainment factor, how the fans react," explains Ferreira. "Disney has been hands-off. There has been zero interference. Eisner never interfered once, never called to ask me why you offered that much to a player. He didn't set a financial ceiling. Tony and I did that before the season. I was under tougher financial restraints in Minnesota because we were losing so much money."

That freedom showed experienced people they had organizational support. It created a confident environment where chances could be taken, where people were not afraid to make mistakes, to try creative, new approaches. "Today, we begin to establish our own traditions. And if we don't think that way, we'll never be a sports franchise that's worth anything. We want to be the best sports organization out there. The moves that we make now will establish what our personality will be as a sports franchise for the future," says Tavares. "We've worked very hard at being a progressive-thinking kind of sports organization. I don't want to break any traditions, but I want our thoughts to be on the cutting edge."

One approach that separated the Ducks from the pack was an in-house study by the scouts and other hockey people about the on-ice and off-ice strategies of four successful NHL teams. This year-long study would create a partial blueprint for the Ducks' future plans. "We've analyzed four NHL teams. They were each selected for a different reason, but there's one consistent thing," explains Tavares. "Each of these teams always seems to be in the hunt. Every one of them is challenging for the Stanley Cup. They're never out of it more than a couple of years. They never fall way off the charts. What we want to know is simple—what do they do that's different from the rest of the league? What makes them special?"

Some of the choices were obvious. The Montreal Canadiens have been the most successful franchise in all of professional sports. Hockey's most recent dynasties, the Edmonton Oilers and New York Islanders, would provide important evidence as well, especially the Isles, an expansion team that made good. The final selection was perhaps most difficult, but the execs settled on the Boston Bruins, whose 26 straight playoff appearances represented consistent performance despite what often seemed an overmatched roster. Over the course of the season, the hockey people would put together the common denominators of the four franchises. A key issue was how many superstars you needed to be a perennial Cup contender. Disney wanted to win, but they didn't want to waste resources. If there was a way to be more efficient in pursuing titles, why not pursue it?

Two universal things that jumped out on first glance were the ability to recognize and secure young talent and front office stability. The Canadiens had only four GMs over five decades: Selke, Pollock, Grundman and Savard. The quartet secured 18 Cups. Harry Sinden should have been renamed Mr. Bruin for his unbroken record of service. Bill Torrey had run the Isles for the franchise's first two decades in the league. Glen Sather *was* the Edmonton Oilers, having held the GM job every day the club had been in the NHL.

Tavares understood that top-notch scouting formed the backbone of his organization. "What are the major assets of this club? The players you put on the ice. If you're not prepared to invest in R & D on the players you're getting, then you're not going to be successful," Tavares asserts. "We've put an enormous amount of time and money into putting together the best computer-scouting system in the league. Our scouts are reporting twice a week. You don't get to see anyone else's opinion of a player or even your earlier opinion once you download your data to the team. We want you to be objective every time you see a player."

After the draft, Ferreira brought in Ranger scout David McNab to be director of pro scouting. McNab's father Max had passed the game on to his sons even when they lived in San Diego during part of their childhood. David's brother Peter had a long, distinguished NHL career. As for David, a backup goaltender at the University of Wisconsin, he tried out at the minor-league level, realized he was overmatched and went on the road to scout at the age of 22. He's given his life to the game.

According to Ferreira, "There isn't a better scouting staff than we have. Pierre spent his whole career scouting. I did it for 16 years; it's still the thing I love best about the NHL. It's the bloodline of any organization. David's done an outstanding job. We have a really good staff. I've tried to keep the staff small. We've got guys that work hard. When you keep your staff small, they become more involved in decisions, closer to the team."

With this talented staff on hand, Ferreira decided to get the jump on the rest of the league by going after players who were ignored at this point of the scouting cycle. During the late summer, most teams begin their preparations for next summer's draft. Along with those efforts, Ferreira sent his scouts to find talent that could be secured sooner. "Jack said he wanted to know who's the best over-age player in the Juniors in Canada for this season and whether there are any undrafted collegiate players that we think can help," says Tavares. The search was on in talent pools the rest of the NHL had unknowingly ceded to the Ducks.

If putting together a scouting staff held one key to success, another had to be selecting the right coach. The Canadiens had been run by legends Dick Irvin, Toe Blake and Scotty Bowman. The Islanders of Potvin, Bossy, Trottier and Smith were Al Arbour's club, much as the Oilers of Fuhr, Coffey, Messier and Gretzky were Glen Sather's team. "What we were looking for when we went on our search for a coach was somebody that had the ability of relating to the talent he was given," says Tavares. "If you were going to insist on playing a certain style of hockey with our talent, the chances of you being successful would be very limited, at least in the short run."

A number of candidates were in the mix, but none of them stood out as the process began. Nevertheless, Ron Wilson, an assistant in Vancouver, had had a feeling he would get the job before he'd even met with anyone. He started to canvas friends around the league, many of whom warned him that a bad experience with an expansion team could be his last job in the NHL. Nevertheless, Wilson prepared for his interview with a whole series of ideas about ways to avoid the pitfalls that new teams fall into. His preparation paid off, according to Tavares.

"Jack interviewed Ron and said, 'Tony, you've got to talk to this guy.' We did the interview and I came out and said, 'I'm ready.' He wasn't designed to be the last guy in, but we were impressed enough with him where we just called it off after that. The thing that impressed me most was what a heady coach he was. He really believed that with the proper system and preparation, you could actually outplay opponents of greater skill. Ron just impressed me with his knowledge of players in the league, his preparation before a game, how he analyzed teams, how he analyzed strengths and weaknesses, and how he designed a game plan to exploit those strengths and weaknesses. Those are the things that impressed me most."

Al Sims, coach of the IHL-champion Fort Wayne Comets, had impressed Tony and Jack, as well. "We also thought that Ron was a bit untested from the standpoint of never being a head coach before," Tavares says. "The only place where we had a question-mark were his defensive strategies—it wasn't necessarily a weakness—but he had been so offensively minded as a defenseman when he played and as an assistant in Vancouver. I said, 'If we could ever get a combination of he and Al Sims, that would really be a fascinating twosome.' Jack and I talked about it and decided it's not our place to tell the guy who he should hire. All we could do is suggest that he give Al an interview. Jack and I both recommended that he find somebody that wasn't like him, that was a bit different than he was in how he viewed the game. He met Al, and though he had three other interviews lined up, and he called us back and said 'you guys are right. This is the right guy. He's perfect for what we need.' The combination is really good and they get along really well and each brings something different to the table."

Wilson needed a second assistant to keep detailed stats, scout future opponents, provide support in coaching the forwards, and put together videos of game action to teach and inspire the players. These were essentially the same functions he'd performed while working under Pat Quinn in Vancouver. For this unseen job, he needed a young coach who was willing to work endlessly yet maintain a positive attitude. Wilson looked to Providence, his alma mater, where Tim Army had proven himself to be a bright, diligent assistant. When he'd lived in Providence as a teen, Wilson had played hockey with Army's older brother and knew Tim aspired to be a head coach someday. He pitched the job as a perfect opportunity to learn the game at the highest level, and Army jumped at the chance.

Tavares, Ferreira, Gauthier, McNab, Wilson, Sims and Army shared an absolute certainty that they had found their dream jobs at that moment. The hours would be long and the pay, while still good, would be below league average in many cases. But the energy of these men, and the people around them, would not recede all season long. Like he had at Disney Studios a decade earlier, Eisner had overseen the assemblage of a group of loyal, diligent employees willing to do more to catch up with the rest of the world. Eighty-hour work weeks became commonplace. The staff would get little rest in creating entertainment for the leisure time of the team's fans.

4

Just Like Starting Over

*All these kids were waving at me, but then I realized they were excited
because I was standing next to Chip and Dale.*

—Todd Ewen

First-year teams often prepare themselves to be lovable losers.
The 1962 New York Mets stand out as a team that forced
observers to wonder at their incompetence. Traditionally, new
teams bring in busloads of marginal players in hopes that the
competition for jobs will separate the men from the boys.

Not the Ducks. On September 10, when the Ducks hit the ice
for the first time, nobody was looking to cast Wilson in the role
of the great manager Casey Stengel, who by 1962 was seen as a
lovable bundle of malapropisms. In baseball, even an awful
team like those Mets won one of every four games. The next
tension-relieving win was only three days away. But a bad
hockey team might win only one in eight and go an awful month
between wins. Nobody in the Pond wanted or expected that.

Before a puck had been shot or a check delivered, a roster's
worth of players with NHL ability or experience was on hand.
Wilson sent eight lines of skaters on the ice, but almost half of
them had little or no chance of making the team. Some of the
players were teens, possible future NHLers, but the rest were

veteran minor-leaguers. These players were little more than extras and stunt men, bodies for the expected starters to skate around and crash into.

Over the summer, Ferreira had acquired four more NHL-quality forwards. Center Shaun Van Allen and winger Peter Douris were signed on July 22 as free agents out of the Edmonton and Boston organizations. Van Allen, a superior playmaker in the minor leagues, had failed to make the transition to the majors. Douris had contributed a little with the Bruins but was seeking a bigger role. On August 10, Jack made his first trade with Montreal GM Serge Savard, his old boss. For a third-round pick in 1994, he was able to secure Todd Ewen, a big, feisty winger, and Patrick Carnback, a young Swedish centerman who had yet to blossom. Ewen and Carnback would have played a limited role in Montreal, but both men made the Anaheim roster instantly stronger. Even after the trades, training camp promised little true competition. "My worst fear is that we don't have much depth," admitted Ferreira as training camp opened.

Bob Corkum and Anatoli Semenov had center spots all but locked up while Van Allen and Carnback would battle with Skalde for the final two positions. Ewen and Douris would be wingers along with Troy Loney, Stu Grimson, Terry Yake, Joe Sacco, Tim Sweeney and Steven King. Thirteen forwards would be just right for the NHL roster, as long as everybody performed up to expectations.

Ferreria hadn't found any defensemen with right-handed shots. Al Sims, who was responsible for the defensive pairings, would have to fiddle with the combinations. On defense, Bobby Dollas, Sean Hill, Bill Houlder, Alexei Kasatonov and Randy Ladouceur had locked up spots while Mark Ferner, Myles O'Connor and David Williams jockeyed for the final spot or two. The only question in the nets was how close Shtalenkov was to being an NHL-quality netminder.

With the roster essentially set, Wilson still had a number of critical tasks. While tinkering with different combinations to see what lines would work best, he had to install his system and create a work ethic. With most players likely to have greater responsibility than ever before and few scorers on the roster, Wilson established a very basic system for breakout and forecheck that would allow the players to concentrate on their defensive responsibility.

His main job, though, was to get inside each of his players' heads to make them comfortable with their roles. From the beginning of the camp, Wilson stressed to the team that he and the other coaches and the front office believed in them. Unlike other places where coaches didn't know what to do with them or didn't think they deserved significant ice time, Wilson told the players he wanted to see what they could do. He knew they would make mistakes, but he assured them that if they would work and learn from their errors that he would support them.

If they had a bad shift or a bad game, they wouldn't suddenly find themselves back in the minors. Wilson thought that each guy could do more than he'd been asked to do up to this point in his career, and he wanted them to go about proving that other teams had been wrong. He also told them frankly that he knew they were not the most talented team in the league, but they could win games by outworking teams. If they were willing to pay the price, it would be a good year for them as a team and individually.

It was the perfect challenge for a professional athlete: "I believe in you even if others don't. Prove that you belong at this level." This message caught on universally with the players, but Wilson also made certain to work with players individually. For the veterans like Troy Loney, coming in from successful franchises, Wilson stressed the opportunity to be a part of creating something new, and the added leadership role they could play on an inexperienced team.

For the players who were about to see their ice time go up

significantly, Wilson worked on building their confidence from the first day of training camp. Wilson projected Bob Corkum as his top defensive centerman, the man who would shadow with the league's best players all season long. He'd be receiving three times as much ice time as he'd gotten in Buffalo and facing stars like Gretzky, Messier, and Yzerman every night. Wilson reminded him of that task every day. When he'd catch Corkum along the boards during practice, he'd remind him that he'd be out on the ice whenever Yzerman was on during the home opener with Detroit. For Corkum, who never knew when he'd be on the ice next in Buffalo, the challenge relaxed him, defining a clear, expanded role that he believed he could perform.

For the week of training camp before the first pre-season game, the players worked their tails off and the confidence in the locker room began to grow. The veterans in the locker room resembled Crash Davis, the minor-league catcher played by Kevin Costner in *Bull Durham*. It's not that they needed to find love with Susan Sarandon. No, most of the guys had happy marriages. But like Crash, they had reached a point in their careers where they understood the subtleties of the game and knew they were at the end of their rope. If they failed in Anaheim, their careers would likely end. The unspoken pressure combined with the intelligence gained through experience to shape the team's character like a kiln glazing a pot, firing an unbreakable work ethic.

When he saw what his teammates were willing to give on the ice, Stu Grimson believed that this team would be better than the experts predicted. Character could make the difference on some nights during an eighty-four game season. They'd catch teams flat and frustrate them. Everybody knew they had the goaltending to stay in a lot of games.

Ferreira, who knew the roster was stronger than he'd had in San Jose, expected to win 25 games. Wilson, who believed 18 wins would constitute a success, took comfort in how well his players were learning the system but knew that he had nowhere near the amount of talent he'd had as an assistant in Vancouver. He didn't see anyone in the locker room in the same class of offensive threat as Pavel Bure or, for that matter, Trevor Linden, Geoff Courtnall, or Cliff Ronning. They'd have to scrape for every point, but every indication suggested that effort would not be an issue.

By the time the preseason opener rolled around against the Pittsburgh Penguins on September 18, the coaches were eager to see the players respond to a skilled opponent. They'd been surprised by the extent of Corkum's strength and Sacco's speed. Mark Ferner had played well in scrimmages and seemed to be a better defenseman than promised. Jarrod Skalde, however, was quickly becoming a question-mark. His puck-handling skills were undeniable and the team could use a second playmaker to support Semenov, but he disappeared on the ice for what seemed like hours at a time.

If the sports market was oversaturated in Los Angeles, you couldn't tell by the crowd of 16,673 that gathered at the Pond to watch the Ducks' trial run. The crowd was more than double the attendance at the Los Angeles Kings' first regular-season opener back in 1967. By the time they took the ice, the Ducks had sold over twelve thousand season tickets and more than half of the eighty-four luxury boxes at about $100,000 a pop. Southern Californians wanted hockey. Wayne Gretzky's arrival had deepened the initial interest, and now the demand was so great that fans were willing to spend $2,000 for a pair of season tickets to watch a team that promised to score rarely and lose often.

The crowd that came for the first game saw smart passes, quick shots, and dynamic moves—unfortunately, all provided by the Penguins. Martin Straka scored a hat trick for Pittsburgh as they cruised to an easy win. The Duck enforcers, Ewen, Grimson and Robin Bawa, played like they'd been kept in a cage the prior week. Training camp meant hockey without fighting and a clash with new Penguin Marty McSorley was like throwing meat to hungry lions. Ewen fought McSorley in the first period, then Grimson and McSorley tangled in the second period. The fights were fairly even, allowing Ewen and Grimson to demonstrate their repertoire to their new teammates. Eisner, sitting in his luxury box, seemed a little displeased as the fights dragged on, but the crowd enjoyed the show, even razzing McSorley, who had been a local favorite with the Kings just a few months earlier.

For two and a half periods, the Ducks could not find the net. Finally, at 11:31 of the third period, Bobby Dollas jumped into the play, picking up a rebound off a shot by Patrick Carnback and jamming it home. Even though the game was out of reach, the crowd went nuts, rewarding Dollas as if he'd scored a game-winning overtime goal in the Stanley Cup finals. When the clock wound down on a 5-2 loss, the players found solace in the warm reception from the home fans. "It's a great crowd," said Terry Yake, who scored the Ducks' other goal. "They cheered every time we had a chance. We'll have a home-ice advantage."

The second exhibition game a few days later featured the first chance to take on their cross-town rivals, the Los Angeles Kings. Unfortunately for the fans, Barry Melrose, L.A.'s coach, had given Gretzky and Kurri the night off. For the second consecutive game, Wilson mistakenly pencilled in Vancouver as the team name on the list of uniformed skaters. His assistants ragged him mercilessly, teasing him that he wished he were back in Vancouver and that he'd never write Anaheim in. Both Melrose and Wilson wrote down the names of their brawlers for the game. Ewen and Warren Rychel squared off a minute into the game to the delight of the crowd. Five minutes later, Grimson pounded Dave Thomlinson. At 7:54 of the first period, Kelly Hrudey went down to cover the puck which had bounced off Dollas' skate and on to Joe Sacco's stick. Sacco stuffed it home, giving the Ducks' their first lead in franchise history. Later in the period, the Ducks scored again when Tim Sweeney rushed the net during a five-on-three advantage and flipped a loose puck home.

Early in the second period, the Kings pulled even on goals by Kevin Brown and Charlie Huddy. Ewen and Grimson each scrapped once more as the rivalry got off to an angry start with the teams picking up almost one hundred penalty minutes. The Ducks outshot the Kings 17-5 in the third period and Yake and Loney had great chances to win the game in the final three minutes but Hrudey was just too good. Early in overtime, Warren Rychel kept his gloves on long enough to put a tough shot on net and Pat Conacher quickly knocked home the rebound. Close, but no cigar.

A few days later, the Ducks went down to San Diego to play an intrasquad scrimmage with the San Diego Gulls, the team's top minor-league affiliate. As an independent franchise, the Gulls dominated the IHL during the '92-93 season with a lineup that featured a number of veteran minor leaguers. With the exception of Houlder, a Buffalo property, none of the Gulls had been able to crack the Duck roster and the Ducks toyed with their fowl brothers, 5-1.

The scoring explosion served the big team well when they returned to the Pond and recorded their first win over a depleted Islanders roster, 3-2, on a game-winning goal by Carnback. The Ducks then flew up the coast to Vancouver where Wilson's new squad played a solid defensive game in tying the Canucks but lost Bobby Dollas to a sprained thumb. The game reminded Wilson of the abilities of Vancouver forward Garry Valk, a tough forward with a strong shot who might be left unprotected by the Canucks in the forthcoming waiver draft. Wilson recommended to Ferreira that he acquire Valk. It was his first real input into the player acquisition process—a case where he knew more than the scouts because he'd been around Valk for years. Wilson also wanted another forward on the roster as Peter Douris was sidelined with a sprained left knee. The same day that Ferreira got Valk, the Ducks closed out the preseason with a game against the San Jose Sharks. Another former Canuck, Anatoli Semenov, scored an overtime goal to beat the Sharks, 3-2.

The Ducks looked competitive as combinations came into focus. On defense, the big kids with the big shots, Hill and Houlder worked well together, especially on the power play. The young guys would carry the offensive load for the defensemen. With Dollas out at the season's opening, the improving Ferner and steady Williams settled in as the third defense pair. The one pair with two left-handed shots would be the two veterans, Kasatonov and Ladouceur, with Kasatonov switching to play the right side.

Up front, Wilson's dreams of putting Yake and Grimson alongside Semenov as a first line dissolved as he watched Stu's stiff skating. Loney, with his mix of skill and physical tenacity, replaced Grimson on the first line . Loney could mix it up and go to the net, giving Yake and Semenov room to be creative. Van Allen would center the speedy Sacco and the powerful Ewen, hopefully creating the same kind of opportunities as the first scoring line. Corkum's checking line would feature Valk on one side and Grimson on the other. Carnback could look to King and Sweeney on his wings. For at least a little while as Wilson tinkered with the mix, Bawa and Thomson would stick around as potential power forwards who could mix it up. When Douris returned, things would change again in all likelihood. Lines would need to gel for the Ducks to have success.

After the last exhibition game, the team enjoyed a four-day break before the opening game, a time for festivities and excitement. Two days before the opener, the Anaheim Chamber of Commerce held a traditional send-off luncheon. Wilson took the opportunity before Anaheim's business and political elite to announce Loney as the team's captain with Ewen, Grimson and Ladouceur as his assistants.

The following day, the Ducks went to Disneyland, not as guests, but as conquering heroes. On a mild Thursday in October when a decent crowd had gathered at the park, something extraordinary happened. A team of heretofore anonymous hockey players received a Main Street Parade.

Led into the center of the park from Tommorowland by a coterie of cheerleaders in Duck attire and on roller skates, Disney's latest product was revealed to the Disneyland visitors. The players stood atop floats, shoulder-to-shoulder with costumed representations of Disney characters. Were these actual hockey players or just cheap fakes? Would anyone in the park know the difference?

Kids in Disneyland love parades, and a crowd gathered along Main Street. As confetti of a dozen different hues bathed the players, most of the adults seemed confused. They really had no idea whether or not they were looking at honest-to-goodness hockey players. In the NHL, teams normally have to win the Stanley Cup before they receive a parade. Without even winning a game, the Ducks had already been the honored guests at such a celebration. Now it was up to the team to justify its honors.

5

Rocking The Pond

GODUCKS
—A license plate spotted in the parking lot of the Pond.

Two days after being dumped by the Red Wings in the opener, the Ducks got a second chance against the New York Islanders. The Isles had struggled coming out of the box, scoring only two goals in losses to Calgary and Edmonton. Wilson rearranged his lineup, putting Myles O'Connor out on defense to replace David Williams, who'd posted a minus-four in the first game and at times looked like he was glued to the ice, while Jim Thomson replaced Steven King on wing, adding a little size to the mix. Ron Tugnutt would get his first chance in the nets. Also gone was the Iceman, booed out of commission by the first night crowd. "It doesn't matter whether or not I like what he did out there," said Tavares. "It's up to our fans."

As the team's first homestand continued, those fans remained a large part of the story. No matter the disappointment of the first night, a good-sized crowd of over fifteen thousand showed up to see if the Ducks could get it right. On a beautiful Sunday evening in Anaheim, the twilight sparkled off the arched green windows of the Pond as couples tailgated Orange

County style in the parking lot, setting up wine-and-cheese picnics along the Santa Ana River.

The less-frenzied atmosphere in the parking lot night lasted until supporters entered the building. The pre-game descent from the rafters of the Duck mascot energized the crowd before the puck had even been dropped. As the music of Wagner blasted from the sound system, and the Decoys waved him in like air traffic controllers, the huge, white duck on skates—soon to be named Wild Wing—dropped to the ice.

After the festivities, the fans could watch the Ducks play one of the teams their management planned to pattern the Ducks after. From 1974 to 1985, the Islanders had made the final eight in the playoffs every year, winning four straight Cups in the middle of the run. Their coach during that era, future Hall-of-Famer Al Arbour, had returned to lead the Isles to the final four just last season. First Bowman, now Arbour. Wilson had to wonder if Dick Irvin and Toe Blake would be coaching his next opponents.

No matter their performance in last year's playoffs, high-lighted by a shocking defeat of the Penguins, the '93-94 Islanders were not near the level of the Isles of Potvin, Bossy, Trottier and Smith. Once the game got started, the Ducks, who'd beaten this team in the pre-season, rediscovered their comfort zone. Playing dump-and-chase more effectively than two nights earlier, the Ducks put pressure on the Isles early. Mark Ferner caught a post with a shot from the point. Patrick Carnback carried the puck into the zone and got off a good shot. The Ducks had come out flying all over the ice, erasing the memory of the first night's effort. The Isles couldn't even get a shot on net in the first five minutes.

When Bob Corkum stripped the puck from David Volek with a wicked check and put the puck on the net, Ron Hextall, doing his best Billy Smith imitation, took a whack at Corkum and drew an unsportsmanlike penalty at 6:29. During the next shift, Troy

Loney got a slashing penalty in traffic around the net to turn the action into an even four-on-four. Given a short power play, the Isles took full advantage, slicing apart the Ducks' penalty-killers with diagonal passes between the Isles' two most skilled players, center Pierre Turgeon and defenseman Vladimir Malakhov. After a quick game of catch, Turgeon flipped the puck by Tugnutt before he could get back into position. Outplaying the Ducks, the Islanders led 1-0.

The Ducks continued to bring the action to the Isles, and exactly at the midpoint of the period, referee Don Koharski hit Ferraro with a charging penalty. The Ducks peppered the net, but Hextall turned aside each effort as the game got more physical. Kasparaitis drilled Grimson, and Volek avenged Corkum's earlier check with an elbow to his head that left the big forward laid out on the ice for 60 seconds. A little later, Semenov moved dangerously through traffic and drew a penalty, setting up a late-period power play. Semenov scored with the man advantage, lighting the Duck's eyes.

The teams went into the locker room tied at the end of one, but the Ducks had dominated. Even so, Isles assistant coach Bob Froese was pessimistic when asked between periods about the quality of the Ducks' roster. "There's no talent out there in the league," said Froese. "I'm surprised they even got someone as good as Semenov."

If the Isles were superior, they hadn't shown it yet. Whatever Arbour said to his charges in the locker room between periods sparked them because the Ducks were a stride behind on every play. Ladouceur eventually had to tackle Turgeon in front of the net and drew a holding penalty. Turgeon made another brilliant diagonal pass but Tugnutt sprawled to stop Volek's shot and keep the game even.

Soon after the penalty ended, Terry Yake got the puck, weaved through traffic and scored as the crowd exploded with joy. The first lead in franchise history came at 7:20 of the second period. Before the fans had a chance to revel in the moment, the Islanders countered when Malakhov put the puck between a Duck defender's legs and set up Ray Ferraro on a three-on-one rush. During the rest of the period, the action slowed. On the rare occasions when an Anaheim defenseman pinched in, the Isles would counter-attack. A low-scoring tie entering the third period resembled what everyone hoped Duck hockey would look like every night.

Ladouceur took another penalty midway through the third period, but the penalty-killers did a better job of denying passes, frustrating the Islander attack. Right after the power play ended, the Isles got a few good opportunities in the Anaheim zone, culminating with McBean's blistering shot from thirty feet out that beat Tugnutt. Despite the deficit, the Ducks did not fold, but increased their attack and searched for the tying goal.

With 97 seconds left in the game, Wilson pulled Tugnutt, creating the first empty-net in Duck history. The Ducks had not even practiced this situation with the combination of players they had on the ice. Semenov won the faceoff and Sacco fired a backhander that Hextall covered up. Time out, Islanders, for Arbour to reset the defense. Semenov won another draw. They worked it around the boards until the puck was sent in front to Corkum who fired into Hextall from fifteen feet away. The puck squirted loose and Corkum dove forward into a pack of bodies, flicking the puck into the net with just 32 seconds left in regulation.

As the players celebrated and the crowd rose to its feet, Wilson urged his forwards to continue to attack, not to settle for a tie. They ended the period with a flurry but Hextall made the key save. As the clock ran down to zero, the remaining fans burst into applause.

Overtime. The Ducks had had a few defensive lapses, but they'd played well enough to deserve a tie. On the first shift, Turgeon skated around almost uncontested but Tugnutt stopped him twice. Van Allen zipped through traffic to put a shot on Hextall before Turgeon's second shift. The Isles chipped the puck loose in their own zone and Steve Thomas found a darting Malakhov who carried the puck into the Anaheim zone before feeding Turgeon, who buried the puck and the Ducks at 2:43 of overtime.

Close could be no consolation on this night, yet Wilson looked ten times better than he did after the first game. "We were more relaxed, we really controlled the play and it showed in our performance," Wilson told reporters in the hallway outside the locker room. He could relax a little, too. The team had played well and worked their tails off to even the game late. Tavares and Eisner made their way through a locker room full of disappointed players.

Tugnutt spoke slowly, his chin dipping at times as if he hadn't shaken off the loss yet. "After tying the game late, losing in overtime is a letdown. It kind of sucks, to be honest. I should have had the last shot. I thought I had it. I saw the puck but it made its way through." A few lockers over, Terry Yake refused to be depressed. "We were more disciplined," said Yake. "We made a big step forward and our games are going to continue to improve."

Three nights later, the Ducks met the Oilers at the Pond with a chance to fulfill Yake's prophecy. The Oilers, another of the franchises the Ducks hoped to pattern themselves after, were no more than a shadow of the dynasty of the mid-80s. Gone were Gretzky, Messier, Anderson, Coffey, Fuhr and Lowe. The new heroes were Arnott, Manson, Ranford and Weight. Edmonton owner Peter Pocklington had gone from one of the most loved men in Alberta to perhaps the most despised man in all of Canada. Pocklington had dismantled one of hockey's greatest teams to fatten his wallet, an act of greed that proved ego and corruption lie on both sides of the border.

The Ducks had two ex-Oilers playing this evening: Tugnutt,

who'd alternated with Bill Ranford, his opponent tonight, and Van Allen, who'd been part of a lost generation in Edmonton. Not good enough as a teenager to crack the lineup of the Gretzky-Messier Oilers, Van Allen suddenly found himself too old for the cost-saving youth movement imposed by Pocklington. With Ranford making key saves and Weight scoring four goals in the first three games, the Oilers had won two of their first three, including a home win over the Isles. Maybe the new version of the Oilers would be ready sooner than people expected.

For the Ducks, tonight was the big chance, with the Flames and Bruins yet to come on the homestand. Wilson put King back in for Thomson, hoping to get more offense. The Oilers already had four players with penalty minutes in double figures, compared to Anaheim's clean slate. They showed why when Ian Herbers got a quick hooking call less than a half-minute into the game, pulling down a rushing Joe Sacco. Sean Hill put the puck on Ranford and Troy Loney jammed the rebound home. Ewen and Scott Pearson mixed it up soon thereafter as the Ducks maintained the pressure throughout the period. Van Allen alone put three good shots on the net.

Late in the period, Ranford unraveled. First, at 18:12, King carried the puck through traffic into the slot and slipped it home. A minute later, O'Connor fought the puck loose along the boards and passed the puck to Sacco circling from the behind the net into the right circle. Sacco fired a shot past Ranford on his glove side at 19:31. As the clock wound down to end the first period, the shots on goal were Anaheim 16 Edmonton 8, and the scoreboard read: MIGHTY DUCKS 3–OILERS 0. A standing ovation recognized their effort.

Between periods, Oiler coach Ted Green changed goaltenders, replacing Ranford with Fred Brathwaite to try to help the team regain its footing. Initially, nothing slowed the Ducks, who continued to pound the net before Terry Yake made a beautiful play, faking a shot to get the defenseman to go down, then skating around him and centering to Billy Houlder who scored to make it 4-0.

Was this too good to be true? Maybe. Edmonton got a power-play goal two minutes later and found new intensity, outskating the Ducks for the rest of the period. Twenty minutes to go and a three-goal lead may sound like a lock, but the Ducks had not won anything yet.

When the Oilers scored just a minute and a half into the third period to cut the lead to two, everyone felt a little tighter. At 7:17, Kasatonov was whistled for high-sticking Shayne Corson in front of the Anaheim net and received a five-minute major and a game misconduct. Now the Ducks were without their top defenseman while trying to protect a lead for thirteen minutes, the first five of which would be spent a man short no matter how many times Edmonton lit the lamp. A minute and a half into the power play, the Ducks fell prey to the diagonal pass as Corson fed Zdeno Ciger, who flipped the puck into the open net. What had been a four goal lead twenty minutes earlier was now one.

The Ducks needed to stop the bleeding. First, the penalty-killers packed in their box, staying home to deny the pass and allowing only long or bad-angle shots. During the remainder of the power play, the Oilers were contained. With under eight minutes to play, the Ducks played only dump-and-chase. Everyone on the ice had their focus on the defensive end as the Ducks tallied just four shots during the period. Meanwhile, the Oilers' scoring opportunities had dwindled as well. With 1:14 to go, Edmonton pulled their goaltender. Without a go-to guy on faceoffs, the Ducks relied on Semenov, who lost key draws in the final minute. Manson and Weight had chances before the Ducks cleared the zone. Suddenly, over fifteen thousand fans rose from their seats and chanted in unison.

10, 9, 8, 7, 6, 5. The Oilers made one last rush. 4, 3, 2. A centering pass, and Sacco got his stick on it and cleared the zone.

1. Bedlam. The bench emptied, players mobbing Tugnutt, the number-one star of the game. Wilson screamed "yes" to Al Sims and broke into a huge smile.

In the hallway outside the locker room, wives and girlfriends of the players laughed out loud and whooped with joy. A little smile kept creeping across Wilson's face as he talked to the press. "You know, our team's not used to a lead like that," Wilson was saying. "Our effort remained high, but our intelligence dropped a little." After he credited Tugnutt for making the key saves at the end of the game, Wilson cut himself short, "Don't talk to me. Go talk to the players. They won it."

Tugnutt's frown of three nights earlier had disappeared. "We had a solid first period, then we sat back a little. We let them get back in. They got hungry, and we got nervous." Discussing the key save on Manson during the final scramble, Tugnutt said, "It was just a reaction. It was a prayer. I had to get up and get over to block it."

Eisner came into the locker room and shook Tugnutt's hand. "Thanks a lot," said Eisner. As always, Eisner drew a crowd of reporters, but he refused the spotlight. "It feels great. Ask these guys," he said, gesturing to the locker room full of players. "They know why and how they won." Eisner hung around the locker room long enough to secure the puck and stick for the game-winning goal from Bill Houlder before ducking out.

Meanwhile, the players talked to reporters about developing the killer instinct to keep teams down once they got a lead. Their minds, however, were drifting to the post-game celebrations that would not end until the following morning. There would be no parties, just lengthy, relaxing post-game dinners with friends, family and teammates. The heat was off. They'd accomplished something concrete. Whatever else happened, they were winners tonight. As they drifted out of the building, a light mist started to fall on Anaheim, the first rain in half a year in Southern California. All the built-up fears and anxieties washed away.

6

The Garden Party

The Rangers will end their 53-year Stanley Cup drought in 1993-94, one year after missing the playoffs.
                    —*The Hockey News Yearbook*, Fall 1993

As soon as the Ducks started to feel comfortable at home, completing the homestand with tight-checking ties against Boston and Calgary, their first road trip sent them cross-country to face the New York Rangers. The Rangers featured gifted young blueliners Brian Leetch and Sergei Zubov and veteran stars Mark Messier, Adam Graves and Mike Gartner up front. Unquestionably, the Rangers would be the most talented team the Ducks had faced since the Red Wings had blown them out on Opening Night.

A year earlier, the expansion Ottawa Senators had earned the nickname "Road Kill" by losing their first thirty-eight road games. GM Jack Ferreira, along for the trip back east, had suffered through a fourteen-game winless road streak at the beginning of his tenure as GM of the San Jose Sharks. Ferreira couldn't help but wonder if the Ducks could be as competitive as they had been during their last four games.

Beyond the test of the team's skills, the game held special significance for Disney and Eisner. Another multi-national communications giant, Paramount Communications, controlled the Rangers. For almost a decade before taking his present position at Disney, Michael Eisner had run Paramount's motion picture studio. During Eisner's tenure at Paramount, his first in films, the studio moved from last to first on the strength of hits that included *Raiders of the Lost Ark, Airplane!,* and *An Officer and a Gentleman.* Nevertheless, new owners at Paramount had grown impatient with Eisner in 1984 which set the table for his eventual installation as Chairman and CEO of Disney. Eisner's only chance to compete with Paramount had always been ambiguously measured, from profit margins to box-office grosses. But when the Ducks, Eisner's surrogates, took the ice against the Rangers, the Disney chief deeply coveted a victory.

The Ducks had already beaten the Rangers in one important contest. When McNab came aboard, Ferreira had sent him out to find the best free agent available in U.S. colleges. Undrafted college players could be signed by an NHL team, but the player immediately lost his college eligibility. McNab and Gauthier both had seen a young defenseman at Western Michigan named Scott Chartier. In fact, McNab knew him because of his former boss, Ranger GM Neil Smith. "We stole Chartier from the Rangers," admitted McNab. "Neil went to school at Western Michigan and the coaching staff begged him to let them have Chartier for another year and he backed off. We made Scott a 24-hour offer and it was his first money offer. He was smart enough to look at the Ranger roster and wonder about his chances there. Pierre got it done before the Rangers even knew what happened." Chartier was sent to San Diego to sharpen his skills with the Mighty Ducks' top farm team. He was expected to be a significant contributor in Anaheim within a year or two.

A road trip to the Northeast held special meaning for many of the Ducks' coaches and staff. Ferreira, Wilson and his assistants Tim Army and Al Sims all had grown up in New England. A full third of the roster had ties to the Northeast as well. Family

and friends came in from three or four hours away to see the
Ducks don their purple road jerseys for the first time. Most
would take another day off from work to stick around and
watch the Ducks play in New Jersey against the Devils the
following night.

For three players, the game promised something extra. Bobby
Dollas had recovered from a sprained left thumb suffered
midway through the exhibition season and would take the ice as
a Duck for the first time. For Steven King, the rusty-haired kid
with the quick shot, the contest offered the first chance to show
the Rangers that they'd been wrong in leaving him unprotected.
Stu Grimson would have an opportunity to strut his stuff in
front of new Ranger coach Mike Keenan, the coach who had
given Stu his first real chance with Chicago.

With so many requests for tickets from players and staff,
Wilson called an old friend to get a special favor. NHL VP Brian
Burke, who had worked with Wilson in Vancouver, secured a
luxury box at the Garden for Wilson's family. When the coach's
friends couldn't make it, Tim Army's parents ended up in the
box, watching their son coach for the first time in the NHL.

Army, a former assistant at Providence College, had been an
All-American center there before playing two years in the AHL
and one year in Finland. Army performed the same duties for
Wilson that Ron had for Canucks' head man Pat Quinn. Tim did
all the advance scouting, breaking down videotape of the opponent's most recent performance and putting together a detailed
scouting report, which Sims and Wilson would use to cobble
together a game plan that could counter the strengths that
impressed Army and attack the weaknesses he'd discovered.

This responsibility, in addition to all of Timmy's other duties,
ensured an endless string of 16-hour workdays during the
season. An arduous but invaluable apprenticeship for someone
who had never been around the NHL before, the tape sessions
served as a doctorate in hockey strategy, circa 1994.

The day before the Ranger game, Army watched a tape of the Rangers' game against the Caps. As he watched, Army took notes and drew up the patterns that the Rangers had displayed on their forecheck and breakout, along with their power-play and penalty-kill. The Rangers had jumped on Washington with a barrage of early goals and cruised home to an easy win.

When he finished watching, Army wrote up his standard two-page report, broken into various components of the game. During the Rangers' pre-game skate the next morning, Army filled in the Rangers' line combinations and completed the diagrams, checking to see if the coaching staff had inserted any new wrinkles. These are the highlights of the report that Army gave to Sims and Wilson about eight hours before game time:

STRENGTHS—*quick starts, excellent PP, opportunistic, work ethic up, great deal of speed and individual talent.* Army saw a Ranger team that was playing harder under Keenan than it had played under Roger Neilson during the prior season. He feared two things: falling behind early and committing too many penalties.

WEAKNESSES—*could get caught up ice, play a 1-on-1 offensive game.* By a one-on-one game, Army meant that they liked to go on solo rushes where theywould try to beat you without passing to their teammates. Army believed that with good discipline, "we could frustrate them, angle them off into the corners." The strategy would not require passive defense, but instead a willingness to counterattack, to exploit the times when the Rangers got caught up ice. "We'll let our defenseman jump up into the play," said Army. "Sometimes a D doesn't get the puck but it forces the opponent to worry about his presence and opens another avenue to the net. It's a big advantage."

BREAKOUTS and ATTACKS—*Leetch can carry the puck.* The Rangers' young defenseman liked to handle the puck all over the ice. Another way to frustrate the Rangers would be to put a body on Leetch whenever he carried the puck.

NEUTRAL ZONE——*They'll send some stretching players in the neutral zone or switch and when a player goes long, they attempt the home-run or breakaway pass often.* The Rangers liked to weave their forwards between the blue lines. They were especially fond of a play where a forward breaks for the offensive zone, or "goes long", at the same moment a defenseman with the puck clears his own zone and fires him a pass, "attempting the home-run." When this play worked, the results were breathtakingly effective, allowing the Rangers to take full advantage of their superior speed. Sims, who was responsible for the defense, had to make certain the team's defensemen kept their heads swiveling all night long, watching for the big play.

When the players arrived at the Garden, the scouting report was posted in the locker room. A little after 6 p.m., the team gathered and Wilson presented the details of the game plan, stressing a quick start and a focus on the defensive end.

Having this detailed plan was valuable, but, in the end, the game itself would rest with the players. And the Rangers seemed to have much better players. While Loney and Sacco, with two goals each, were the only Ducks to have scored more than once, Leetch, a mere defenseman, had already recorded three for the Rangers. Wilson and Sims could make little adjustments on the bench, but in the end, Bobby Corkum would have to fight Mark Messier off the puck in the corner. Each of the Ducks would have to win or at least break even in dozens of similar small battles if the team were to stand a chance.

Army spent the game even further removed from the action than the other coaches, watching from the press box and tracking the two teams' scoring chances. In a sport that's been immune to the explosion of statistical data that surrounds football, basketball and baseball, the Ducks were trying to find a more precise way to measure the performance of their players. What the team was looking for was a better plus/minus system which would calculate opportunities created and could be used to measure both individual and team performance. Army counted any opportunities below the face-off circles, breakaways, and unpressured shots from further out as scoring chances. He classified the chances in seven categories: rushes, offensive zone plays, forecheck, neutral zone chances, faceoffs, power play, and penalty kill. While he recorded the action, Army noted key moments that he wanted to show Ron and Al between periods on video. During stoppages in play, Army talked to Sims about things he'd observed.

When the game started, the Rangers tried to carry the action to the Ducks, expecting their weaker opponent to panic under early offensive pressure. The Ranger coaches must have seen a tape of the Detroit game and were hoping for more of the same. Instead, the Rangers found a patient Duck team that relied on good early work by goalie Guy Hebert who frustrated both Mike Gartner and Tony Amonte, and then waited for their own chance to strike. At 8:25 of the period, Hill and the Rangers' Esa Tikkanen got their sticks tangled up and were sent off with matching penalties. No danger there, but twenty-five seconds later Terry Yake got caught pulling down a Ranger behind the play and was rewarded with a two-minute hooking call.

The Ducks had weathered the early storm, but now the Rangers had the first man-advantage of the game. Corkum and Valk kept their poise at the top of the Duck penalty-killing box, keeping the puck out of danger during much of the power play. What little the Rangers got, Hebert handled easily. When Yake skated out of the box eleven minutes into the game, the Ducks received a shot of adrenaline. They'd survived the game's two most serious crises: the Rangers' explosive start and their devastating power play.

Shortly after, Ranger defenseman Jay Wells got nailed with a hooking penalty at 11:56 and Wilson sent out Semenov with Loney on his left and Yake on his right to take advantage of the opportunity. Keenan sent out Messier and Tikkanen, the two old

Oilers, to kill the penalty. Semenov, the team's most gifted playmaker, sprung Yake loose for an instant with a cross-ice pass. Yake flipped the puck towards the net where Loney had camped out. Troy outmuscled the defenseman and sent the puck past Mike Richter at 12:22. 1-0, Ducks.

Four minutes later, Bobby Dollas made his first appearance on the stat sheet, tagged with interference when he tried to slow the Rangers down during a dangerous sequence. The Anaheim penalty-killers again rose to the occasion and the period ended with the Rangers picking up another minor.

Between periods, the Ducks' coaches told their players simply to maintain their intensity. For one period, they'd been able to keep to the game plan. Although the shots were close, 12-11, Ducks, the Rangers had spent three-and-a-half more minutes on the power play. Between them, Leetch and Messier had just one shot on goal. The Ducks had controlled the first period but would need more of the same during the second if they wanted to stay in control of the game.

The Rangers began the second period by shutting down the Duck power play. A few minutes later, the Ducks were given a bench penalty for too many men on the ice. Free to choose any player to serve the bench minor, Wilson sent Grimson to the box. Whatever Stu's value, it generally didn't include penalty-killing. As Stu watched, Valk, Corkum, Semenov and Loney shut down the Ranger power play again. While Grimson and Dollas had not played any special roles in the game, King, the ex-Ranger, continued to put the puck on the net, forcing Richter to make one big save after another. Midway through the period, when Billy Houlder popped the puck free in the neutral zone and found Bobby Corkum jumping up into the play, Terry Yake sped down the wing. Corkum flipped the puck to Yake, who quickly slid it by Richter at 10:21. 2-0, Ducks.

Down two goals, Keenan directed the Rangers to increase their forechecking to try and create more offensive opportunities. Of course, at the same time, this would give the Ducks more opportunities for counter-attacks. In fact, Duck pressure forced a Ranger penalty just a half-minute later. The Duck power play fizzled out when referee Richard Trottier quickly issued a make-up call, an inevitability with the home team down two goals and one man, calling Carnback for interference at 11:18. The two teams skated four-on-four for the next minute-and-a-half, and the Rangers increased the pressure, with Tikkanen getting numerous chances. The up-tempo game worked to the Rangers' advantage. Shortly after the teams were back at even strength, Leetch stole a pass at center ice and skated through traffic. Deep in the Duck zone, he drew the defensemen towards him and found Amonte alone in front. Tony slipped the puck past Hebert at 13:38. 2-1, Ducks.

After the goal, Leetch stayed on the ice for the rest of his shift, but the Ducks' line of Semenov, Yake, and Sacco took advantage of their fresh legs to slow the Ranger rush. Semenov broke up a home run pass and drove to the net. At the last possible second, he dropped a pass to Yake, who flipped the puck into an open net at 14:37. 3-1, Ducks.

The period ended uneventfully, but the Ducks had maintained control. Army looked at his scoring chance chart. The Rangers had gotten no scoring opportunities off rushes and only a couple of chances off their power play. The Ducks had outchanced the Rangers, 14-10, through two periods. Hebert had certainly played well, but the real reason for the lead was that the Ducks were outskating the Rangers.

Between periods, Army, Sims, and Wilson went through tapes of the goals and exchanged thoughts about the likely course of the third period. Two things seemed certain: the Rangers would take even more chances and Keenan would ensure they played with more fire in their eyes. A two-goal lead was nice, but the Rangers were an excellent team. The game was far from over. Anaheim couldn't afford to just run out the clock.

The Rangers came out high, but maybe a little too juiced. They were getting lots of chances but also wasting energy on their physical play. At 4:14, Nemchinov got a penalty and the Ducks tried to add to their margin but were barely able to keep the puck in the Ranger zone. To the untrained eye or even to one of the coaches caught up in the excitement of the game at ice level, things might have seemed under control, but Army saw things more clearly.

"When you're on the bench, you miss stuff. The action's so fast, and you follow your part of the team more, making sure you're getting guys on and off the ice properly," notes Army. "If somebody gets hurt, then you have to change it. Guys are asking you questions. You're trying to watch the clock and the other coach as he's making changes. It can be chaotic. There's an awful lot going on down there—so many split-second decisions that you don't get a clean overview of the game. You can see it more objectively up-top."

What Army saw was the Rangers wearing down the Ducks. Late in the power play, the Rangers kicked the puck loose and began to counter-attack. Sensing danger, Steven King held up the nearest Ranger and drew an interference call. This time, the Ranger power play was able to move the puck easily. With his legs wearing down, Sean Hill was unable to clear Messier out from in front of the net, finally tripping him. As Trottier signaled the delayed penalty, Richter skated off for an extra attacker and the Rangers kept moving the puck, denying the Ducks a chance to touch up the puck. Kovalev sent a pass cross-ice to Leetch, who was pinching in, and put the puck by a screened Hebert. The Rangers had cut the lead to one and remained on the power play for another two minutes.

Leetch and his defense partner Alex Karpovtsev continued pouring shots on net from the point, but Hebert rose to the occasion, keeping the rebounds away from the front of the net. The Ducks struggled to clear the zone, and with the game resting on Guy's shoulders, he was magnificent. Shortly after the Ducks killed the penalty, Gartner was caught in an act of frustration. The Duck power play lacked potency, and the clock continued to tick down. With Gartner's penalty winding down and only eight and a half minutes left in the game, Tony Amonte got caught high-sticking right in front of referee Trottier.

On their second power play in a row, the Ducks started to get their wind and legs back. Late in the power play, Hill left the puck for Carnback who found Yake, who slammed the puck home at 13:39. Yake's linemates mobbed him. The goal completed his first career hat trick and the first hat trick in Mighty Duck history. The taut battle had turned into a comfortable Duck lead. The Rangers continued to press, pulling Richter at 18:40, but no further scoring occurred.

In their first road game, Anaheim had beaten the mighty Rangers, 4-2. There would be no awful, agonizing wait for the breakthrough. The game plan had been well-designed and the players had performed beyond expectations. The team had also reached the .500 mark for the first time in their short history. Yake was the hero of the night, but the game had been more than a one-man show. Semenov, King and especially Hebert had played brilliantly. "I can't imagine a bigger win," said an overjoyed Wilson right after the game. Army and the rest of the New England natives had shown their friends and relatives the best of what the Mighty Ducks had to offer.

When the team showed up flat the next night in the Meadowlands and got handled by the Devils, 4-0, nobody was happy but everyone understood. The afterglow of the win over the Rangers would linger pleasantly around the team for months, a reference point during highs and lows. If they played hard, if they got a big game from Guy or Tugger and if they got a break or two, they could beat anybody. They'd believed it before, but now they knew.

7

In the Name of the Father

Break up the Mighty Ducks!
—Ron Wilson, after four games in Western Canada

By the time the Ducks started a road swing through Western Canada in mid-November, they had slipped significantly in the standings. After the win over the Rangers, the team had lost eleven of thirteen, including six one-goal losses, and were on pace for a 45-point season, better than many first-year teams but far from historic. The pressure of losing so many close games could have worn the players down. The coaching staff had the players going to school on their defensive lapses and maintaining a healthy attitude about coming to the rink.

Wilson saw no benefit in turning up the heat on his team. He wanted to instruct, not intimidate. His players would perform better if they understood their assignments and corrected their mistakes. Such lessons required on-ice repetition and video breakdowns, not brimstone and fire.

"You wake up in the morning, you still look forward to coming to the rink," said Bobby Dollas during a bad streak. "I've been on teams where you dread coming to the rink. You know you're going to get yelled at if you screw up in practice. You come in here and the coaching staff never rips us. They're always positive. I tip my hat to them. It rubs off on everybody."

"We enjoy everything we do this year," says assistant Tim Army, "even after you lose, you don't come in with a long face, bitter or still sulking. It's a new day. Learn from the game the night before and go on. The players feel comfortable. There isn't a mopiness or a gloom in the locker room. They enjoy coming to the rink every day. Coaching is people. If you can't relate to your players, then you can't have success. Ron does a marvelous job of relating to the players."

Wilson's techniques seemed a world apart from those available to his father when he had coached Detroit seventeen years earlier. The video equipment and lap-top computers in his office at home and on the road allowed a more scientific approach to coaching and game preparation. The importance of keeping an element of playfulness and a sense of joy among the players would have been foreign to the coaches of an earlier era.

Certainly, players have been playing three-on-three pickup games and games with tape balls in locker rooms since the beginning of organized hockey, but the old school required a coach to be disciplinarian and taskmaster. A tyrant like Eddie Shore who strapped his players in harnesses and yanked them off the ice when they failed to perform a task in practice was successful for decades in that earlier era.

As a boy, Wilson had watched innumerable games that his father had coached in the minors, keeping shot charts and studying the players. His father's mandate to develop talent had to fit the needs of whatever organization he was working for. Ron remembered brutal teams that his father coached in Richmond, then the Flyers' top farm team. Even in Richmond, Virginia, Larry Wilson had developed his players' non-pugilistic skills, but the coach was expected to maintain his emotional distance and Ron's dad was no different. Even older present-day coaches like Scotty Bowman gave their players no indication about how they were feeling and showed little interest in how "their boys" were. They ran the team and that was that. But not in Anaheim.

"Every day, the coaches try to talk to everybody to see how they're doing," says Army. "I think they were pretty good with us. Guys would come to us if they have something major to deal with. If coaches aren't accessible, players won't come to you." By no means were the players running the team, but any frustrations could be aired, injustices addressed and tensions released instead of being allowed to fester.

Perhaps because Wilson and his assistants provided a reliable sounding board, players didn't use the media to voice their displeasure with coaching decisions, and the coaching staff didn't single out players for the press, either. In a city where Barry Melrose ran his Kings—at least, the non-stars who lacked any leverage—in and out of the dog house, Wilson's methods created an air of calm. "It's not my nature to single anyone out," says Wilson. "I would never do that. I don't think you should. Everybody's got his own way. Barry's style worked last year for the Kings."

Wilson's heightened sensitivities could be traced partially to his quixotic playing career. The career scoring leader at Providence as a defenseman, Wilson enjoyed dual citizenship in Canada and the U.S. He'd represented the United States in a number of international competitions, playing against the brilliant Soviet teams of that era. He started in the NHL under Roger Neilson in Toronto. When Punch Imlach took over in 1980, Wilson left the Maple Leafs to go play in Switzerland because he didn't believe Imlach was allowing him to utilize his offensive skills.

He'd planned on staying in Europe only a year and then returning to join a different NHL team. But he enjoyed the European game and his family liked the lifestyle so much that it took a call from Brian Burke, his old roommate and a player agent, to drag him back to North America after five years away. For the next two seasons, Wilson played for a Swiss team before joining the North Stars for the tail end of the NHL season. His experiences enabled him to understand the difficulties facing transplanted European players while giving him insight into players who felt discouraged by a limited role. By playing in the NHL, the NCAA, a major European league and numerous international competitions, Wilson had been exposed to every style of hockey being played on the planet. As a coach's son, he'd watched closely. Whatever game strategies one used, team cohesiveness was a prerequisite to success. A coach had to work to keep his players happy within the team concept.

Wilson's desire to solve problems directly reflected an in-house consensus. "One of the things I really like about Ron is I have yet to see him come out and criticize a player publicly," notes team president Tony Tavares. "Lots of coaches get frustrated and make that mistake. Even if you don't like someone, when you run that player down in the newspapers, you tie your general manager's hands. Everybody knows who's in the doghouse. Ron never does that. He keeps his feelings well-camouflaged. We have internal discussions about who he's happy with and who he's not and where he thinks he needs help and where he doesn't."

Even as the team slumped, the players never panicked because the coaching staff never showed any signs of distress. "We have a bunch of guys who were third or fourth line," says Bobby Dollas. "You can't fault a team that gives its best. With the talent in this league, sometimes it's not good enough. I think Ron knows that. That's why it's been a really relaxed atmosphere around here. We lose a couple of games in a row, nobody's freaking out, nobody's losing it. Everybody's pretty confident we'll turn it around."

That confidence was essential as the team went on the road to try to break out of the slump. Road trips in the NHL often create the territory for turning points, whether positive or negative. On the road, the members of the team are away from family and friends and together with each other for long stretches of time. Work and play bring together teammates who either bond or fragment apart as on-ice performances trigger off-ice behavior.

The first game in Vancouver set the tone for the whole trip. Five days earlier, the Ducks had lost defenseman Mark Ferner and captain Troy Loney to serious injuries. Orthroscopic surgery on his right knee would sideline Loney for five weeks. Despite a chronic sore shoulder, Steven King went on the trip to replace Loney. Ferner was replaced by David Williams who was recalled from San Diego where he'd been playing exceptionally well.

In their second chance to play their former Canuck team, Semenov and Valk hoped to repeat the excellent performances of their first encounter a week earlier. And they did. Todd Ewen scored before the Vancover fans had reached their seats and Semenov followed. Goals by Geoff Courtnall and Cliff Ronning kept the Canucks close midway through the game. Consecutive shifts by Douris, Semenov and Valk late in the period produced goals by Peter and Garry to put the game out of reach at 5-2. The line had scored thirteen goals in the past nine games.

Seven seconds after Valk's goal, Grimson and Canuck brawler Shawn Antoski pounded each other for a while. At the end of two periods, the Ducks led by three despite being outshot 31-21. The third period produced more of the same. Gino Odjick drew David Williams into a fight, the Ducks and Canucks traded goals and Tugnutt made one huge save after another to preserve a 6-3 win. Pavel Bure went without a point despite putting six shots on net. To a man, the Ducks were thrilled by their ability to close the door on Vancouver in the third period. They'd checked hard and demonstrated the ability to maintain their intensity, even with a big lead.

Wilson, although happy to gain a win over his former boss Pat Quinn, modestly refused to take too much credit for his players' performance. "I always think the players win and lose the game and the coaches have a little input, but it's what the players decide they're gonna do when they step on the ice," said Wilson.

The second game of the trip would be at Edmonton, the first meeting with the Oilers since they'd beaten them in mid-October to gain the franchise's first win. Seeking to gain bragging rights over their ex-mates were Semenov, Van Allen and Tugnutt, who was playing back-to-back games for the first time since a dismal home game against New Jersey during which he'd been pulled. Van Allen, who had proved to be a surprisingly effective backchecker, scored his first goal of the season in the first period. As one ex-Oiler enjoyed a moment in the sun, Tugnutt faced a barrage of long-range shots. During his days in Quebec, Oiler defenseman Dave Manson had beaten Tugger with a shot from beyond the blue line. Tonight it seemed every Oiler wanted to crank up one slapshot from that range.

Later in the period, Ewen scored for the second game in a row and continued to stand up for his teammates by squaring off with whomever was sent after him. The Ducks never trailed as they cruised to a 4-2 victory. The first winning streak of the year began on a night that featured the prettiest goal of the year to date. Bobby Dollas jumped up into the play on a three-on-one and carried the puck in tight before giving a head-and-shoulder fake that caused Ranford to drop to his knees, then Dollas roofed it. Tugnutt made 46 saves, but many of the Oiler shots came from far away. He'd played well, but the defense had been solid. "Maybe I shouldn't say this, but that was our easiest game of the year," Wilson admitted afterwards. "I felt like we were very much in control all night."

Wilson later credited that dominance to his players. "In hockey, a coach's job is to try to keep the players motivated and interested in the games in the face of the travel and the physical grind, and to provide a general game plan—for example, one man or two men on the forecheck." Wilson smiled as he continued. "I probably shouldn't say that because you print this and they'll have it when I go in and ask for a raise. I think a good coach can make a difference in a good team. A bad coach can screw up a good team. Can a really good coach improve a bad team? By how much? Not that much. You are what the horses are. That's essentially true in any sport but more so in ours."

For coaches who are control freaks, hockey's the wrong business to get into. "A lot of people say to me, 'We watch you and you're not yelling stuff on the ice.' Now, if you've ever been on the ice, you know you don't hear a thing from the bench," Wilson explained. "The only time you hear a thing is during a stoppage of play. The only time in hockey you can run anything set is off the faceoffs. If we win, we do this. If we lose, we do that. That's black-and-white, but the rest of the game is a lot of gray. We don't call plays the way you call them in basketball. We don't dictate."

"Look at the NBA. You watch a practice. I watch [New York Knick coach Pat] Riley and they run 15 plays depending where the ball is. It's a very set offense. Coaches in those sports are pulling strings," Wilson continued. "We don't tell pitchers what to pitch or the batters which pitch to take. You have a system and then the players go on the ice. In our sport, there's more improvisation than any of the others. In football, the offensive coordinators and head coaches are calling the plays so they're directly responsible. All the players have to do is execute. But, in our sport, the players have to read a lot of situations. There's no time to communicate from the bench. You get a two-on-one and I'm not running down the sideline with my fist up telling the guys what to do. You have a basis to fall back on and a defensive system. The rest of the game's up to the players. You make some little adjustments on a night-to-night basis. In our situation, if the other team works as hard as us, 99 percent of the time they should win the game because they have more talent."

The true test for the Ducks' work ethic would come the next night in Calgary. Although it was less than two hundred miles down the road from Edmonton, the game twenty-four hours later promised to be difficult. In two previous games without rest, the Ducks had lost by a total of seven goals. The team with the second best record in hockey, the Flames, had had a day off and would not look past Anaheim after having struggled to come up with a one-goal win and a tie in their two earlier match-ups. Like the team Ferreira had helped put together a decade earlier, the current Flames boasted skill and size.

What the Ducks needed was an early goal. What they received was an interference call on Garry Valk on the first shift of the game. Hebert survived a few good shots, and the Ducks killed yet another power play. They'd killed 24 of the last 25 they'd faced. With a new lease on life, the Ducks started to challenge the Flames' breakout. Increased pressure forced a Calgary penalty. On the first shift of the power play, Semenov continued his hot streak, beating Mike Vernon. Six minutes later, the Ducks scored an unlikely goal when Kasatonov powered a slap shot by Vernon from the point. The goal itself was unremarkable, but the assists from brawlers Robin Bawa (who was replacing a flu-ridden Peter Douris) and Stu Grimson were Bawa's first in the NHL and only Stu's second of the year.

From that point on, the Ducks' offense created few scoring opportunities. The game became increasingly physical, as both teams took advantage of replacement refs filling in for the striking regulars. Van Allen suffered a cut to the face, which cost Ronnie Stern a double-minor, but when Ted Drury broke Sweeney's nose out of the view of the officials no call was made. Early in the second period, German Titov scored on a deflection. For thirty-five minutes, it was left to Guy to protect the one-goal margin.

In the third period, MacInnis, Fleury and Titov had good opportunities to score. When Valk was called for holding Gary Roberts at 18:09 and Calgary pulled Vernon fourteen seconds later, the pressure increased. Hebert made four tremendous saves down the stretch to preserve the team's third consecutive win on the road in Western Canada. Wilson was furious about the non-call on Drury; he believed the refs, replacement and regular, had already missed a number of intentional high-sticks inflicted on his players. But his disgust at the officiating did not overwhelm the joy that flowed from a win over a top opponent. The Ducks had gone from four wins in nineteen games to playoff contention in four quick nights. Only Winnipeg stood between the Ducks and an unblemished road trip.

Back in Anaheim, Ferreira credited the coaching staff. "Right from the beginning, the players bought into their system," said Ferreira. "They've never allowed the players to get down. They're as prepared for every game as any team that I've been involved with. Ron's been very consistent, very upbeat and the team has always been prepared."

A key to that preparation had been the work the team did between games. Wilson ran the bulk of the practices, delegating to Sims control of the defensemen and having Army jump in where either man needed help. "The practice schedule's ready before we go on the ice. There's no wasted time. We're there to troubleshoot," explains Army. "You may take a guy to the side and talk to him about the last game. You try to get involved with all the guys but after practice you'd always do some one-on-one stuff. In hockey, you can work with mechanical things on guys but they're subtle. It's more about aggressiveness, reactions, more those types of errors, like how quick the release is. You can work on technical things, but it's not like a hitter in baseball. You won't have those types of flaws in a hockey player. They don't get into a rut like that."

With the Ducks flying high, Wilson canceled practice during

the day off before the Winnipeg game. By giving his players a day away from the ice, it allowed them to share their positive feelings for each other away from the ice, talking over meals, going to movies and bars. Friendships would be cemented at the best time possible. That same day, Winnipeg coach John Paddock held the longest practice of the season, trying anything to snap an awful slump.

The Ducks suddenly had a bandwagon to climb aboard. Eisner, who had to take a business trip to the East Coast, set up his charter to stop in Manitoba so he could see his hot team. The Ducks had not faced the Jets yet, but Winnipeg had put together yet another underachieving team. Their offense was potent, but their defense seemed incapable of protecting any lead. Despite Hebert's brilliance in Calgary, Wilson went back to Tugnutt. The plan for the night was to take advantage of the prior day's rest to play their most aggressive game of the trip.

During the first three games, the Ducks had never trailed. Thomas Steen took care of that at 14:54 of the first period on a goal set up by Teemu Selanne. The deficit caused no panic in the Ducks who countered the wide-open style favored by the Jets with aggressive checking all over the ice. The discipline paid off in the second period when Van Allen won a faceoff back to Billy Houlder at the point. Houlder scored his fifth goal of the year by firing into the crowd of bodies in front of Essensa. Early in the third period, Douris and Semenov worked the puck free deep in the Jet zone. Essensa tried to put the puck out of danger. Instead, it ended up on Houlder's stick and Billy tallied his second goal of the night. Late in the game, the Jets pulled Essensa and Darrin Shannon had a great scoring opportunity. Tugnutt shut him down, and the Ducks held on to sweep the trip through Western Canada. "It's unbelievable," marveled Wilson. "When things are going well, the team starts running itself."

Wilson's too modest. During these four games, the team found itself because each of the players continued to believe they could compete despite getting beat night after night the previous month. Wilson's confidence kept up the players' self-assurance. Guy and Tugger had been no less than brick walls. The goalies had saved 152 of 159 shots for an amazing .956 save percentage during the trip. Wilson's first line of Semenov, Valk and Douris had been involved in more than half of the team's goals. At Wilson's urging, even the defensemen were getting into the offensive act. Ladouceur, Hill, Dollas, Kasatonov and Houlder scored, Houlder scoring twice. By playing better than anyone in the league for a week, the Ducks had climbed back into the conference race. Games with three rivals in the next week would tell more about that picture, but now Wilson rested on solid ground. Nobody had ever expressed any dissatisfaction or impatience over the past month, but results created insurance. He would get a fair shot to show his NHL coaching ability, something that his father had never received.

8

The Great Neighbor

I brought a team here because half a million Canadians live in Southern California. Now I know why they left Canada. They hate hockey.
                    —Jack Kent Cooke, original owner, LA Kings

After too many years of staring that reality in the face, Jack Kent Cooke sold his team to Jerry Buss, who later sold it to Bruce McNall. Then the man who'd made a piece of his fortune by smuggling antiquities out of the Old World in his shoes stole a national treasure with everyone watching. The story of the deterioration of the relationship between Wayne Gretzky, the greatest player hockey's ever seen, and Peter Pocklington, the man who owned his labors, has been told so many different ways that finding the truth no longer seems possible. No matter, McNall stepped into the breach and courted Gretzky in the summer of 1988 like a college basketball coach trying to convince the next Michael Jordan that his program was the best. McNall was willing to pay any price for Gretzky because he believed the Great One would increase the value of his franchise exponentially. A happy Wayne, that is.

Unhappy with Pocklington's willingness to move him, Gretzky was easily wooed by McNall's exuberance. The important part of the deal had been done. The other pieces—compensation, for instance—were mere formalities. McNall sent Pocklington three first-round picks, Jimmy Carson, Martin Gelinas and $15 million in exchange for Gretz, Mike Krushelnyski and Marty McSorley. Though the Oilers won another Cup and Wayne has yet to bring a title to Los Angeles, the deal was a bargain. Wayne's arrival sparked the interest of non-fans. Hockey took off in Southern California, a key market in the potential TV audience that the NHL wanted so desperately. Four years after Greztky came to town, the success of the Kings and the personal relationship between McNall and Eisner made another area team possible.

Overcoming a herniated thoracic disc that cost him half the regular season, Gretzky had led the Kings into the spring '93 Stanley Cup finals for the first time in club history. Rookie coach Barry Melrose was given a lot of credit for the head games he worked on his players as they battled their way through series with Calgary, Vancouver and Toronto. When they came up short against Montreal, assisted by the curve in McSorley's stick, one look at the roster made it clear that most of their key players might not have the wheels for more playoff runs. Gretz, Jari Kurri, Kelly Hrudey, Charlie Huddy and Dave Taylor had been in the league since the days of Rocket Richard, or so it seemed.

Despite the presence of three gifted young blue-liners—Blake, Sydor and Zhitnik—the Kings' future was now. Instead of bolstering the present, the Kings took a step backward when they decided in the off-season they couldn't afford to keep free-agent Marty McSorley. They started out well enough at home, opening 4-1-1 while scoring six goals a night. But once they hit the road, the team went into free fall, able to win only 2 of its first 13 on the road. Tim Army, for one, believed the Kings had failed to replace McSorley. "Rychel's a game kid, but he's not Stu or Todd or Marty McSorley," Army believed. "That hurt the Kings. When they went on the road, teams took liberties with their skilled players. You start losing games, it begins to spiral, you lose confidence. Their first two road trips they lost their confidence. They'll have to fight all year to prove themselves."

The team's offense had died, too, but Melrose's solution was to bring in more hacks to even the physical confrontations. Over the seventeen games before meeting the Ducks, Los Angeles had held their opponents under three goals only once. To win with a porous defense, the Kings needed more firepower, but they traded for Doug Houda and recalled Phil Crowe from the minors. Within a month of arriving Houda had the worst plus/minus numbers on the team. His skating and puck handling abilities were almost non-existent. He could not play the point on the power play nor be relied on to kill penalties. When he gained control of the puck in his own zone, he'd ice it at the slightest sign of pressure. Crowe was similarly one-dimensional.

The magic of McSorley had been that he provided a physical presence without detracting from the team's skill level. The Kings' roster, which had seemed rife with talent a few months earlier, now utterly lacked depth. The top half of the team had to go out every night and carry the other half. When the team failed, the work ethic of the better players was questioned. Melrose's whisking of players in and out of the dog house did nothing to restore team harmony. No help would soon be available. The Kings ended November in the midst of a six-game losing streak.

When the Ducks and Kings met for the first time at the Forum on December 2, the two teams were tied for tenth in the conference with 20 points apiece. Just like the pre-season clash that featured one fight after another, the two teams took the ice with a little extra to prove. Cross-town rivalries in sport can often be special, but in Los Angeles, that excitement had failed to develop. The Rams and Raiders only met occasionally and played in different conferences. If anything, the rivalry between the Dodgers and Angels was worse. Playing in different leagues, they'd never competed in a game that had any meaning despite over three decades in the same town. The Clippers and Lakers could have cemented a nice rivalry but the Clippers failed to become a competitive team.

The Angels, in fact, represented everything in a sports franchise that the Ducks did not want to become. In operation for thirty-three years, the Angels had reached the postseason just three times. Ironically, the Angels had competed immediately, garnering the highest winning percentage of any first-year expansion team in pro sports history. Their original roster was the first of a series of short-range plans in which their front offices repeatedly acquired famous and not-so-famous players who were past their prime.

The Ducks wanted to do a better job of long-range planning than the Angels, but, more importantly, they wanted to avoid that team's inferiority complex. Sure, the Kings had Gretzky now, but he couldn't play forever. After all, he wasn't Gordie Howe, was he?

If the struggle between Anaheim and Los Angeles was going to become the hot rivalry of the future, you wouldn't know it by the Kings' fans, many of whom showed up late for the opening stanza. The Ducks started the game chippier than normal, with Hill and Kasatonov each drawing minors in the first three minutes. Rob Shick, the referee, was well-known around the league for protecting stars. Any idiot could see who had the stars in this game. The Ducks killed the penalties off and then Crowe and Grimson got into a fight. When Rychel drew a high-sticking call and Blake got charged with roughing, the Ducks had a 69-second two-man advantage at 9:10. The Kings' penalty-killers erased the first minute before Peter Douris scored shortly after stripping the puck away from Sydor. The Ducks led, 1-0, despite taking far fewer shots through the first ten minutes.

The celebration didn't last long. Ewen and Rychel squared off and Ewen received the extra minor. Then Garry Valk got hit with a double-minor less than a minute later and Bobby Dollas followed him to the penalty box 40 seconds later. The refs had just come to terms on a new collective-bargaining agreement that ended a three-week strike. In his first game back, Shick seemed to be trying to make up for lost time by getting his whistle back in shape.

Hebert had been priceless so far but this was too much to face. Gretz hit Kurri in stride, who in turn found Robitaille open. Luc drilled the puck past Hebert at 14:00 and the game was tied. The Kings retained their two-man advantage but failed to score. Before the period had ended, Shick nailed each team with one more minor penalty. Nobody scored but the Kings continued to attack Hebert. The period ended even, with the Kings leading 18-3 in shots. Only five minutes of the first period had featured five-on-five hockey as an endless procession of Ducks and Kings wound their way in and out of the penalty box. Wilson was furious with the calls but warned his players to adjust their game between periods. If Shick was going to call it tight, they'd have to adapt.

The Ducks drew another minor early in the second period and Hebert continued to sparkle. Midway through the game, the Ducks had been outshot 26-4. Somebody needed to wake up King goalie Rick Knickle. Often, the toughest night for a goaltender occurs when he's untested for long stretches of a time before an opponent's flurry. Mid-period, the momentum shifted as the Ducks became involved offensively. Carnback put a good backhander on the net from ten feet away. Knickle, who apparently had found a way to keep his focus, gloved it. The Ducks continued to attack during two short power plays late in the period. Valk got a chance and then Houlder fired a bomb from the point but Knickle was sharp. The second period was scoreless despite pressure from both teams. The scoreboard read: KINGS 1–DUCKS 1 with shots on goal 33-10 in favor of the Kings. The crowd was tense, worried that the Kings would not be able to beat Hebert again. Between periods, the Ducks geared themselves toward an even more disciplined third period.

The Ducks came out blocking shots and forechecking more aggressively. Hebert made a couple more big saves before Gretzky held the puck behind the net long enough to draw Sean Hill's attention. Hill tried to separate Gretz from the puck, and, on the borderline call, Shick, true to form, gave Gretz the benefit of the doubt and sent Hill off. A few seconds later, Kurri had the puck thirty feet out and skated in as Kasatonov continued to back away before the Finn drilled a shot that went in over Hebert's shoulder. 2-1, Kings.

The Ducks then got a power play of their own. Van Allen appeared to score during a pileup in front, but the goal was waved off because Steven King had hit the puck above his waist. Though a good call, it inspired the Ducks to increase their forechecking to get even. The play became more end-to-end. When Robitaille dug a puck out of the corner and slipped it back to Kurri at the same spot he'd scored from earlier, Kurri went high again. With Carnback blocking his view of the play, Hebert never saw the puck. 3-1, Kings.

The Ducks had actually outplayed the Kings during this period,but the talented top half of the King roster had converted their few chances. The Kings killed two more penalties as Knickle made more big saves. Robitaille took another penalty at 18:32 and Wilson pulled Hebert. Houlder fired another big shot and Van Allen got a piece of it to cut the lead to 3-2 with a minute to go. For the last 60 seconds, the Ducks turned the heat up. Rob Blake played like a Norris winner during the last shift of the game, blocking passes and shots, poking the puck away and digging in the corners to help run out the clock. With the 3-2 victory, the Kings had broken their losing streak. Kurri, the number-one star of the game, was relieved. "If we keep working hard, it will come around," Kurri said, hoping this win was the light at the end of the tunnel. "This rivalry's good for hockey."

Melrose was relaxed, too. "It's gonna be a great rivalry for our fans. They're playing basic, Roger Neilson-style hockey. They're not that far away from being competitive." Down the hall, Wilson grimaced at questions about the calls. "The refs sucked the juice out of the rivalry," Wilson said sarcastically. "Five-on-five was a pretty even game for the ten minutes we got to play it." It hadn't been quite that bad, but Rob Shick could leave the arena knowing he'd affected the play of the game, if not its outcome.

By the time the Ducks got a chance for revenge during a Sunday afternoon game the day after Christmas, the Kings had slipped into another tailspin, losing six of eight. The Ducks, meanwhile, had won four of their last seven, even though Grimson accidentally crashed into Semenov along the boards during a contest with Tampa Bay, injuring the Russian's elbow. The team's leading scorer was expected to be out at least a month and Ferreira's concerns about a lack of depth would be fully tested.

Jarrod Skalde, the inconsistent young center called up from San Diego in the absence of Semenov, had given the team a lift by scoring the game-winner in overtime at home against St. Louis and then scoring two goals in a win at Dallas. Even more impressively, the Ducks beat an excellent Toronto team at Maple Leaf Gardens, 1-0, on the strength of Tim Sweeney's short-handed goal and Guy Hebert's shutout, both team firsts. The Ducks entered the game two points ahead of their cross-town rivals as both teams hung around the edge of playoff contention. Hebert, who'd played well the first time out against the Kings, was back in the nets. Knickle had been sent back to Phoenix and Kelly Hrudey and his trademark bandana stood tall between the pipes.

The crowd on hand in Anaheim was a lot more excited about the rivalry. Scalpers worked the parking lot as the fans gathered early. The Kings scored quickly when Pat Conacher stuffed home a nice pass from Tim Watters at 2:58. A good number of Kings fans enjoyed the moment. The Duck offense started slowly, testing Hrudey with one lone shot in the first nine minutes. The Kings' offense struggled to mount an attack because of bad transitional passes by their defensemen. The game seemed to be little more than a series of neutral-ice turnovers.

Then Corkum got a breakaway, Hrudey stoned him and the Ducks came to life. Skalde skated by Rychel who was forced to take him down. Williams, back in from San Diego to replace an ailing Mark Ferner, took a big shot. Kasatonov hit the left post and Valk missed an open net during the power play. Gretzky countered with a great pass to Donnelly who fanned on the one-timer. Sweeney fought off a body check and made a pass to Yake, who slammed home his thirteenth goal of the year at 16:03. The pace of the game continued to rise after Sydor drew a penalty. The Ducks peppered Hrudey before Hebert faced down short-handed chances for Shuchuk and Conacher. The period ended even at one. And Rob Shick, in for an encore performance, had called just two first-period penalties.

During the first half of the second period, both teams seemed to be skating through slush. Despite two King power plays and one Duck man-advantage, shots stood at just 5-2, Kings, twelve minutes into the period. Neither Hrudey nor Hebert had been tested in any significant way. A few seconds later, Douris and Shuchuk got free on breakaways at opposite ends of the rink, with both goalies rising to the challenge before the sellout crowd of 17,174. Ladouceur had done such an effective job on Gretzky that the Great One raised his stick in frustration while finshing a check late in the period. The Kings were about to lose their cool, but the bottom half of the roster chipped in. McEachern scored on an assist from Rychel just before the period ended. After two periods, the Ducks had played the Kings even but could only look up at the scoreboard to find themselves down a goal again.

The Ducks escalated their attack early in the third period. Hrudey foiled a number of excellent chances. The ultimate working-class King, Pat Conacher, scored an amazing goal off his own rebound as he was being pulled down by Ladouceur. Down two goals, the Ducks opened up their game, going non-stop from end-to-end. Hrudey stopped Ewen and then Sacco before Douris poked the puck free and fed Corkum who nailed a one-timer to cut the lead back to one. Despite unceasing pressure, the Ducks would get no closer. The two relentless centermen, Corkum and Conacher, would finish the game as the top two stars. With the workers running the tempo, the pace continued to surge as the Ducks outplayed the Kings for the rest of the period, while Donnelly, Kurri and Blake continued to do fine defensive work to preserve the one-goal lead. Even an extra attacker proved unimportant as Hrudey held on. KINGS 3–MIGHTY DUCKS 2.

Melrose was generous again after the win. "They get excellent goaltending every night and they can beat anybody." Wilson gave credit to his opponent, as well. "We outchanced them tonight. At the end of the first period, we were all over them. The difference in the end was Hrudey. They capitalized on the only three mistakes we made in defensive coverage tonight. We were competitive, although we didn't have as much enthusiasm as I would have liked."

The players in the Duck locker room were disappointed. Down the hall, Hrudey was praising the strength of Anaheim's attack and the skill of the players, but the Ducks were dissatisfied with the level of their play. The rivalry was underway now. "We've felt the rivalry from Day One," said Ewen, before escaping the locker room. The Ducks had four more chances to gain the victory everyone so desperately wanted.

9

Lords of Discipline

People say Disney's in the forefront suggesting fighting be taken out of the game. We have never raised that at a Governors meeting. Does Michael object to fighting? If he had his druthers, fighting would be out of the game, but he recognizes that many times a fight occurs because someone else has taken a liberty. Given that other teams have rough-and-tumble players, the Ducks are going to have rough-and-tumble players. We're not going to be run out of any rinks.
                                            —Tony Tavares

On Thursday January 6, 1994, the night wind howling off Lake Michigan cut deep into the bones of Chicagoans making their way from the parking lots to the sixty-five-year-old Chicago Stadium. The crowd hoped to see their beloved Hawks swamp a weak new team. They also came for blood. The second and final appearance of the Mighty Ducks at the soon-to-be-replaced Stadium insured the return of their old friend Stu Grimson, the Grim Reaper.

"The people of Chicago enjoy their hockey. It's almost a cult activity for them," says Grimson, who played for three years in Chicago before joining Anaheim. "The crowd noise at the Pond doesn't reverberate like it does in Chicago. The Stadium's a real confined area, it's smoky, it's dark, there's no sports atmosphere like it that I'm aware of. Every player, whether you're the home team or the visiting, feeds off the energy that that building generates."

The energy in the house that night would have made Jim Norris, original owner of the Stadium and long-time owner of the Blackhawks, proud. Beyond his ties to hockey, Norris had used his ownership of the Stadium, plus Boston and Madison Square Gardens and Detroit's Olympia Stadium, to corner a large chunk of professional boxing a half century earlier. Tonight's matchup promised a healthy dose of the fisticuffs that Jim and his son Jimmy had so dearly loved.

"Anytime you go into that building, you know you're going to have to go shoulder-to-shoulder with those guys," says Grimson. "Our guys rise for games like that. We can play as physical as anyone in the league. Those are the kind of games that really play to our benefit when it's brute strength against brute strength because we don't have the elite level of ability that a lot of teams in this league do."

In the Stadium tonight, the Blackhawks and Mighty Ducks had a true conflict of interest. The Ducks' tough guys, Grimson and Todd Ewen, who'd been nicknamed "the Animal" when he broke into the league in St. Louis, prepared to square off with Chicago's many physical players. Despite the presence on the roster of the two enforcers, occasionally referred to by Wilson as "Stuey and Ewey," as if they were two of Donald Duck's little nephews, the Ducks had stayed near the bottom of the League in penalty minutes.

Before the season started, Stuey and Ewey made a pact not to take any unnecessary penalties. They believed their team lacked the offensive punch to come back from any deficit created by opposition power-play goals that resulted from their excesses. This sensible agreement occurred unbeknownst to management, coaches, or even many teammates. Unspoken codes are a long-standing element of hockey tradition. In a game that demands more improvisation than any of the other major sports, players must know their roles without even being told. Ewen and Grimson had both played for better teams that could overcome cheap penalties. This NHL experience enabled them to realize they would have to demonstrate their leadership by being more selective in their physical play.

Told later about the secret agreement, Team President Tony Tavares was pleased with his players' intelligence and sensitivity. "What I like about that is that they recognize who their owners are as well. They'd be putting pressure on Disney if they were out there instigating every night. That's very considerate on their part."

Proponents of fighting looking for the long arm of Disney chief Michael Eisner, outspoken in his desire to cut down the violence in the game, in the Ducks' relatively peaceful ways would be disappointed. Eisner had not nixed the drafting of Grimson or the trade for Ewen, and their restraint on the ice was self-imposed. By contrast, the Blackhawks, continuing a tradition from the era of Grimson and Mike Peluso, tried to intimidate many teams and stood high among the league leaders in penalty minutes. If the Blackhawks could goad the Ducks into losing their composure, perhaps they could increase their significant talent advantage.

When the game started, Kasatanov took an early tripping penalty and Chicago jumped on the Ducks with a power-play goal in the first minute of play. The teams exchanged even-strength goals later in the period, but, for the most part, the first period was a quiet one: sticks remained down, checks were clean and tempers stayed cool.

Early in the second period, the mood changed when Blackhawk defenseman Neil Wilkinson scrapped with Shaun Van Allen. Mick McGeogh, the referee, gave the offenders minors for roughing, a mere slap on the wrist in the hopes that the tussling would end there. The Blackhawks gained by trading the creative and normally even-tempered Van Allen for the mediocre Wilkinson. The teams battled scoreless for a few more minutes, but the play got chippier. When Wilson sent out Patrick Carnback's line with Grimson and Ewen on the wings, Chicago coach Darryl Sutter countered with his nastiest defense pair, Wilkinson and Russell.

"When the coaches put Stu and I out on the ice together, the opponent either has to face that problem head on or let us go," says Ewen. "If they want to hit us head on, we sit a lot of time in the box." Adds assistant coach Tim Army: "Stu and Todd feel the tempo of the game and decide when it's right and when it's wrong. I would never tell anybody—and I know Ron and Al feel the same way—to go get somebody. I wouldn't want someone to tell me to do it. They know when they have to do it."

A few seconds into the shift, Russell ran Ewen and the two men squared off for a long series of blows. The fight seemed even, but the sentencing decision hurt Chicago. Ewen received a five-minute major for fighting, but Russell, perceived as responsible for the blow-up, received not only a major but also was hit with an instigation minor and a game misconduct.

Hockey is a game of transition and turnovers. Momentum can be as important as control of the puck and that momentum changes dozens of times during a game. Often, after a game, coaches will struggle to pinpoint the crucial moment in a game full of potential turning points. In many contests, according to Army, "a fight can change the momentum of the game."

Tonight was Exhibit A for Army's view. Before Ewen and Russell squared off, Chicago had dominated physically, getting better scoring opportunities and taking a 2-1 lead through the first half of the game. Twenty seconds after the fight, Tim Sweeney flipped in a power-play goal from the right circle to tie the game at two as the Ducks gained control.

A few minutes later, the game got so physical that the normally mild-mannered Sweeney was tossed for an intentional high-stick, his first major penalty in the NHL. Nevertheless, the Ducks scored twice during the ensuing five minutes. First, a slapshot by Garry Valk beat Eddie Belfour on his glove side during a four-on-four. Then hard-checking but clean Bobby Corkum beat Belfour shorthanded with a bomb from the blue line, his second goal of the night, assisted by Valk. When the second period came to a close, the Ducks had three goals on four shots and the normally devoted Blackhawk fans had turned on their All-Star netminder. Anaheim took a 4-2 lead into the dressing room thanks to the change in tempo.

Each night, Grimson and Ewen perform a clear, well-defined role. "I'm trying to create a situation of physical superiority for my team, having the physical momentum go our way," says Grimson. "When you see me out there involved in something, it's either coming to the aid of a teammate or trying to create something for my club."

They make a good salary and receive all the attendant benefits of being a player in the National Hockey League. Becoming an enforcer seems like an easy ticket to the good life, right? No, not so fast.

If you look at the teen years of superstars like Gretzky or Lemieux, the whole experience seems like a mad, happy dash to the NHL to test their world-class skills. Frenzied perhaps, but joyous nonetheless. For Stu Grimson, the transition from goal scorer early in his Junior career to enforcer proved so difficult that he went back to the University of Manitoba for two years.

"It's a role that as a seventeen and eighteen year old I struggled with. I was asked to be responsible for the physical play, the fighting. That's fine, but I was playing a very limited amount," Grimson remembers. "When you're asked to do only that, you feel one-dimensional. I was still at a point in my life where I was growing accustomed to the role. It's taken some time and some experience to be comfortable with it, if anybody can become completely comfortable with it."

Despite being drafted by the Calgary Flames, Grimson got off the straight-and-narrow path to the NHL, escaping to college where he could gain perspective. "I was just at a point where emotionally I wasn't ready to turn pro. It took a couple of years for me to step back and realize what I wanted," says Grimson, who continues to take classes in his pursuit of a degree in Economics. "Being away from something for an extended period gives you a chance to reflect and determine whether it's what you really want or not. I wouldn't be in the NHL today if I hadn't made that decision to go back to school."

"At this point, I accept the job willingly," Grimson, scoreless through the first half of the season, admits. "The best part of the game is still scoring goals. I'm always in a situation where I want to take on more playing responsibility but the physical part of my game will always be a part of what makes me an NHL player. That's one thing I do at NHL caliber so it would be foolish for me and unfair to the people who employ me to abandon that part of my game."

Ask Todd Ewen, whose six goals before the Chicago game placed him among the team's leading scorers, whether he enjoys sitting in the penalty box and giving up shifts when he could be on the ice. "Sometimes, it can get a little frustrating but I know what got me in the National Hockey League," says Ewen, "and I know what's going to keep me here. That's something I have to isolate on every time I go on the ice."

"I wish guys didn't have to fight like that. They take an awful beating. Their hands are beat up," says Army. The injuries are a price that two good guys are willing to pay to be a part of the game. Ewen's offensive skills allow the possibility that he could survive in the game if fighting were abolished; the same cannot be said for Grimson.

Away from the ice, Grimson and Ewen defy their brutish images. Ewen, a prodigious artist and devoted father who's hard at work on a children's book, often finishes games with his gifted hands so beat up and swollen that he can't even draw caricatures of his teammates. Once, at the end of a practice, Ewen and a few teammates took on Wilson and friends in a pick-up game. When Wilson scored the winning goal, Ewen play-fully wrestled his coach to the ice and then stripped Wilson's shirt from his back to the amusement of everyone involved, including a smiling Wilson.

More than a reflection of Wilson's unusually easy rapport with his players, the incident demonstrates another aspect of the enforcer's role, that of superior teammate. A scorer or a top goalie can get away with a few eccentricities. Enforcers have to fit in because GMs always believe there's another one available. Brawlers don't get picked in the first few rounds of the entry draft unless they have other abilities.

"Todd has been the backbone of the team in a lot of ways," says Tavares. "Anytime we need to get going, he figures out a way to get us going. His hands have been in unbelievably bad condition, but he still responds to the challenge. He's a great character guy."

Stuey and Ewey serve as Assistant Captains, and they're also two of the funniest men on the team. When a reporter asked a player who was suffering from chicken pox if there are any modern techniques to enable a faster cure, Stu jumped in. "Lasers," he joked. "They've got laser surgery now for chicken pox."

Later in the year, after a big road win, the club's loose but tired of waiting for Wilson, who's late for the bus because he called Ferreira in Anaheim to get players sent out to replace injured bodies. Stu tries to goad the reluctant bus driver to blow the horn to speed up Wilson. The driver won't go for it, but when Wilson finally emerges from the locker room and walks in front of the bus, Stu races up the aisle and gives the horn four quick blasts, sending Wilson almost off his feet and the players into the aisle in fits of laughter. What took you so long, Coach?

Army, who was an All-American at Providence, believes that Ewen and Grimson serve a purpose beyond their leadership role. "I think fighting protects players from the stick work. College hockey has no preventive factor so the stick work's worse. The masks have bred this. In pro hockey, if you want to run at somebody, you're probably going to get in a fight or get a stick in the mouth. Everybody that plays is willing to sacrifice their body, but not like that. Fighting creates a sense of deterrence. Gino Odjick protects Pavel Bure. He gives Bure room. It's good for the game for Pavel Bure to have room to operate."

Of course, the Cold War is over and one could argue that the Ducks have few, if any, skilled players to protect. Some analysts believe that they sought out big players to create a different kind of competitive advantage. "There aren't enough skilled players to go around. Imagine that you're an expansion GM. You don't have a lot of player talent and you've got to see who you can get," theorizes Rick Gruneau, co-author of *Hockey Night in Canada*. "You just know if you draft some big, tough guys and you play a defensive style of hockey and really go after some of the skilled players on the other teams, you're going to win a few games. Sophisticated hockey fans know that when you expand, the nature of the game changes. After an expansion, we have a lot of clutch-and-grab, big guys trying to neutralize skilled players. That creates a market for big, tough players."

Gruneau's theory seems to be confirmed both by the many Duck victories produced by frustrating a more talented team and the huge jump in penalty minutes over the course of the Expansion era. "Some expansion teams don't just lose, they get humiliated physically," says Ferreira, who should know after suffering through a terrible first season with the Sharks. "In San Jose, we got embarrassed night after night and that would take an emotional toll on your players. That's a big part of why we brought Stu and Todd in here."

Knowing your role and performing it night after night are

two entirely separate things. Ewen and Grimson are clearly among the best fighters in the NHL, but even that isn't enough. "There aren't a lot of enforcers in the league that are 40-goal scorers, but you have to be able to go out and contribute," says Grimson. "You can't be a defensive liability. If every time you're on the ice, your team's in jeopardy of being scored on, you're going to become a dinosaur in a hurry."

Centering a line with two enforcers on the wings made the transition from Sweden to the NHL even more difficult for rookie Patrick Carnback. He spent much of the year struggling with reduced ice time and wondering how he could demonstrate his offensive skills when his linemates were spending so many shifts stopping the opponent from taking liberties. "Carns is used to playing in a puck-possession game. It was difficult," says Army. "His role could change next year with Kariya and Karpov coming in. I think he's controlled his frustration pretty well. He's proven that he's more adept in a skilled situation. But, you know, there were times during the year when he was our fourth-line centerman. If you want to be on the second line, you have to play better than Corkum and Van Allen. You can't let it fester inside. You've got to earn it."

During tonight's game, Carnback had missed a number of shifts in the first two periods. By the time the teams came out for the third period, the Blackhawk fans had rediscovered their faith and were roaring in support of their team. Billy Houlder quieted the crowd when he slammed in a shot at 2:16 of the third period, putting the game out of reach at 5-2. Three seconds later, rookie winger Tony Horacek went about earning his first big-league paycheck and reawakening the bloodlust in the stands by attacking Ewen. As Chicago's finest hollered their approval, Ewen and Horacek, two big Canadians, swatted each other for a while before tiring. Horacek, the instigator, got tossed out of the game. Despite two fights, Ewen reclaimed the ice after serving his major.

For ten minutes, the game went along quietly, as Chicago actually tried to attack the net and beat goalie Ron Tugnutt. Eventually, though, they got bored with this approach and Patrick Poulin squared off with the smaller Carnback. Poulin's actions finally called Stu to action. Grimson pulled Poulin off Carnback and started pounding him before the officials jumped in. Stu received a game misconduct for being third man in, but he had performed his job and protected his linemate. The referee also ejected Poulin and Carnback, the Swede's first NHL ejection. In the next few minutes, four more players, three Blackhawks and one Duck, took penalties that ended their nights.

With less than a minute left in the game, Chicago defensemen Smith and Kucera were sucking wind as the Blackhawks tried to kill the five-on-three, but Sutter had only one defenseman left on his bench. As for Wilson, with Valk, Grimson, and Sweeney gone, he was down to one left wing, Troy Loney. When Loney needed a breather, Wilson sent Van Allen, a centerman with a left-handed shot out to the wing. Van Allen got on the ice just in time to watch Sean Hill slap home the final goal of the night, with the empty benches next to the two coaches testifying to that night's 105 minutes worth of penalties.

Since the league's inception, the number of penalty minutes per game has risen. In the twenties, thirties and forties, teams averaged about eight penalty minutes per game. In the fifties and sixties, that number increased to just over eleven minutes a game. In the earlyseventies, a nascent franchise, the Philadelphia Flyers, or "The Broad Street Bullies", pushed the penalty envelope, claiming the NHL lead for a decade with per-game averages over twenty and even thirty minutes a night. The thuggery worked to their advantage because they got away with even more cheap stuff than they were called for. They'd exploited the impossibility of refereeing this fast and violent game to become one of the NHL's major powers just a half-decade into their existence. Other teams soon copied their success, pushing the penalty minute per game average up around twenty where it leveled off during the eighties. It has remained at this level over the last few years.

Oldtimers often question the legitimacy of Gretzky's scoring records because of the increase in goals per game today, but few notice the even greater increase in penalty minutes. Scoring has increased significantly, but not by 250% like penalty minutes. Red Horner, a prolific fighter for the Maple Leafs in the Thirties, led the NHL in penalty minutes in eight straight seasons but is no longer even among the top 50 in NHL history. In seven fewer seasons, Ewen already has surpassed Horner's career mark although he's never even been close to a league-leading total.

Violence is so much of a part of the NHL game that it's hard for many insiders and fans to even imagine its absence. Those who defend and profit from the brutality are among the game's most powerful figures, including Don Cherry. Cherry's way of thinking has been challenged in recent years by two of the game's greatest players, Ken Dryden and Wayne Gretzky, who have called for immediate ejection of players who fight. That position has support from perhaps a third of the league's players, as well as NHL governors Eisner, McNall, and Harry Sinden of the Bruins.

The way the hockey world is today is not the way it's always been, no matter what the traditionalists tell you, or the way it needs to be, according to Wilson, who sees a natural substitute for the fighting. "People like one-on-one confrontations. Hockey's one-on-one confrontation is fisticuffs. So turn it into a goalie and a shooter," argues Wilson. "There's the battle right there and that's what going to be on sports highlight shows at night. The shootout that won the game, not the fight that happened in the first period. Normally, the fight's the highlight of the night. In basketball, they can show the slam dunk or the three-point shot. We don't have those things in hockey. Wouldn't it be great to see Wayne Gretzky coming in on a breakaway?"

The game highlights on TV that night did not feature Corkum's two goals and two assists, but instead the numerous brawls. In Europe, hockey—the complete game with sticks, skates, and pucks—is played without fighting. Despite Don Cherry's xenophobic attacks on what he considers the dirty stick work of the Europeans, they play the game more cleanly than their North American brethren. Many of the new powers in the NHL believe that fighting keeps their sport from expanding its U.S. audience and receiving a national network TV contract.

The popularity of cartoon violence—from Schwarzenegger to Beavis and Butthead—in American society strains the credulity of this argument. At the same time, spousal abuse and corporal punishment of children are no longer tolerated like they were just a few years ago. Mainstream American society may be inching away from the acceptance of violence, but the trend is far from overwhelming. In the world of pro hockey, a tense equilibrium has been reached on fighting. The NHL will let it go, as long as it doesn't get really ugly.

If the NHL eventually becomes serious about expansion to Europe—the next expansion will likely be to Atlanta and Houston—then the League may finally purge much of the pugilism from their sport. Such a result will necessarily mean the extinction of Grimson and many of his fellow Canadian enforcers. The game would undoubtedly be better to watch, but the locker rooms a little colder, a little less interesting places to visit after a practice or a game.

10

The Russians Are Coming

The Soviets had come so far so fast. Time was clearly on their side...If they were this good now, after our seventy-one-year headstart, how good would they be in just a few years? And what about us?
—Ken Dryden and Roy MacGregor, remembering the 1972 Canada Cup series, in *Home Game*

While the Ducks scattered to the four winds to enjoy the All-Star break holiday, Alexei Kasatonov, the team's lone representative at the festivities, flew on to New York. Kasa had certainly performed well enough in Anaheim, but, despite his relentless work ethic, he was starting to slow down as he edged toward his mid-30s. Corkum, Yake, Hebert and Bobby Dollas probably would have been better choices. Kasatonov's selection was in part a reward for a career's worth of meritorious service. By that measure, he remained head-and-shoulders above his teammates. A two-time Olympic gold medalist in 1984 and 1988, he'd been an all-star defenseman in the Soviet Union for the Red Army team for the better part of a decade.

He'd even been involved in something of a milestone confrontation for Russian players in the NHL. For years, the Russians, like other Europeans, were baited by their North American counterparts. The Canadians believed they could bully

Russians used to a game where fighting was outlawed. These incidents became a key part of the adjustment, and the strategy employed by the Russians had been exclusively to turn the other cheek. In 1991, Kasatonov had changed all that. While playing for the Devils, Kasatonov was challenged by Ron Francis of the Whalers. Francis was no heavyweight, but, nonetheless, he must have been amazed when Kasa dropped his gloves and squared off with him. The fight itself was fairly even and unmemorable, but Kasa had blazed a trail. Now kids like Darius Kasparaitis and Boris Mironov showed a willingness to scrap that was unheard of only a few years earlier. Such behavior would have clearly been unthinkable two decades before during the first Canada Cup. Team Canada took penalty after penalty while the Russians refused to respond in kind.

When Team Canada miraculously came from behind to beat the Soviets in that series, the national celebration could not stave off a period of intense self-examination. To those who had watched the series, either as fan or player, one thing seemed clear: the Soviets would rule hockey. The question was not if, but when. Whether a function of xenophobia, insecurity or both, the worry that Canadians would no longer lord over hockey was very real.

But the Soviet dominance never happened, in part because Canadians, consciously or otherwise, adopted some of the best elements of the Soviet game. The speed and creativity of the Edmonton Oiler dynasty was reminiscent not of an earlier NHL team, but instead of the Soviet national team. Two decades after '72, the newly-democratic Russians seemed stalled in their progress on ice while Canadian hockey's new synthesis had raised its game a notch.

The European influence had been positive, sparking a new, more creative approach to the game from its original practitioners. Individual brilliance found its rewards as the NHL game emerged, bloodied but resilient, from the years of Flyer dominance. But was the perceived crisis really over?

Canadian participation in the NHL has declined from 92% of the league's players in 1972 to 64% today. American-born players tripled their presence to a 17% level during that period. Many of those players were inspired to stick with the game through their teen years by the 1980 U.S. Olympic team's Miracle at Lake Placid. The total non-North American presence in the NHL had blossomed to one in every five players. The Russians have only been entering the league in significant numbers for a few years but already own eight per cent of the roster spots. This kind of statistical evidence provides fodder for Don Cherry's Canada-first tirades. Although his complaints about the nasty stick work and lack of production of the Europeans are baseless, he holds considerable sway over a large audience.

The breakdown of the former Red giant sent an outrageous amount of talent into the NHL, and the implications for the game were profound. Kasa represented the older generation, players who'd been allowed to come to the NHL once they hit their decline phase and the Central Red Army team could no longer use them in featured roles. Kasa's generation included Vyacheslav Fetisov plus the famous KLM line. Vladimir Krutov failed to stick in the NHL but Igor Larionov and Sergei Makarov rediscovered some of their old chemistry upon being reunited in San Jose. None of these players had taken a place among the league's elite, but the generation just behind them—some defectors and some sold by their Russian teams for hard currency—promised more.

The impact of the Russians was there to see at the All-Star Game in Madison Square Garden. During a second-period shift, Barry Melrose, coach of the Western Conference team, sent five former members of the Soviet Union out on the ice together. San Jose goalie Arturs Irbe was in the net, with his teammate and fellow Latvian Sandis Ozolinsh next to Kasatonov along the blue line and Pavel Bure and Sergei Fedorov up front. Brendan Shanahan, the only interloper, played on the left wing.

The game resembled hockey slightly more than other recent All-Star contests. The goals still came early and often as the East won 9-8 on a game-winning goal by Ottawa's gifted Russian rookie Alexei Yashin, his second goal of the game. For the West, Ozolinsh had performed spectacularly with two goals and an assist. An American, Ranger goalie Mike Richter, walked him with the MVP trophy for his one solid period of work.

Kasa's efforts at the All-Star game were workmanlike, fitting with his character and the failure of the Russians to develop truly brilliant offensive defensemen. For all the Kharlamovs, Makarovs, Bures and Tretiaks, Russia had produced no Orrs. Their creative players almost always played up front.

In fact, the player who most belonged in New York representing the Ducks was Kasa's fellow Russian, center Anatoli Semenov. In the Soviet Union, Semenov had been a second-level star, playing for Moscow's second-best team, Dynamo, a weak cousin to the Red Army team that won the league title every year. Semenov was to the Red Army's Makarov as a player like Mike Gartner was to Gretzky. You could see the quality in the lesser player but there was no question that he was on a lower tier.

In Anaheim, Tony had been a fan favorite from the beginning of the year after scoring a game-winning overtime goal against the Sharks in the final exhibition game. It was hard to believe Orange County residents had changed so rapidly from the days of the Cold War. Thirty-five years earlier, Khrushchev had thrown a tantrum when he'd been denied a chance to visit Disneyland because Walt Disney didn't want a communist leader in his park. Before the season began, Semenov and Kasatonov, Russian hockey players who had beaten the United States in international competitions, had received unhesitating applause while participating in parades at the park. Apparently, it's a small world after all, at least if you can produce for the home team.

Before he'd dislocated his left elbow in an unlucky collision with Grimson along the boards in early December, Tony had been the team's dominant offensive player, scoring almost a point a game. The team hoped to have Semenov back in the lineup soon after the All-Star game, but no one knew for certain when he would return. After Tony went out, the Ducks were held to three goals or less in ten of their next eleven games.

Tony's injury created a lot of difficulty for trainer Blynn DeNiro. Most hockey players, European or North American, have a high pain tolerance. "They'll play dead," asserts head scout David McNab. "Hockey players are much tougher than football players," claims DeNiro, who worked as a trainer for the Rams for four years prior to joining the Ducks. "Players in college football who get hurt receive immediate attention from eight student trainers and a number of doctors. They report their pain because they expect to receive attention. In Junior hockey, you've got one trainer and maybe an equipment guy who knows a little first aid. Guys learn to handle injuries on their own."

Unfortunately, a dislocated elbow is one of the most painful injuries an athlete can suffer. The tendonitis in the elbow remains painful for weeks after the time when it's safe to start playing again because the risk of re-injury is minimal. Despite almost fifteen years in the game, Semenov had never suffered a major injury and he became gun-shy. The tendonitis scared Semenov into believing that he was not well enough to play. The cross-cultural differences exacerbated the situation.

DeNiro patiently struggled for weeks to get Semenov to take a shot with an anti-inflammatory that would accelerate the healing process. Tony had never taken a shot before and wasn't about to start now. Eventually, DeNiro was able to get Semenov to appreciate the difference between being hurt and hurting.

When Semenov finally took the treatment, his elbow improved much more rapidly.

Insiders claim there's an unwritten rule around the NHL that teams won't have more than two Russians on the roster because of the problems they supposedly create off the ice. The belief is that Russians stay to themselves and won't integrate into the team. With the exception of Winnipeg, Canadian teams have been especially reluctant to draft Russian talent. One thing that made the young Russians attractive was their relative financial naivete. Despite being among the top players in the league in '92-93, Fedorov had made less than the league average. Given their levels of experience, Kasatonov and Semenov came cheap for the Ducks, although the time missed by Tony was no bargain.

If the Ducks were rocked by the injury to Semenov, the league was stunned by a story that broke in Montreal's *La Presse* a few weeks later that claimed that Fetisov was being targeted for extortion threats by members of the Russian mafia who had promised bodily harm against his family. The article claimed that many Russian player agents living in North America were in fact little more than small-time mafiosi. Fetisov hotly denied the charges and said that none of the forty-four Russians in the NHL were paying anything. Many other top Russians issued denials but others remained strangely quiet, including the two veteran Ducks.

One thing could not be denied. The situation in Russia was becoming increasingly dangerous. What the NHL players were facing was a product of societal deterioration. While the Communist system was far from perfect, there was a certain respect for the government that kept black market activity underground and far less violent. Ironically, many former bureaucrats for the Soviet police state had moved to new positions of power in an even more corrupt society where rampant capitalism and extensive bribery supported by cheap violence flourished in tandem.

The loss of civility in the former Soviet Union had affected the Ducks during the preseason when a civil war broke out in Moscow. Semenov and Kasatonov, along with Mikhail Shtalenkov, the veteran Russian goalie, scrambled to reach relatives who reassured them that the conflict was occurring in a limited downtown area. The phone lines burned in the other direction when the fires and then the Northridge quake hit Southern California.

Whether Semenov, Kasatonov or any of the other Russians wanted to admit their fears about the violence and extortion, NHL teams had already begun taking steps to protect themselves. When Sergei Fedorov signed a four-year, $11.7 million deal with the Red Wings, Detroit brought all of Fedorov's family out of Russia.

Despite the brilliance of young Russians like Bure, Fedorov and Mogilny, the perception among many NHL insiders was that the talent gap in Russia, along with the weekly broadcast of NHL games, had turned the Russian game meaner and taken out much of the skill. Instead of emulating the Kharlamovs, Makarovs and Bures, young Russians now patterned themselves after the Proberts, Domis and Grimsons. This trend was real. When the Central Red Army team toured the IHL during the prior winter, they lost badly almost every night. Even so, the Russian games remained much cleaner than Canadian Junior games, according to the young Russians who'd competed in both places.

The Ducks had looked into an arrangement to work with the Penguins to share ownership in the Central Red Army team, but they hesitated for a while until they could properly assess all the risks. For about a million dollars a year, the Penguins had bought some control of the Army team to facilitate their ability to find talent in the newest mother lode. In their first entry draft, the Ducks had drafted five Russians with their eleven picks and continued to believe the place held a huge amount of talent. A toehold with the Red Army team would allow the scouts to develop trustworthy contacts to provide first-hand information, the heart of any talent-seeking enterprise.

A concern in bringing Russian players into the NHL continued to be cross-cultural differences. Even a veteran like Kasatonov still encountered hurdles. When Alexei turned thirty-four years old the day after the franchise's first win, a few of the Ducks celebrated by sneaking up from behind and hitting him in the face with a whipped-cream pie. Kasa was not amused, finding the whole incident confusing and perhaps even troubling. Semenov told his teammates that his Russian buddy was a little insulted. A harmless bit of fun, perhaps, but a dangerous line had almost been crossed.

A pie in the face was a far cry from "the shave". During that initiation ritual, hockey players tie down new teammates and shave off their pubic hair in front of the collected whole. This long-time practice was far from pleasant for North Americans, but at least they knew what to expect. It had been especially horrifying for many of the early European players who thought they were being singled out for harsh treatment. Such practices were no longer common. Gretzky, among others, had used his informal power to eliminate it from locker rooms he was in. The Ducks specifically forbid their veterans from shaving new players.

While things were becoming more humane in NHL locker rooms, the same could not be said for Russia. A few weeks after the All-Star game, Alexander Mogilny accused his agent of making extortion threats against him and his family. Unhappily, nobody was surprised.

11

Doing The Right Thing

Disney's gonna do youth hockey programs. We're gonna bring hockey to the inner city. We're gonna make it affordable for kids to play. We're gonna change the complexion of the kinds of people that are allowed to play hockey. Our effect is gonna be something that the NHL never expected. Our effect is what we do for the community, not what we do for the sport.

—Michael Eisner

The early residents of Anaheim faced a brutal series of natural disasters during the community's first ten years. In the first three months of the Ducks' inaugural season, Southern Californians coped with three of their own. The fires came first. In early fall, at the end of the dry season, brush fires raged out of control from Altadena to Malibu to Laguna Hills. None of the Ducks lived in these areas, but a fire in the Anaheim Hills stopped just yards from Terry Yake's property. Some of the Ducks' Orange County fans and a few of the Kings suffered severe damage.

The floods were next. When the first rains in six months hit a short time after the fires, the subsequent flooding triggered horrific mudslides. In the never-ending struggle between humans and nature, those living too close to the edge paid the price. Fortunately, there was little loss of life, but the property damage was estimated in the hundreds of millions.

Just two months later, on January 17, the Los Angeles area was devastated by the Northridge earthquake, an awful early-morning tremor centered in the San Fernando Valley. In the worst quake in Los Angeles in decades, dozens were killed and thousands left homeless as buildings and freeways collapsed. Even some fifty miles away in Anaheim, the quake woke and scared everyone in town. A team full of players from Northern latitudes who'd been happy to play a little more golf in the dead of winter had a glimpse into the other side of California life. A lot of people seriously considered moving out of Los Angeles once and for all. It had been a nightmarish winter.

The Ducks survived the three terrible events intact. A game with Vancouver had finished just six hours before the big quake. Shortly after it hit, building inspectors at the Pond found few signs of damage. Everybody considered themselves lucky. Just down the block, the scoreboard at Anaheim Stadium fell during the quake and tore out a chunk of the left-field stands.

Communities come together most readily after natural disasters. Owning the Mighty Ducks had already reshaped Disney's relationship with Orange County. Once a source of land and labor for a Disney product designed for out-of-towners, Orange County had become a marketplace for Disney. Its citizens were the primary Mighty Ducks customers.

And, as the cliché goes, the customer is always right. Being a resident of Anaheim without working for Disney is probably a lot like being a Canadian glancing warily south of the border. If the giant, whether Disney or the United States, does something substantial, all one can do is watch. Resentments build up over time as a powerful force determines the shape of smaller, nominally independent communities. With the Ducks at the Pond, the locals suddenly became enfranchised. Disney had been involved in the community in some positive ways in the past, but now it had a new sense of connectedness. When fires raged across Southern California, the Ducks jumped into action.

Synergy for Disney means more than just employees sitting around finding ways to maximize profits through shared ventures inside the multi-billion dollar company. As the fires burned out of control for the better part of a week with floods and mudslides soon to follow, Joe Santilello, a senior vice president for corporate legal affairs for Disney in Europe, had an idea. He believed Disney should put together a celebrity hockey game to benefit the Red Cross for its volunteer efforts during the fire. Santilello passed his thoughts along to Eisner, and Michael asked Tavares to see what he could put together.

Tavares found a date, December 9, when the Kings and Ducks would both be off at home and the Pond was open. Tavares talked to his old friends with the Kings who were more than happy to get involved. The two teams would play with a few additional teammates. "Ice the Fire," as the game was called, attracted a huge, enthusiastic crowd.

The Hanson brothers of *Slapshot* fame played for both teams, or, more accurately, seemed to be a team unto themselves, a trio of comic thugs mugging players, refs and even mascots. For the celebrities—Chad Lowe and Jason Hervey, among others— fantasy was brought to life, a chance to skate with their heroes. For world-class women players like Manon Rheaume, Tony's sister Cammi Granato and her Team USA teammate Erin Whitten, the opportunity to play with the boys, even in a light comedy, was a treasured moment. Even the Eisners got into the act, with Michael driving the Zamboni between periods and his sons playing in the contest.

The NHLers skated around without their helmets and got to show off a little. The goalies tried end-to-end rushes. The defensemen pulled out their spin-o-ramas. In the end, the Ducks won the game, 9-8, a rare home victory, whether real or imaginary. The crowd had been given a great evening of entertainment. More importantly, the night raised $250,000 for the American Red Cross.

As Disney reconsidered its relationship with Orange County, the team struggled to win on home ice. By late January, they had only six wins in their first twenty-four games at the Pond. Triumphs over Dallas in November and St. Louis in December represented the only victories over teams with winning records.

Theories for the struggles at home abounded. Some players blamed the pressure of trying to please the home crowd, which made the team a little tight. Others wondered if the distractions at home—family, friends and golf—took the players' focus away from their job, causing them to come out flat many nights. Someone even wondered if the opposition was playing harder in the Pond because coaches often rewarded victorious teams with a day off to goof around in Southern California.

Whatever the problem, the Ducks had to find a way to bring their road game home. After a win over a weak Winnipeg team, the Ducks would get a more serious test. The Rangers, the best team in the NHL and headed for the home-ice advantage throughout the playoffs, were coming to the Pond seeking revenge for Anaheim's early-season win at Madison Square Garden. One advantage the Ducks occasionally benefited from at home would be catching teams the night after they'd played the Kings across town. Not only had the Rangers played at the Forum the prior evening, but the game was a wild overtime affair with both teams leaving everything on the ice in an effort to win for Messier and Gretzky, the old friends who were the respective teams' captains.

Mike Richter had beaten the Kings the prior night, but Glenn Healy got the call to square off against Hebert and the Ducks. The most animated crowd of the season was on hand to try to send the Rangers home unhappy. In the first period, solid checking, a few brilliant saves by Hebert and goals by Corkum and Sweeney helped the Ducks secure an early two-goal lead. When three fights broke out late in the period, the fans joined in, energetically chanting "Rangers Suck" as the clock wound down. The Ducks, up 2-0, had just completed their best period of hockey at the Pond all season.

In the second period, the Ducks continued to take the game to the Rangers. Only Glenn Healy's brilliance kept the Rangers within range. When Messier jammed home a rebound midway through the period to cut the lead to one, the Rangers came to life and began exchanging rushes with the Ducks. With under a minute left, Messier got loose again, outskating Ladouceur on a breakaway and flipping a backhand over Hebert's glove. The period ended with the two teams even and Wilson worried. "When we scored the first goal, I had a pretty solid feeling," Wilson said later, "but I was concerned how we would start the third after we gave up that goal to end the second."

Both teams came out flying to begin the final period. The Ducks got the first break early when Sacco ducked behind the net and set up Bobby Dollas, who easily beat a defenseless Healy. Now the Ducks worked to hold on to the slim lead. When Yake drew a double-minor at 11:44 for high-sticking Alexei Kovalev, the Duck advantage was jeopardized. Time to return to Tim Army's scouting report and attack the Ranger defensemen at the point. In over a hundred minutes of hockey, the Rangers' power play had failed to click against Anaheim. With Corkum and Hill leading the charge, the Ducks allowed just one long shot on net during the entire four minutes. The Rangers never got close after that, and the crowd counted down the final seconds in unison as Messier came up empty on one last rush.

Wilson was ecstatic. "To win against the best team in hockey at home is special for both our fans and our players. To get a win and to play well in a couple of wins since we've been home is important and sort of gets the monkey off your back. We've swept the best team in hockey. It's a special night for Stu because Mike Keenan gave him the break that he needed to get in the league, and they were doing a little trash-talking during the game."

Eisner, the former Paramount executive, wandered around the locker room with a smile on his face, shaking the hand of every player in the locker room. "That was the second-most important game of the year, after the first win over the Rangers," Eisner told Tavares.

Hebert believed the team had started to turn it around at the Pond. "We're not getting the nerves at home anymore. The fans were great, the loudest they've been this year. We're starting to settle down at home, not panicking in the third period and playing good, sound defense. Beating the Rangers is tremendous. They're so strong and have so much talent. Them playing in LA definitely helped us—we reaped the benefits of the schedule and we'll take every advantage we can get."

With the team starting to succeed at home, Eisner and Tavares were free to look for other avenues to make a contribution. Another idea came from a different arm of Disney. Disney-owned Buena Vista TV produced a TV show called "The Crusaders," a one-hour weekend news magazine show. The show had featured a story about a merchant who asked his customers to exchange their guns for the toys he sold. Guns turned in were destroyed.

In mid-February, after the show's producers contacted the team's front office, the Mighty Ducks announced a "Guns For Tickets" program. Working in tandem with the Anaheim police department, the Ducks offered two tickets to a home game for each handgun surrendered to the police at the central station on one Saturday morning. Tavares saw the program as a chance to remove handguns from the streets and homes of Orange County. That morning, 106 guns were turned in to the police, including sawed-off shotguns, rifles and handguns. In a country where there's one gun for each resident, the program was a mere step on a cross-country journey, but it was nevertheless a step in the right direction.

The Ducks rewarded those who turned in their guns with

212 tickets to upcoming games. The Ducks sold out their last twenty-five home games which ensured the scramble for extra tickets would create more work in the ticket offices. No one complained. If the only thing that stood between the Ducks and a goal was hard work, you knew the goal would be reached soon. The effort in every part of the Mighty Ducks' office from day one had been phenomenal. And now that the office had shown the ability to put together large-scale community relations projects, the time had almost come to go after the project Eisner had dreamed about.

One huge on-ice goal remained, a win over the Kings. The night after the win over the Rangers, the Ducks had gone up to the Forum to try and beat the Kings. The Ducks outskated the Kings for sixty minutes, but Hrudey was brilliant. More importantly, midway through the second period, recent call-up Don McSween was hit with a five-minute major and game misconduct for high-sticking Wayne Gretzky. The Great One convinced a linesman he'd been cut. It was a bad call that turned a tie game into a blowout as the Kings scored twice during the penalty.

After the game, Wilson was livid. "All of you should go in and ask Wayne to see the cut," Wilson told the gathered reporters. "A five-minute major for high-sticking is when you cut someone maliciously. I didn't see it. At the time, (linesman) Shane Heyer claims he did. When you watch it on the replay, it's not even a two-minute penalty. Unfortunately, it completely changed the game because we had dominated them up to that point. That's a mistake. You can't have a linesman make a call when he's not 100 percent sure. He said he saw the whole thing and I know he didn't. Wayne must have made the call himself. And they said his gum was bleeding. Give me a break. Shaun van Allen's got a ten-stitch cut over his eye from the other night, and no call. If Stu gets hit in the mouth, no call. Wayne gets hit in the mouth, and there's gonna be a call. I don't blame them for that, but at least make sure there's something there."

When the Kings and Ducks met again at the Pond a few weeks later, tempers had not cooled. Terry Yake was quoted in the papers saying that the Ducks had outplayed the Kings in five-on-five action, implicitly laying the credit for the Kings' three wins with the refs. Tony Tavares went one step further, leaving nothing to the imagination. He said that superstars get the calls in the NHL and that Gretzky got the benefit of calls none of his players would receive. He even accused the Great One of whining to get those calls. It was the only public statement Tavares regretted all year, although some of the more cynical reporters covering the team believed the incident was a deliberate attempt to add fire and interest to a new rivalry.

Whatever the motive, Wayne was well aware of Tavares' remarks when he hit the ice in Anaheim in mid-February. The game was even more significant because the two teams were tied for ninth in the conference, three points behind the surprising San Jose Sharks. The first period featured completely wide-open Kings hockey, but the Ducks were forcing the issue, outshooting the Kings 19-8. Nevertheless, Gretzky penetrated the Duck defense twice in the first twenty minutes, scoring off a no-look pass by Mike Donnelly and then returning the favor by setting up Donnelly on a two-on-one. Yake and Corkum scored late in the period to pull Anaheim even. As the period ended, the home faithful rewarded the team's efforts with a standing ovation.

In the second period, the Ducks continued to apply pressure, but failed to contain Wayne. He set up two Jari Kurri goals with passes that other players don't even dream of making. In the middle of the third period, Bobby Dollas scored to cut the lead to one, and the Ducks, if it was possible, raised their intensity. Hebert foiled a Gretzky breakaway, and the crowd started a "Beat L.A." chant. The Ducks got great chances, but Hrudey was everywhere, stopping blasts by Valk, Dollas and Douris in the final minutes. When Wilson pulled Hebert to get an extra attacker on the ice, the Kings gained control of the puck. Gretz broke loose behind the defense and flipped home the empty-netter that iced the game.

It was the seventy-ninth five point game of Wayne's career. He seemed to enjoy it more than any of the others. "I saw Mr. Tavares had a lot of kind words. I guess people never learn that those kind of things push me. I'm very surprised at Mr. Tavares' comments. They were uncalled for so they lit a fire under me. I felt that his comments were very unprofessional for a man that's supposed to be president of a hockey club. I guess if he's got nothing more to worry about than Wayne Gretzky, something's wrong. We read an awful lot all week. We can't play five-on-five against them and they're a better team than we are. I think they learned a pretty valuable lesson tonight—that you do your talking on the ice, not off the ice."

Wilson refused to blame Tavares, instead noting on-ice failures. "I think we've been unlucky against them. This time it was 49 shots and Kelly Hrudey played spectacular. We made some mistakes. Above all, our defensemen weren't very alert when Gretzky was on the ice and it cost us. Our defense's job when they see Wayne out there is to make sure he doesn't have any open ice and we were caught up the ice three times with him on the ice and it's inexcusable. Those are things we talk about before the game. Our little mental mistakes in the end cost us."

While the Ducks were still searching for a victory against the Kings on the ice, they had decided to go ahead with their primary off-ice endeavor. The Walt Disney Company established a charity called Disney GOALS, which stood for Growth Opportunities through Athletics, Learning and Service. The idea was Eisner's with support from Tavares and the team's in-house attorney Kevin Gilmore. The charity stated its mission was to "seek to create positive social alternatives, in an atmosphere of tolerance and understanding for disadvantaged children."

The Ducks set up a program to start in the summer of 1994 that would make a serious effort to try to bring hockey—both on-ice and with in-line skates—to communities where the game simply was not played. The program would be modeled after a successful effort in Harlem in New York City. On first glance, Anaheim and Harlem could not be more different, but Anaheim's underside included broken homes, dead-end jobs, and kids without hope. Disney could make a difference, even in Orange County. With no cheap tickets and no good reason to expect demand to weaken, putting something into this part of the community was far from a self-interested act.

By making this effort, Disney indirectly raised a sensitive issue for people around hockey: race. There's no question that hockey's fans remain predominantly white. As do its players: Grant Fuhr, Dale Craigwell and Fred Brathwaite are still exceptions to the rule. Despite low TV ratings, hockey programming is valued for its demographic: up-scale young white males. While not exclusively white, the crowd at the Pond reflected that league-wide reality.

What the charity needed was a jump-start in funding. In his time working for Spectacor, Tavares had been involved in a charity fund-raiser with the Flyers that allowed the fans to connect with the players. In the midst of the Guns for Tickets program, the team announced FanFair, the first of many annual fundraisers for GOALS.

A key to making this promotion run was the unique arrangement that the front office had arranged with the players where they shared in the team's memorabilia business. It was one of many ways the Ducks were made to feel welcome. Players' needs and special moments were recognized. When a goalie recorded a shutout, a Disney artist produced a caricature commemorating the night. Perhaps it sounds trivial, but the atmosphere of partnership made the Ducks willing participants in those promotional events the front office felt were important.

Wilson, his coaches and players would take extra time to greet special guests.

FanFair occurred on Sunday, March 20. A general-admission ticket got fans a chance to take photos with players, get their autographs, try to dump them in a dunk tank or beat them with a shot. The Ducks set up a casino on the club level where players would serve as dealers and run blackjack, craps and roulette tables. With the team starting to win at home, thousands of fans leapt at the chance to meet their favorite players.

Prizes included cars, uniforms, masks and a meal or a round of golf with a player. Over a quarter-million dollars were raised for GOALS, and fans and players enjoyed the day together, further cementing the bond between the team and its community. If a little self-interest colored the desire to create goodwill, so be it. The Ducks had done the right thing.

12

Guy and Tugger

Nothing is as good as it used to be, and it never was. The "golden age of sports," the golden age of anything, is the age of everyone's childhood....For me, the greatest goalies must always be Hall, Sawchuk, Plante, and Bower.
—Ken Dryden, *The Game*

Hasek, Vanbiesbrouck, Brodeur, Richter, Roy, Belfour, Irbe, Potvin and Joseph. In China, 1993 was the Year of the Monkey. In North America, it was the Year of the Goaltender. During the '92-93 season, teams had combined for an average of seven and a quarter goals per game. A year later, each game featured an average of six and a half goals a night, the lowest goals-per-game average in two decades. Scoring was down by about ten percent, a statistically and historically significant amount.

Prior expansions had often been linked to a slight increase in scoring. During the past quarter-century, scoring had risen from about five goals per game to over seven. And, with the addition of five new teams in only three years, most NHL insiders believed that scoring would rise because weaker goalies and less-experienced defensemen would be forced to play. This year, however, the trend had been reversed.

The performance of four of the five new teams accounted for much of the statistical improvement. The Ducks and the Panthers were holding opponents to three goals a game, well below even the stingy league average. In their third year, San Jose had cut their goals allowed by almost two a game, as Irbe sparkled in the nets and veteran import Jeff Norton stabilized a gifted young defense corps that included Ozolinsh, Mike Rathje, Vlastimil Kroupa and Tom Pederson. Tampa Bay's acquisition of Darren Puppa from Florida in Phase II of the expansion draft had spurred them to cut by one full goal their goals allowed per night. Only Ottawa failed to improve in this area.

The key question was why. The Ducks' solid performance in the first fifty games of the season had people around the league searching for reasons. Many credited the neutral-zone trap. Somehow, the trap became the dirtiest four-letter word anyone in the league could utter. There was nothing illegal about using this defense against breakouts, but it was seen as immoral because it was so efficient when performed effectively.

"People are a little bit insulted by the success of the first-year teams. So people used the trap as an excuse for why we were having success, but we didn't even play it," explains Army. When established teams lose to a new club with a roster full of has-beens, never-had-beens, and wouldn't-t-bes, they search for excuses. "There's a general lack of respect for us around the league," says Tavares. "There have been many nights when we've won because we've outplayed the opposition."

"It's the new fad in hockey now to play the trap. But teams have been playing it for years. It's been around forever. The Canadiens used it in the '70s when they had all their success. They limited teams to very few scoring opportunities," Army remembers. "Team Canada used it to slow down the Soviets. It's been around for two decades. This isn't a new thing established by the Anaheim Mighty Ducks and the Florida Panthers this year. But it was used in hockey circles to say 'that's the reason they're having success' instead of giving some credit where credit was earned."

The teams that played the trap consistently included its long-time practitioner Montreal and two teams coached by former Canadiens, Bob Gainey's Dallas Stars and Jacques LeMaire's New Jersey Devils. The Panthers certainly played it, but, allegations to the contrary, the Ducks didn't.

The Ducks played a "one and a half" forecheck as opposed to the trap. The differences between the two systems aren't that great. In the trap, the lead forechecker attacks the man breaking out to one side with the puck. The second forechecker locks the man awaiting a pass on that side on the half-board. The third forechecker dangles in the center of the zone, making any cross-ice pass very dangerous. With his two easiest passes denied, the man with the puck often chooses to send the puck directly into the neutral-zone. If the pass is poor, a turnover will occur and the trapping team will dump the pack back into the zone it had just left. Even if the pass is good, the two forwards will have little support and will be forced to dump-and-chase all by their lonesome, a less-than-threatening situation.

In the "one and a half," the Ducks lead forechecker also attacked the man with the puck. The difference was that the second forechecker did not seal off the man along the boards, instead waiting about halfway between that man and the center of the zone. If the lead forechecker had any success, the second forechecker would go deep into the zone, instead of passively waiting for the first pass. If anything, the Ducks were playing a little more aggressively than the trappers around the league, but no one seemed to notice.

Another explanation for the lower scores fit all the evidence available—the goalies were playing better. For all the griping about traps and clutching-and-grabbing, shots on goal around the league remained at a near-identical level to the prior season. Those teams that tracked scoring chances, admittedly a more subjective record, believed that the number of scoring chances around the league had remained constant. Scoring had decreased ten percent, and goaltending had improved by ten percent. During '92-93, goalies allowed 11.5 percent of shots to score. In the year of the goaltender, only 10.5 percent of shots ripped the nets.

As good as the league was, the Ducks' goalies were even better, as Tugnutt and Hebert allowed just over 9 percent of shots to score during the first half of the season. Outsiders felt the Ducks had an advantage over other expansion teams because the old teams could only protect one goaltender. Wilson didn't buy it. After all, each team had protected their number-one goaltender.

The Oilers wanted to keep Ranford and the Blues preferred CuJo, right? All the Ducks had were two players perceived as number-two goalies a year earlier. How much of an advantage was that? Furthermore, Ottawa and Tampa Bay were free to take goalies in Phase II of the Expansion Draft. They had access to a decent goaltender in their second year of existence.

Unfair or not, the Ducks had taken full advantage. The tandem of Hebert and Tugnutt had kept the team in a number of games in which they were outplayed, and had each won games single-handedly. From the moment he picked the two goalies, Ferreira assumed one of them would take over the number-one job. He never intended them to share the position ad infinitum. Once Guy or Tugger had established himself, then the other man would be available in the right trade.

During the first half of the season, Tugger performed magically on the road with a save percentage in the .930s and wins over the Canucks, Isles and Blackhawks. But at home he struggled, losing night after night. Hebert had started slowly, losing seven of his first ten games with a save percentage in the low .890s. By late November, Tugnutt had inched a little ahead in the competition for number one.

Goalies are free to separate themselves from the rest of the team. Guy and Tugger roomed together on the road. Tugger, a husband and new father, wore glasses away from the ice and spoke deliberately, like Ken Dryden, the game's most renowned intellectual. Guy, a bachelor with a ready laugh, controlled his answers to the media like rebounds, projecting the image of a guy whose life had been nothing but hockey. That was in fact true of Tugger, who'd gone straight from Juniors to the pros, but Guy had gone to Hamilton College in upstate New York, securing a degree in studio art. Despite their differences, the men got along well. "Ron's a good friend," explains Hebert. "Goalies always stick together, anyway."

Although he'd performed miracles on the road, Tugger's home performances left the team in a bind. Ron had been having trouble with bad bounces on the less-than-perfect home ice mix. The Ducks were still working to get the right mixture, but they could not wait for Tugnutt to come around. When the Ducks got great goaltending, they would win. With good work in the nets, they had a chance to win. Anything less and the skaters might as well hit the showers early.

For Tugger, the key home loss came against Vancouver on January 16. The Canucks won the opening face-off and Trevor Linden fired an unobstructed shot from the blue line which beat Tugger easily. The Canucks went on to get three more goals—two from Courtnall and one from Bure—before the period ended to all but put the game away. Between periods, Wilson asked Tugger what had happened on the first goal. Tugger complained about the lights not being fully up and claimed he'd never seen the shot. While the mercury vapor lights that had been darkened for the two national anthems were not fully operational at the start of the period, that was one alibi too many for Wilson, who immediately pulled Tugger and replaced him with Guy. The Ducks almost came back to salvage a tie that night.

During this time, Tugnutt and his wife Lisa celebrated the birth of their first child, a boy named Jacob. Neither goalie had started more than three games in a row, but now Tugger spent game after game on the bench. When Hebert started against the Kings late in January, that made six straight starts. After the Kings broke the game open, Tugger finally got some ice time and played at home, losing to the Flames.

Guy was back in the nets for the next game against Vancouver, a team that Wilson seemed to take extra pleasure in trying to beat. The former Canuck assistant had even posted some Mighty Ducks bumper stickers in the Canucks' offices when he had first heard he'd been named Duck head coach. The afternoon of this game, the Vancouver staff got their revenge by covering Wilson's new car with Canuck bumper stickers. Vancouver's attack, however, stopped in the parking lot as Guy shut them down in a 3-0 victory. The Ducks' first home shutout delighted Wilson.

"Guy's played well for us. The shutout's special for him. This is our best game of the year. In the last five home games, we played as well as we do on the road. Our guys finished their checks, did the job in the neutral zone and cut down on those silly mistakes. It's very special to beat my old team, especially after what they pulled. It took me half an hour to get all the Canuck bumper stickers off my car, but payback is sweet."

Hebert hadn't had that much to do because Wilson had matched lines all night with his old boss Pat Quinn. When the Russian Rocket was on the ice, so were Corkum, Valk and Douris. Their forechecking had shut down the league's most gifted scorer. Guy was grateful. "Every night, we're prepared for each team," Hebert explained. "It's not just one system for all teams. We knew exactly what we wanted to do, and the guys did a tremendous job. They never stop working out there."

Wilson hadn't made his intentions clear with respect to the goalies, but he was direct after a loss to Chicago. The Ducks' next game against the Kings was a big one because of the rivalry and the building playoff race. When asked who would start, Wilson pulled no punches. "I think Guy's played solid," Wilson told the gathered reporters. "His record is much better than Tugger's. In the big games, I think he's the guy who should be in there right now. It's as simple as that."

Strangely enough, Hebert had no idea that Wilson had changed his status. Asked if he believed he was the number-one goalie, Hebert responded, "Not at all. We don't even really speak in terms of a number one or two. Nothing's taken for granted. Ron could end up with a bunch of games. You just try to take each game as they come and play well enough to make them put you back out there. Ron's way of showing confidence is by starting me. That's a good enough vote of confidence right there."

With a clear number-one goalie, Ferreira was now free to see what he could get for his back-up goaltender. He'd seen Shtalenkov play down in San Diego, and the Russian looked ready. One team in need was Montreal. Patrick Roy, of course, remained perhaps the best goalie on the planet, but the team's backups caused GM Serge Savard a number of long nights. If, God forbid, something happened to Roy at playoff time, the Canadiens had no good options. Old friends Ferreira and Savard began to work the phone lines.

Meanwhile, Tugger got another chance between the pipes at home against his old Quebec team on February 18. No goalie had missed a revenge game, and the Ducks had won five of the six contests. On this night, both teams played a sloppy game. Late in the second period of a scoreless affair, with the Nordiques on a two-man advantage, the Ducks lost a draw in their own end and Quebec got it back to the point for a shot by Alexei Gusarov, yet another veteran of the Central Red Army team. The puck found the net, the goal light came on, and, as he cleared the puck away, Tugger looked up at the scoreboard clock. It read 0:00.5. A half-second later and the goal would have been disallowed. Those were the breaks, and, on this night, that was the only break. The third period was scoreless, and the game ended 1-0, Quebec.

"I don't think we were as sharp as we should have been for a game like this. We had seven or eight passengers on board tonight who weren't ready to play and we got taught a lesson tonight. We have to be ready, everybody has to be ready. We had three or four defensemen who were awful and a number of forwards who just didn't participate tonight. We had a bunch of guys playing the game in neutral, not contributing either way," Wilson said sharply.

Ron had played well, but he was unable to make the save that counted. "I didn't see the shot. I'd seen the beginning when he was first winding up. As the play progressed, there was more men that went to the front of the net. I found out later it was tipped. I didn't even see that. I saw it at the last second and, by then, it was too late. When you're screened like that, it's not so much guessing, it's anticipating. You go down and cover the low part of the ice. You just hope it hits you or goes wide. The ice was fine. Ice has been really good lately. The lights have been good. Everything's been great. It was a pretty even game. You take half a second out of the game, it's a 0-0 game. It's weird how it is."

What made it even weirder was that it was Tugger's last appearance in a Mighty Duck uniform. One save, and he'd have registered a shutout. Could the Ducks have traded him right after a perfect game? Nobody knew for sure, but everyone was glad they didn't have to confront the situation because the Habs were ready to make a deal. They had an abundance of forwards, including wonderful young talent in their system. Stephan Lebeau had not even turned twenty-five and had over one hundred NHL goals. A tough little centerman who was always among the league leaders in shooting percentage, Lebeau struggled to fit into the Canadiens' system where defense was all. His offensive gifts needed room on the ice to flourish. Whether the Ducks would give him that room seemed doubtful, at least in the immediate future, but Ferreira could not pass up the chance to acquire a talented young veteran like Lebeau. The front office would just have to find other talented players to put alongside Lebeau.

Ferreira and Savard finally consummated the deal as the Ducks were about to hit the ice at the St. Louis Arena on February 20 for their pre-game skate. The coaching staff had been kept abreast of the trade talk, and the players became aware something was up when they saw Mikhail Shtalenkov in the locker room dressing for practice. Mike had only appeared in two Duck games back in November, losing a late lead at Vancouver and then getting pulled after Toronto beat him three times in the first period three nights later.

Nobody explained to the players what was going on. The three goalies skated out for practice as if it were the most natural thing in the world to have an extra goalie around. Just before Tugger was to go face shots from his teammates, the coaches were ordered to pull him off the ice. They told Tugger he'd been traded. Ron was stunned.

"For the first time in a while, I was really enjoying playing," Tugnutt reflected. "I think that that had to do with the California lifestyle. It took my mind away from hockey and it kind of made me play better. I had a lot of other things going on away from hockey. In Montreal, it's hockey, hockey, hockey. In California, it's hockey and whatever follows. The only hard part of it was the shock. For the first time in my career, I didn't expect to be traded. All of a sudden I'm gone. It really caught me by surprise. I liked the LA lifestyle because I think it suited me. It's always easy to go into a game saying 'well, you're not expected to win.'"

That relaxed attitude may have been one of the factors that led to the trade, but when it happened, the players were taken aback. Outside of the Russians, no one really knew what Shtalenkov could do. Furthermore, Guy had never been a number-one in the NHL before. And the numbers showed that

Tugger had performed nearly as well as Hebert. At the time of the trade, Guy had 13-17-3 record with a .906 save percentage and a 2.80 goals allowed average. Ron was 10-15-1 with a .908 save percentage and had allowed 3.00 goals per game. Nobody thought poorly of Lebeau, but goaltending had been the strength of the team.

There were doubts and fears throughout the locker room. When Hebert had two weak games in St. Louis and Buffalo, the media heat was on for the first time. The Ducks rebounded to gain three points in Pittsburgh and Quebec to finish off the trip, but they would be under the microscope in their next game. The first home game after the trade would be Montreal's lone appearance at the Pond all season. The starting goalies would be Guy and Tugger.

That day, before the Canadien practice, Tugger talked some more about the trade. "I definitely felt myself shaking a little bit when I first saw my name on the back of the jersey. When I put it on, I had to walk to a mirror to take a look. It's gonna be fun to play against the old boys. I know when the game's over tomorrow, I'll be able to walk across the hall and say hi to a bunch of friends. Boy, is it ever different in Montreal. First day there, I did three hours of interviews. Those guys are serious, no ping-pong table. It's just hockey, hockey, hockey."

Across the hall, Lebeau was sporting a sunburn he'd picked up on the golf course the day before. (For the record, he shot 91 while playing with Yake, Dollas and trainer Blynn Deniro.) Despite having left the area where he'd been raised, Lebeau seemed to accept the trade.

"I sold my house five days after the trade. I was happy in Montreal, but it's time for me to turn the page. It was great to win a Cup for Montreal. I grew up in Montreal. I was lucky enough to play five years in my city. Of course, leaving my family was hard. Next year, I will get a satellite for them. I bought them a house just down the block from my house, but that's the way hockey is. It's gonna be strange. Everything's going so fast. I'm happy to be playing against Montreal so fast. I have nothing to prove to them. Both parties were happy with the trade. I have no hard feelings. Because of the way they play hockey, I didn't expect to stay there forever. I was not really surprised. I was expecting it because my ice time was reduced. It's a great opportunity for me. I was very pleased when Serge told me I was coming to Anaheim. Everybody loves the Mighty Ducks in Montreal, especially the kids."

"I'm very excited to get more ice time. Carbonneau and Muller are playing about 20 minutes a game. It was tough for me to get going. I just want to be a big part of the team. I like more responsibility. Ron's system is pretty similar, but I'm gonna have more freedom offensively here. The pressure is really tough in Montreal, even more for French-Canadiens who grew up in Montreal. I dealt with that for five years, but I'm not going to miss it. Maybe I'm going to have a normal life here."

In a Duck locker room rich with Swedes and Russians, Albertans and Bostonians, Lebeau was the first French-Canadian to put on the jersey of *Les Canards Méchants* (The Mean Ducks), as they were referred to by Canadiens' broadcaster Claude Quenneville. Despite the new-found trés chic pronunciation of his name, Guy Hebert, a resident of upstate New York, is about as French Canadian as Guy Lombardo.

Canadiens' head coach Jacques Demers stressed to his players to play extra hard in front of Tugger on this night. They did just that. Vinny Damphousse scored from about thirty feet out at 5:23 before the Ducks had even put a shot on Tugger. A few moments later, Tugger faced a long wrist shot by Valk which he sticked aside easily. Midway through the period, Corkum rushed the net and Douris followed the rebound to even the score. The rest of the game was all Canadiens. For the first time in a while, the fans got a little restless. Some even booed the effort of the players. One group of six had spelled out K-A-R-I-Y-A on their t-shirts and started a chant of "we want Paul" during a timeout. Late in the second period, Hebert gave up a bad-angle goal to Ed Ronan to put Anaheim two goals down. In the third period, Tugger stoned Yake, his old golfing partner, and Sacco twice. Carnback scored a late goal to make the score 5-2. With a minute and a half left in the game, Lebeau got free and skated in Tugger. At the last second, he flipped the puck to his backhand and fired it into the post. When the final seconds ticked away, the Canadiens mobbed Tugger, celebrating his first win at the Pond since December 1. Ron enjoyed the moment.

"This was one of the toughest games I've ever played," he said. "Guys were poking the puck out and we wouldn't let them do it. I'm an experienced goaltender that can handle the pressure in Montreal. If I do get any playoff action, I'll definitely be more than willing to play."

In the hallway, Wilson was far less upbeat. "Guy just wasn't very sharp tonight. I'm not overly concerned. He's gotta stop three or four of those goals, but those things happen to goaltenders. They're not perfect. We got caught up in the impatience of our fans. We weren't driving our feet wide or going to the net hard. We were too fancy. I'm just gonna throw tonight's game out. Sometimes your first game back from a long road trip is your worst game. You relax a little because you think things will come naturally to you at home. But it takes you time to adjust to the time-zone changes." Then Wilson allowed his former goalie some praise. "Ron played well. They played tighter with Tugger in there."

Hebert did not seem at all disturbed by the soft goals he'd allowed. "I think we're gonna settle down and get back to the way we were playing earlier. I try to keep an even keel, but March is a great time of the year for hockey. The last time I was a number-one goalie was three years ago in Peoria. You go through transitional periods when you feel tired and mentally burned out. I don't really think that's playing a major role for me right now. Everybody gets tired, of course. It looked like an intra-squad scrimmage to me. Tugger won out tonight, but I think he got a little lucky. I was screened on the first two goals. That's what happens. You'll drive yourself crazy if you worry about every goal you give up."

Complacency or an attempt to create a wall behind which to store a bad performance? Wilson would have to judge that as each game grew in importance. Since the trade, Hebert had played poorly in three of his four starts. He would get a few more chances, but time was running out. In the year of the goaltender, two bad weeks could cost a great goalie his job.

13

What Disney Wants

*I don't want the public to see the world they live in while they're in Disney-
land. I want them to feel they're in another world.*

—Walt Disney

When Paul Kariya skated in on Tommy Salo for a penalty shot
that would decide the Olympic gold medal in hockey for 1994,
all of Canada held its breath. With the shootout making its debut
on the world stage, no one was watching more closely than the
Ducks.

Eisner wanted a shootout in the NHL during the regular
season. "One thing Michael talks about is eliminating ties.
Shootout supporters only exist because they're looking for a
way to end ties," explains Tavares. "Is a shootout the right way
to do that? We don't know yet, but one of Michael's biggest
concerns is we are dealing with time-sensitive audiences. We're
not the Dodgers."

In other words, Disney wanted a clean result without adding
any length to the contest because they didn't believe fans would
stay through sudden-death overtime. Unlike the baseball team
up the road that expected its fans to arrive late and leave early,
the Mighty Ducks wanted their supporters' attention from the
opening faceoff to the final horn. They believed the energy of the

crowd could at times translate to the players on the ice. Those same players would hardly want to add to their already burdensome regular-season schedule with long games whose uncertain finishes would destroy travel plans.

To further their efforts to secure the shootout, Disney appealed directly to their youngest audience. The script for the sequel to the first Mighty Ducks movie, "D2", had no real ending. Brill, the writer of the first film, was no Stan Fischler. Without a great background in hockey, he struggled to come up with a conclusion that would be original yet credible. Disney directed him to settle the title game with a shootout. Kids that have seen the movie more than once still get excited at the end of the film when the Americans win after their goalie's last save.

In Lillehammer, the result had been scripted, too, at least in Kariya's head. Amazingly, Kariya had visualized himself scoring the tournament-winning goal in overtime against the Swedes. Paul played a key role as the Canadians waltzed through their draw. Sure enough, in the gold medal game the Swedes and Canadians played to a tie in regulation. Kariya had two excellent chances in the overtime that followed but he could not put the puck past Salo. Time for a little improvisation.

When he and Petr Nedved gave Canada an early two-goal lead in the shootout, it looked like the Canadians would win their first significant international tourney in decades (with the exception, of course of the numerous victories by the world-champion Canadian women's team). The Swedes, however, evened the score and sent the shootout into sudden-death. Their first shooter, Peter Forsberg, the wunderkind whose NHL rights belong to the Nordiques, scored on Canadian goaltender Corey Hirsch with a breath-taking move when he faked hard to his forehand before pulling the puck back at the last possible second and flipping it in the net.

Down a goal, the Canadians had one last chance: Kariya. Paul came in straight and fast. He tried to wrist a shot up high.

Salo knocked it away. The Swedish team swarmed the ice as Kariya turned away from the net, heart-broken. His dream had turned sour. The game had been well-played, and neither team had deserved to lose. The shootout held viewers' hearts in their throats and created a rare chance for the goalie to be a hero, but, for the losers, to be denied a gold medal this way was infinitely cruel.

What Canadians wanted after this devastating moment was an end to talk about installing the shootout in the NHL. As the NHL put together a committee to study the possible use of shootouts to settle regular-season ties, Disney would have to be patient. With other powerful opinions around the league, Disney could not simply get what it wanted.

What everyone wanted was for Kariya to heal, to rediscover his joy in the game and find a way to erase the pain. He had not been responsible for the loss by any means. But with the puck in his hands at the final moment and with the demands he placed on himself, he was devastated.

Despite the awful conclusion, Kariya did not rail against the shootout. "I think shootouts have a place in hockey. They're very exciting for the fans. I don't think there is anything more exciting than a shootout to decide a game. But the time and place has to be looked into. I don't think the final game of the Stanley Cup or the Olympics is the right place. Certainly during the regular season it might have a place in the game. I'd like it."

Beyond the shootout, Kariya and the Ducks also agreed that it would be nice to see Paul in an Anaheim uniform now that his commitment to the Canadian team was over. Just as Paul was about to return to the University of Maine, the athletic department got hit by a scandal. The hockey team had played an academically ineligible player and was going to be stripped of all its wins and put on probation for the rest of the season, eliminating it from post-season competition. Rejoining a program in free fall was the last thing Paul wanted. Maybe Don

Baizley, Kariya's agent, and Ferreira could find a way to bridge the multi-million dollar chasm between them.

The difficult negotiations between Baizley and Ferreira suggested in microcosm the tension inside Disney between becoming a top-level sports organization and spending the money required. Everyone wanted Kariya in a Duck uniform. Clearly a gifted player, Kariya's good looks, humility and intelligence would be a magnet for fans. Even his Japanese-Canadian ancestry fit perfectly with the attempts in the Mighty Ducks movies and through Disney GOALS to make hockey more inclusive in its appeal.

The problem was money. Disney wanted hockey to grow and knew they needed to promote the game's stars to increase their fan base, but there was a catch. Increased popularity created greater leverage at the negotiating table. Animated characters, no matter how popular, could not ask for a raise. If you poured money into promoting *The Lion King*, you owned those characters for life. They couldn't ask for free agency or demand a trade to Warner Brothers.

Fictional characters could do little damage to your company's goodwill. Hockey players might embarrass your organization with off-ice problems. Witness Bob Probert's struggles over the past few years. Furthermore, as a player aged, popularity would exceed productivity.

Although Ferreira didn't want to pay Lindros or Gretzky-level wages to an unproven commodity like Kariya, the front office wanted Paul around because they knew the importance of superstars in the game. "You lose a star in this game, and it affects your team dramatically. You have to have superstars," Tavares admitted. "The question is how many. That's what we're trying to analyze right now. You cannot be a great team without great players. *How many* great players you need on one team *is* questionable. Do you need to have the talent that Detroit has now, by example? Or do you look at a Montreal and say they typically win with two or three superstars and a real good supporting cast. What's the magic? What works the best? We don't know that yet."

Even players expressed skepticism about Kariya's impact. Pro hockey players have the team-before-individual concept drilled into their heads from the time they first lace up their skates. Terry Yake's reaction to the attention the negotiations received was typical. "They can do all the hemming and hawing they want. Lindros is supposed to be the best pick ever and they're not in the playoffs. One player seldom if ever will make the difference. I don't believe in the savior theory. Gretzky and Lindros aren't in the playoffs. I'm not going to say that he wouldn't help because any kind of boost from the offense would help us."

Players in other sports have reached a level of awareness where they realize that if one guy gets a good contract, then every player benefits. In a sport where Gordie Howe, the game's greatest icon, scraped by for decades, never asking for or knowing if he received the best salary on his team, players' financial attitudes remain in the Dark Ages. "It's not necessarily better if he gets more money. It won't change the salary structure," Yake claimed. "It's all based on what everybody thinks of the player. What he gets has nothing to do with the rest of our players. Do you think if he gets two million and scores forty goals and somebody else in here scores twenty goals that they will give him one million? I don't think so."

Kariya's agent was asking for about two million dollars per season, and no Duck on the present roster was making more than $650,000. Was Kariya really three times better than anyone on the team? Probably not, but a better way of looking at the deal was whether or not the Ducks could afford to sign rare talent.

By any financial measure, the season had been a wild success. The team had played to close to ninety-nine percent capacity, and Mighty Duck-wear was selling better than that of any other professional sports franchise. "From an attendance standpoint, it's far in excess of what we projected. In advertising, we've got huge upside next year. Certainly, merchandise has been far and above anyone's wildest expectations. Across the board, I'm very happy," Tavares said near the end of the season. "Are we having a good financial year? Yeah, you bet. You don't have to be a genius to figure out with one of the lowest payrolls in the league and one of the highest-grossing arenas that we're doing pretty well."

Surely, Disney could share a larger portion of its profits with the players. Eisner's friend McNall had recognized the Great One's importance to the Kings' profit-and-loss statement by making Wayne the highest-paid player in the game. Gretzky is perhaps the most generous superstar in the world of professional sports, both on and off the ice. That made a season that should have been his most glorious the most difficult he'd ever endured. During the year he was trying to break the Record—Gordie Howe's 801 goals scored—his team struggled, his wife and kids suffered through an awful earthquake with Wayne on the road in Philadelphia, and his mother-in-law was injured in an auto accident in St. Louis. Wayne somehow persevered on the ice, again leading the league in scoring.

Howe, who'd always been Gretz' hero and had become Wayne's friend, refused to ratify the forthcoming achievement, arguing that his goals in the WHA should be counted towards the all-time record. More difficult than that, some players around the league were attacking the Kings, believing that celebrating Wayne's individual achievements during team losses had caused the Kings' collapse. Accusations of selfishness had followed Wayne since his days in midget hockey, but he'd always been able to answer by pointing to the success of his team. This season, he was great, but his team wasn't. It wasn't Wayne's fault, but the losing nagged at him, making it impossible to fully enjoy his race to break the game's most cherished record.

As Wayne approached the record, the rest of the sports world yawned. Hockey remained on the periphery, and the chase drew far less attention than Henry Aaron's pursuit of Babe Ruth two decades earlier. This lack of status was what Bettman needed to change. "This is a critical time for the league," said Tavares. "Gary has the foresight and the guts to bring the NHL out of the dark ages and raise values for everyone, owners and players alike. We don't do enough to promote our superstars. That would help the game immensely."

What Tavares, Eisner and Bettman wanted to do to increase the popularity of the game was three things: increased promotion of superstars, better TV broadcasts, and expansion to other key American TV markets. Sure, the shootout and reducing violence were still on the agenda, but nobody believed tinkering with the game was as important as improving its presentation.

Bettman's model for better promotion was the NBA he'd just left. In the NHL, there was a problem in the effort to mold guys into superstars. The culture of fans, front office, and players made it very difficult. Hockey players were all supposed to be equals. This was not a one-on-one game with an in-your-face attitude like basketball. In the NBA, Magic Johnson and Larry Bird stood out because they made their teammates better while showcasing their individual brilliance. Their talents would have separated them in the NHL, too, but not their unselfishness. The culture, particularly for Canadian players, demands modesty—a requirement to always be one of the boys. Yake was right: Gretzky's Kings and Lindros' Flyers were underachieving tremendously. Accurate or not, the Ducks could look at franchises with superstars and see character flaws.

Tavares also wanted everyone to take a hard look at the way the product was being presented on television. "There's got to be some enhancements made. From a live standpoint, you can't find a sport that's much more exciting. The challenge is translating that to television, making it just as exciting. What Disney

Pierrre Gauthier, Tony Tavares and Jack Ferreira select players at the 1993 Expansion Draft in Quebec.

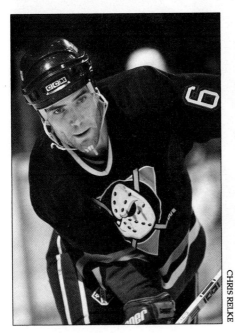

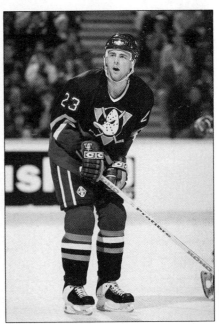

Sean Hill scored the first goal in franchise history.

Bill Houlder led Anaheim defensemen in goals and assists.

Troy Loney, a Cup winner in Pittsburgh, captained the inaugural edition of the Mighty Ducks of Anaheim.

Stu Grimson made an agreement with Todd Ewen to not take unnecessary penalties.

Around the NHL, Duck fans come out in force to cheer their team.

Bob Corkum surpassed everyone's expectations, leading the team in goals scored.

CHRIS RELKE

Todd Ewen led the team in artwork and penalty minutes.

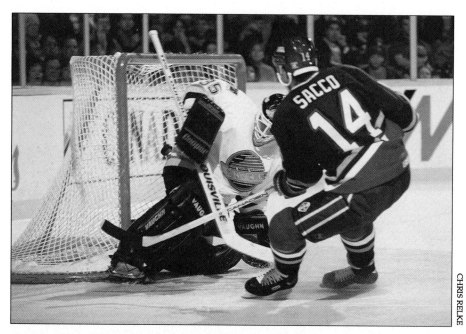

Joe Sacco's breathtaking speed freed him for breakaways throughout the season.

Terry Yake, who led Anaheim in total points, recorded the team's only hat trick in the road win over the Rangers.

Garry Valk supplied solid two-way play, finishing third in points and penalty minutes.

Veteran defenseman Alexei Kasatonov represented the Ducks at the NHL All-Star game.

CHRIS RELKE

Shutouts of Vancouver and Toronto highlighted Guy Hebert's twenty wins.

CHRIS RELKE

Don McSween scored his first NHL goal a few months shy of turning 30.

Randy Ladoucer, the steady veteran, led an outstanding defense.

Igor Larionov, with his old linemate Sergei Makarov, led the Sharks in a six-game sweep of the Ducks.

A shining moment in a dismal King season: Wayne Gretzky and Bruce McNall celebrate goal number 802.

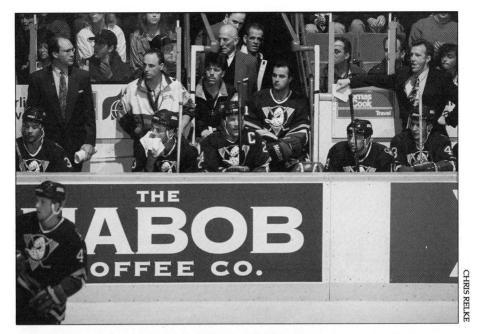

CHRIS RELKE

Al Sims, left, and Ron Wilson watch the Ducks secure another road victory.

TED SOQUI

MIGHTY DUCKS OF ANAHEIM

Despite attending almost every Duck home game, Disney CEO Michael Eisner did not interfere in the operations of the team.

Assistant Coach Tim Army put together the scouting reports.

The Swedish rookie Patrik Carnback got hot late in the season.

The Ducks and their fans celebrate Stephan Lebeau's game-winning goal during the first-ever victory over the crosstown rival Kings.

1993-94 Mighty Ducks of Anaheim

Front Row (sitting) L-R: Mikhail Shtalenkov, Alternate Captain Randy Ladouceur, Head Coach Ron Wilson, Assistant General Manager Pierre Gauthier, President Tony Tavares, Governor Michael Eisner, Vice President/General Manager Jack Ferreira, Director of Hockey Operations Kevin Gilmore, Captain Troy Loney, Guy Hebert.

Second Row L-R: Trainer Blynn DeNiro, Equipment Manager Mark O'Neill, Assistant Coach Al Sims, Terry Yake, Bobby Dollas, Alternate Captain Stu Grimson, Alternate Captain Todd Ewen, Stephan Lebeau, Assistant Coach Tim Army, Goaltending Coach Brian Hayward, Assistant Equipment Manager John Allaway.

Third Row L-R: Bob Corkum, Peter Douris, Joe Sacco, David Williams, Bill Houlder, Anatoli Semenov, Jim Thomson, Shaun Van Allen, Tim Sweeney, Don McSween.

Top Row L-R: Scott McKay, Sean Hill, Scott Chartier, Maxim Bets, Steven King, Garry Valk, Mark Ferner, Patrik Carnback, John Lilley.

Did not finish the season in Anaheim: Alexei Kasatonov, Ron Tugnutt.

After the final game of the year, the Mighty Ducks salute their devoted fans.

CHRIS RELKE

Ron Wilson hopes to have Paul Kariya playing for the Ducks as soon as possible.

B. BENNETT/BRUCE BENNETT STUDIOS

Celebrating at the 1994 NHL draft in Hartford: Gary Bettman, David McNab, Oleg Tverdovsky and Pierre Gauthier.

and Blockbuster add is an expertise in that field. So do the people Gary's hired. You're getting the right component parts to be able to figure out a solution to this long-standing problem. There are some simple answers: don't insult your audience, but don't use insider terms. We have an opportunity to reach out to the masses."

According to Tavares, the product could be improved immediately. "Using equipment like the telestrater is critical to help explain the game. We have more cameras at the Pond than other teams. When we put X-55s up close to the ice, we get nice, tight shots," explains Tavares. "With close-ups, we really can start to address the identity problems with our superstars.

The Duck broadcasts differed from others in the quality of their pictures, but the issue of shot selection was still a league-wide problem. If you just used tight shots to follow the puck, you would maintain the sense of action, but frustrate a viewer who wanted to follow the flow of all the players on the ice. If you pulled back so that a play could be seen from start to finish, you ran the risk of losing sight of the puck. One thing the Ducks were trying hard to do was develop the players' personalities to increase their connection to the fans. Tavares believed the product was ready for national consumption. "If we're serious about getting this product in the marketplace," he asserted, "we ought to consider buying our own network time and selling the advertising ourselves, like baseball."

More than anything else, Tavares believes that franchise location would be critical. "The dispersal of teams—all cold-weather marketplaces—was a problem. Every new franchise has to answer two questions. How will it do in its local market? Will it help in the NHL's overall TV strategy? Unfortunately, in the past, other than this most recent expansion, they didn't approach expansion intelligently. This is no shot at Ottawa, but when you look at an Ottawa, from a strategic standpoint, television-wise, does this help you? Ottawa does nothing to help get an American TV contract."

"The last expansion has some strategy behind it. These are both warm-weather franchises that can make a difference in seeking a television contract," Tavares elaborated. "As far as Anaheim's vote goes, if I have to make a choice between Atlanta and Saskatoon, that's a no-brainer for me. Will Saskatoon support an NHL team? Sure, but you're getting a large 'A' market in Atlanta. It shouldn't be who puts up the first fifty million. It should be who's got the best marketplace."

As Disney and Bettman were considering the league's long-term future, two immediate crises flared up. While Gretzky was chasing the goal-scoring record, his owner Bruce McNall was reaching new depths in his finances. What was rumored for months erupted in the media, embarrassing the NHL as its preeminent owner dealt with personal allegations of theft, and the corporate stigma of being a bad credit risk. The Kings' already fragile state became even shakier. Rumors of an impending sale whirled around the team as Gretzky tried to complete a three-year contract extension.Within months, McNall would be dislodged from his position as Chairman of the NHL Board of Governors and sell off controlling interest in the Kings.

Across the country, Viacom, which was tied to Blockbuster, purchased Paramount. The owner of the Panthers now controlled the Rangers as well, although, for the moment, MSG continued to run their day-to-day operations. The NHL needed to take some action soon if they were to avoid the conflicts of interest that had weakened the league a half-century earlier.

By the end of World War II, Jim Norris had used his brute strength to gain effective if well-disguised ownership of four of the original six NHL teams . Unfortunately for Chicagoans (as well as New Yorkers and Bostonians), Norris loved only the first team he owned, the Detroit Red Wings. His devotion to the Wings skewed the competitive balance of the League. The Blackhawks under their original owner made the playoffs consistently and won two Cups in eighteen years. The Norris-era Blackhawks fell apart, missing the playoffs by finishing fifth or sixth in twelve of their first fourteen years. During the quarter-century of the "Original Six" from 1942 to 1967, Detroit and her only true competitors, Montreal and Toronto, won all 25 Stanley Cups save one.

Norris' behind-the-scenes ownership haunted the franchises in Boston and New York. The Bruins suffered through the worst period in the franchise's history. In New York, the team collapsed, beginning the so-called Curse of 1940, the Rangers' half-century Stanley Cup drought. Hardly a curse, it was neglectful management which doomed the Rangers, a testimony to the negative power of monopoly and conflict of interest.

Although Disney's only hockey team, the Mighty Ducks was far from the Walt Disney Company's only major venture during the '93-94 winter. If Eisner wanted Disney to gain an even greater share of the worldwide entertainment dollar, he had to venture into the sports field, tentatively at first and then, if everything went well, full speed ahead.

The Mighty Ducks represented Disney's experiment in pro sports. If they were successful, entry into other, more expensive pro leagues was soon to follow. So how were they doing? The results were clear. Even before Bettman and Disney had tweaked the product to make it more marketable, the Mighty Ducks were an outrageous financial success. While Disney would continue to work to push the NHL down certain paths, its horizons had broadened.

The worlds of the NBA and major league baseball beckoned. Rumors spread during the summer of 1994 that Disney was investigating buying the California Angels from Gene Autry for slightly more than a hundred million dollars. In his eighties, Autry, the Singing Cowboy, had already sold off most of his estate, including desert resorts and radio stations. Once a new collective-bargaining agreement was put in place in baseball,

Disney would take a closer look at the Angels' financial numbers.

The nature of Disney's lease with Ogden at the Anaheim Arena made it almost impossible for anyone but Disney to bring an NBA team into the building. Disney's control of the luxury suites and the signage in the Arena had made the deal one of the best in all of sports. "Would I object to another team in here? No. Is it difficult? Yes," admitted Tavares. "We negotiated well to get a reasonable lease, and the first guy in always gets the best lease. One could argue that the only way an NBA team gets in the building is if Disney owns it. I don't think the lease was designed that way, but since we have control over so many items, it would be easier to come in if we own it."

Did Tavares have any hesitation about entering the world of basketball? "I never ran a pro basketball team, but I never ran a hockey team before this either. Take the mystique away, and it's a business. If you'd be good at running a business, you'll be good at running a franchise," Tavares explained, his eyes clearly trained on the near future. "My thought was we'd give this a few years before we'd jump into other leagues, but we built this so fast we have certainly established peoples' confidence in our off-ice team. They've done a phenomenal job, and I believe could do a phenomenal job in other sports."

As Disney Sports Enterprises explored the worlds of professional baseball and basketball, Anaheim's professional football team moved one step closer to departure. The construction of the Pond had given the Rams an escape clause in their Anaheim Stadium lease which required a lump-sum payment. When the Rams gave Anaheim a few million dollars, it freed suitors across the United States to begin a tawdry mating dance in an attempt to bring the National Football League to their city.

Anaheim had learned that perhaps they could not have everything they wanted, at least in the way of professional sports franchises. Even as they moved to expand their sports empire, Disney was being taught the same lesson in the NHL. Whether the desired change was a shootout or a network TV contract in the United States, progress would be gradual. What Disney wanted might happen someday, but it would not occur overnight.

14

Good Surprises

It's just by accident that he's here, but it's going to take a bomb to get him out of the lineup.
—Ron Wilson on Don McSween

A medium-sized pair of wooden doors hang on the office walls of both Jack Ferreira and Tony Tavares. Open the doors and inside you find a surface for writing down elaborate plans. On the inside of the right-hand door, you will also find "the board," a place where the men tinker with their roster, looking at combinations, dissecting weaknesses. The names on the board rise and fall all season long. In mid-December, Jarrod Skalde's name is found on the second line, a testimony to the twenty-two-year-old's hot play. After he slips back to the minors a month later, he's vanished from the board like the victim of a political purge.

If you're not on the board, you don't exist in the Duck present. That might not be so chilling for a kid working his way up through the minor-league system, but for a career minor-leaguer approaching his thirtieth birthday, out of sight is, in fact, out of mind. When the Ducks invited two teams' worth of defensemen to training camp in September, they could not find any room for San Diego Gull blueliner Don McSween.

It wasn't as if they hadn't seen McSween. He'd played alongside Bill Houlder all year along. His numbers were good, although not as good as Houlder's, but they looked right through him. Unwanted by the Ducks, McSween signed another minor-league contract independently with San Diego. He'd enjoyed playing there the prior year and figured he'd play a couple more years before getting a nine-to-five job full-time. He still hoped he could get back to the NHL so his sons could see him play there, but he didn't think it was very likely any more. After all, it had been more than four years since the second of two token appearances for the Sabres. He'd played nine games and recorded one assist.

Midway through the season, McSween's numbers looked solid, but he hadn't called attention to himself. When in need, the Ducks had recalled David Williams or Anatoli Fedotov. In early January, a string of injuries hit the Duck lineup. Mark Ferner remained a little banged up, which meant that Williams had reclaimed a place on the roster. Williams' improved play—he went plus-ten over his first month back—secured a spot on the team. In quick succession, Sean Hill and Randy Ladouceur went down. Both men were expected to be out for at least a couple of weeks. In San Diego, Fedotov was injured. With few options, Ferreira decided to bring in a pro instead of rushing one of the kids.

Gull GM Don Waddell tracked down McSween late on the night of January 10 after talking to Ferreira. "Don woke me up in the middle of the night. I assumed something bad had happened back home," McSween remembered a week later. "They asked me if I could get in a car and be at practice in Anaheim at 11. I said that I could do that. At first, you're nervous. You're 29 and you think opportunity's passed you by—and then your chance is here."

McSween was signed to an NHL contract and added to the roster on January 12. That night, McSween played against San

Jose in the Pond. After four low-scoring one-goal losses, the Sharks' GLM line, Garpenlov-Larionov-Makarov, finally detonated, pushing the Sharks to a three-goal lead early in the second period. The Shark defense clamped down on the Ducks to secure a 5-2 win. McSween's night was unremarkable as the Ducks slid to a record of 4-15-2 at the Pond.

The next day, Wilson led the Ducks through one of the longest practices of the year. "I'm not a big believer in punishment practices," Wilson admitted, "but it seemed like the players wanted it." The next night, playing against Hartford, the Ducks found themselves down three goals again early in the second period, long practice or not. Ready to explode, Wilson restrained himself because his players were actually much more competitive than they had been a few nights earlier.

Instead of folding up their tents, the Ducks attacked Whaler goalie Jeff Reese, peppering him with eight shots in three minutes. At 10:47, McSween drove the net hard, crashing through traffic. Carnback jammed the puck into the net and the goal light came on. Reese exploded in anger, complaining that the Ducks pushed him and the puck into the net. The video goal judge confirmed the goal and the lead was cut to two. The flurry continued. With Reese visibly sagging under pressure, Bob Corkum scored a short-handed goal two minutes later. And a few minutes after that, Carnback made a beautiful blind pass to Sweeney who scored on the one-timer. When Carnback got loose on a breakaway and scored again two minutes later, the sellout crowd rose as one to celebrate. Four goals in six minutes and four seconds turned another disappointing home effort into a night to be remembered.

Before McSween arrived in Anaheim, only Bobby Dollas among the defensemen had shown any real ability to create scoring chances. Hill and Houlder occasionally hurt teams with their shots, but otherwise the defensemen were not really an offensive factor. The concentration on defensive responsibility often made them appear rooted at the blue line, unable to get their legs to churn forward and jump into the play. This weakness made the forwards' job even more difficult. In San Diego and throughout his minor-league career, McSween always looked to jump into the play.

At 3:23 of the third period, he did just that. Carrying the puck, McSween skated forward from neutral ice through traffic and drew the defense to him before dropping a pass to Tim Sweeney all alone in front. Sweeney nailed his second goal of the night and the issue was settled. In one game, McSween had tripled his NHL point total. An empty-netter made the final score 6-3. Wilson could not have been happier. "Donny's not feeling any pressure," the coach asserted. "He may crash and burn, but he's really helping us now with his skating ability."

As it turned out, Ladouceur missed just three games despite a deep charley-horse. While trainer Blynn DeNiro marveled at the veteran's healing capacity, Wilson found a way to keep McSween in the lineup. Returning to his home state of Michigan, McSween got two assists against the Red Wings in a hard-earned tie. Wilson was effusive. "He's playing outstanding. I can't say enough about McSween. He plays for years in the minors, gets a cup of coffee in the NHL and comes through with flying colors. He's won himself the job."

With a large share of the credit to McSween, the Duck offense had come to life. A week later in a game at the Pond against Winnipeg, McSween had a chance to play against his old room-mate and teammate at Michigan State, Jet goalie Bob Essensa. Working the point on the power play late in the first period, McSween took a pass from Peter Douris and fired a slap-shot towards the net. The puck dipped in the air and got by Essensa giving the Ducks a two-goal lead. After serving a six-and-a-half year minor-league apprenticeship, McSween scored his first NHL goal against perhaps his best friend in the league. The two men had been ushers at each other's wedding.

After the 3-1 win, McSween reflected on the moment he thought would never arrive. "I've been getting some shots, and been trying to join the offense, and I thought maybe I will get one, and, you know, tonight was the night, and it's just a great feeling. Now I can tell my sons about this, and I have the puck to prove it," said McSween, who was looking for a video record as well.

"Peter won the draw right back to me. And, as soon as I went to wind up, their guy was starting to go down. I tried to get it off in time, and as he went down, it grazed against his shin-pad. It put some spin on it. As it came to Essensa, it kind of skipped on him, and he couldn't handle it." Laughing, McSween added, "it was probably going in anyway. It was all net. It probably would have put a hole right in the back of the net if he hadn't touched it."

A few yards away, one of the other players joined in the fun, shouting out, "You own him, Donny!" Beating Essensa added to the moment. "It means a little extra because Bob's a good friend of mine. I've got bragging rights this summer on the golf course. In the scuffle after the goal, I gave him a friendly jab and asked him if he'd sign the puck after the game. I told him I'd even buy him a soda. He gave me the typical brush-off in the heat of the battle. It was fun, something I'll remember for a long time."

Unlike the majority of NHLers who've scored before they've had much chance to dream about their first goal, McSween had had plenty of opportunity. "You think about beating four guys and scoring, but the great players don't even do that," said McSween. "Most of the time, it's goals like that, getting the puck and putting it on net. That's hockey. In a few years, I can tell a story and make it sound like it was the prettiest goal ever."

Sorry, Don, let the record reflect that your first goal was hardly the most aesthetically pleasing of the season, but few moments were more cherished. McSween reflected on his role with the Ducks. "Whatever offense I can give them is a bonus.

I don't have the hardest shot in the world, maybe not the greatest hands. I've always been able to carry the puck and make a few passes. That's what I've done down in the minors, and I've always thought that if I got a chance to do it up top, I would. My main concern is staying in my zone, getting the puck, moving it out, taking the body and trying to limit them in their scoring chances. I'm a good plus/minus player, at least I have been in the minors, and that's probably what they're looking for from me. This is a defensive-oriented team. I'm just trying to blend in and help out."

The only regret that McSween had was that his family could not see his first NHL goal. "Unfortunately, my wife and kids are down in San Diego. She wasn't able to get in," explained McSween, but they joined him in Anaheim a few days later. "It's so hard with two little ones and then you have to make the drive back late at night, getting home at one in the morning. Logistically, it just was not really possible. But I called her."

When asked if he'd called between periods, McSween laughed. "No, I waited. I think I'd take a little bit of flak from the guys if I'd have done that. After the game, I just made a quick phone call and she was very happy. She's waited a long time for it, too. It wasn't easy to persevere, but one thing about it is I've always loved the game. You just gotta take pride in what you do. I've always gone to the rink with a smile on my face, happy to be able to make a living just playing a game. A lot of people would give their right arm for that. My wife's been behind me. That's important when you have a couple of kids. It's hard for her because she's by herself a lot when we're on the road. She knew I had a dream to play in the NHL. She always said, if you have that dream, keep playing."

Now Don McSween, among the team leaders in plus/minus in scoring chances, had found a prominent place on the roster boards in the offices of Tavares and Ferreira. While McSween came out of nowhere to ascend to a contributing role, the Ducks' two other good surprises came from the original roster. Bobby Corkum, who got little ice time in Buffalo behind LaFontaine, Hawerchuk and Bob Sweeney, had scored ten career NHL goals coming into the season. From day one, Wilson had expected him to do one job, shut down the opponent's top scorer. Anything else would be gravy.

All Corkum did was lead the team in scoring most of the year. By February, he had netted twenty goals, more than he'd scored in any college or pro season. He continued to play his defensive role so well that the team played its opponents even when he was on the ice going against the league's best. Wilson was not that surprised. "Before the season, I thought Bob might get ten to fifteen goals," Wilson said in February, "but that all changed when I saw how hard his shot was."

Jack Ferreira was really glad that the kid out of Salisbury, Mass. and the University of Maine had gotten a chance to discover what he could do. "Bobby Corkum's a great athlete. He had all the tools and now he got the ice time and took advantage of it. The biggest thing with Bobby Corkum was that he never had to come to the rink and wonder how much he was going to play," Ferreira explained. "He could really develop his skills because he knows he's going to play. Even if he made a mistake, he knew he was still going to be out there."

Peter Douris and Garry Valk, Corkum's linemates for much of the season, contributed to his success. "The pair of Peter and Garry both work, work, work and whoever the center happens to be, Tony [Semenov] or Bob Corkum just fit right in and work equally as hard," said Wilson. "I think it's the pair, Garry and Peter, and their tremendous work ethic that rubs off on everybody else. They really go together like hand and glove. They read each other well, and the center iceman can sit back and see how hard they work down low in the corners."

Douris, uncomfortable in receiving that praise, was more than willing to acknowledge Corkum's efforts. "He's worked so hard," Douris said, "and he's been just as productive as Tony." Other teammates were effusive in their praise. "Corkum's unbelievable, he's just tearing it up," said Todd Ewen. "He can snap that puck, and he's been consistent all year."

When he reflected on his increased productivity, Corkum refused to take much credit. "Ron's been very good all year. He's been telling me to shoot. He's definitely a players' coach," Corkum said after a victory. "The game is at least 75% confidence. It has a lot to do with my success this year. He's a guy that you can approach and talk to about anything and that's certainly helped."

That night, Corkum had scored on a spin-o-rama move and was asked to describe what had gone through his mind on the play. "I'm still not exactly sure what I did there," Corkum said, still wondering about the skills he occasionally displayed. "I have a little more patience on the ice now. I'm doing stuff I never did in Buffalo."

What Corkum had become was the perfect center for a tight-checking, low-scoring team. He could put the puck in the net, fight in the corners, set up his wings and frustrate the opponent's best playmaker. Corkum also took most of the key faceoffs, winning more than half of them. Many people around the NHL could hardly believe that this part-timer from Buffalo could be the Ducks' best forward. To them, it was just more evidence that Anaheim's roster was short on talent. As the trade deadline approached, the GMs that had watched Corkum closely tried to take him off Ferreira's hands. Out of curiosity, Jack would listen to the offers, but he wasn't really interested. Corkum looked to be one of the team's long-term assets.

If Corkum surprised because he reached a level few believed he could, Bobby Dollas stunned everyone by finally fulfilling the promise that had been seen more than a decade earlier. Playing for Laval as a seventeen-year-old, Dollas scored sixty-one points in sixty-three games to attract the attention of all the scouts. In the 1983 entry draft, Dollas was the second defenseman selected when he went to Winnipeg as the 14th pick of the draft. Expectations were high, but the Jets and Dollas struggled as the front office rotated coaches as if they had them on an egg timer. After four years in the organization, Dollas was traded to Quebec. He had scored no goals and played in only 55 games.

"I used to be really offensive in junior," remembers Dollas. "In the long run, it helped me and it hurt me. It hurt me because they expected a lot from me. I didn't have a lot of time to mature, but when I did mature there was no room for me. That was the hard part. I was always coming in as a free agent to a new team. When you come in like that, they're hoping you're a good player, but they're not calculating you to be one of their top guys. Where it's helped me, people are always looking at me and saying he's a first-round pick and he's been doing pretty good, getting better year after year, maybe we'll take a chance on him. That's probably what's kept me in the game so long. From what I heard, they didn't expect a lot from me when I first got here. They thought I'd just be a steady defenseman."

If anything, his experience in Quebec was even worse. The Nordiques went through three coaches in two years, none of whom believed in Dollas. He got into just twenty-five NHL games and was unable to score. When he was offered a spot on the Canadian National team during the 1989-90 season, Dollas leapt at the chance to escape the NHL and work on his skills.

"Defense is the hardest position to learn. You have to learn the game properly. Coming out of junior, it's very run and gun; when I came out of the Quebec league, that hurt me. When I came to the NHL, they asked me to play more defensively and I had a hard time," Dollas recalls. "I did not read and react. I didn't have my head on a swivel looking around at what was happening. I was just concentrating on one guy at a time. The year with Team Canada, we did so much practicing that it really helped me."

One weakness of the NHL schedule and, to a large degree, the minor-league schedule, is that the demands of a game almost every other night leave little time for teaching. With Team Canada, Dollas had reaped the rewards of practice and attentive coaching. When he joined the Red Wings in the fall of 1990, everything looked good. Bryan Murray wanted him on the team and found room for him in the lineup, but the situation deteriorated. 56 NHL games in his first year under Murray became 27 in year two and, finally, just 6 during the 1992-93 season. None of Dollas' coaches seemed to get the best out of him.

"It's been a long and winding road. I've been on some teams where you dread coming to the rink. I belonged to teams— Winnipeg, Detroit, Quebec — where I'd get a little ice time, but it was tough. I finally feel like I've found a home here. It took me 10 years to find this. I've always had a problem playing for coaches that rant and rave. You don't feel comfortable, you're always on edge. On those teams, there are cliques."

The atmosphere around the Ducks had breathed new life into Dollas' career. "In this dressing room, everybody gets along real well. I just hope everybody stays content. They're really happy with the way things went for me this year. All I can accredit that to is the confidence in letting me play, letting me do my own thing. As long as you keep people happy, people will play for you. A lot of guys here are happy, and a lot of guys had a career year. I'm just happy to be here. I'm 29 years old. I gotta make money sooner or later because nine to five's coming up."

Ferreira agreed that a little freedom had worked wonders for Dollas. "Bobby has gotten a shot and he's found his niche. He knew he was going to be in the mix. He really settled down and did a lot of things. It's circumstances. Some guys get a label and then you don't really watch them because there are guys that are younger, but when you're putting a team together, you'll look anywhere."

Coming to an expansion team recharged Dollas' batteries. He was excited from the moment he heard he'd been drafted. "I came in with an attitude like I've never had before. I came in expecting to make the team. I had a good year last year in Adirondack and I didn't get rewarded very much. I was a little disappointed. So I came in here taking a few more chances. In other years, maybe I was too scared to make a mistake. With a little more confidence, everyone tries things. I'm just thankful I got picked up."

Other Duck defensemen, including Hill, Houlder and Kasatonov, scored more frequently than Dollas. Ladouceur was perhaps more consistent in his positioning, but no defenseman had a better all-around year. His brilliant play was reflected in his team-leading plus/minus numbers, both in goals and scoring chances. Bobby Dollas rarely made a bad play and never had a bad night. He had mastered the league's hardest position after an impossibly long apprenticeship.

"You learn by playing against these guys. If a guy's got one good one-on-one move, he's not gonna try something new. If a guy likes to shoot all the time, you know that and you take him away and let the other guy shoot the puck. You weigh your odds," explains Dollas. "Let's say we're playing Dallas. They get a two-on-one with Modano and Churla. What am I gonna do? I'm gonna move towards Mike Modano. I'll let Shane Churla shoot the puck. If he scores, he scores. If he doesn't score, I did my job. I get away with a lot. It's called cheating. Sometimes you cheat the right way, and sometimes you cheat the wrong way. There's no time to think. Sometimes I make a move and I don't know what the guy's thinking, but I predict and it happens quite a bit. You think 'nine times out of ten, a guy'll do this' and you're there. You have those gifted players where you can't predict anything. The other 90 per cent are pretty predictable."

Ten years after being drafted, the game had become if not exactly easy, at least manageable. The best way to understand how long it took Dollas to get a firm toehold in the NHL is to realize that the only defenseman taken before him in the 1983 draft, Normand Lacombe, retired from the league three years ago. Dollas had come a long way indeed. He watched his younger teammates a little bit wistfully. "Look at Sean Hill. Sean's got a lot of potential," Dollas asserted. "He's a good young defenseman. Sometimes he plays real well, but sometimes he might be lackadaisical out there. That's the key thing for a defenseman: consistency."

If one characteristic defined the season's three best surprises, it was consistency of effort and performance. Don McSween, Bob Corkum and Bobby Dollas made every game a difficult struggle for the opposition. Like the best of their teammates, they created a pride in wearing their jersey that had nothing to do with merchandising. Each had a few moments of brilliance, but they would not be the featured players in a highlight reel. What they delivered instead was sustained excellence that could only be seen on repeated viewing. As the season moved forward, each man found his way up the ladder on the boards in the offices of Ferreira and Tavares.

15

Shark Hunt

I know Sergei's going to find me. If he sees me in good position, he'll get me the puck.
—Sandis Ozolinsh, on teammate Sergei Makarov

Canadians must find this nearly impossible to believe, but the state of California is now home to more NHL teams than any Canadian province. Among the fifty states, only New York, with the Isles, Sabres and Rangers, could claim as many teams as the Golden State. As the Western Conference playoff race took form, the Sharks, Kings and Mighty Ducks found themselves in more than just a battle for statewide bragging rights. The teams were locked in a fight for the eighth and final playoff spot.

When the Ducks took the ice at the San Jose Arena on Sunday afternoon, March 6, the race shaped up as follows. The Sharks led with 58 points, the Ducks were three points behind, and the Kings, playing a day game in Chicago, trailed by five. For the first time in their fledgling existence, the Ducks faced a game with a playoff atmosphere, and, to add to the pressure, the Sharks had beaten the Ducks five straight games. Wilson was not fazed by the losses. "The first four games, we generally outplayed them and Irbe won the games," Wilson said. "The last one they kicked our butts. We just couldn't manage to handle

Igor's line, and they dominated us."

Igor's line was Igor Larionov, Sergei Makarov and Johan Garpenlov, two Russians and a Swede of Russian descent. They often were on the ice with the defense pair of Jeff Norton and Sandis Ozolinsh. The five almost always took the first power-play shift together. With Irbe in the nets, the Russian/Latvian invasion in San Jose was made easier by two members of the staff. Coach Kevin Constantine hired Vasily Tikhonov, the son of legendary Red Army and Soviet National coach Viktor Tikhonov, as an assistant coach and Sergei Tchekmarev, a trainer with that Red Army team, as an assistant trainer. Language and other barriers would be handled smoothly.

Most importantly, Constantine had the courage to let the Russians play their own game. Larionov and Makarov carried the puck all over the ice, unlike almost any other players in the NHL. Other NHL coaches had tried to force them to play dump-and-chase like their teammates. Constantine taught his other players one style, but he set his Russians free, and each man rewarded their coach with their best season to date in the NHL.

During Wilson's pre-game talk, he stressed defense. On the road, he would not be able to match lines with Constantine and he expected the Sharks' coach to keep the GLM line off the ice when Corkum and company were out there. Wilson wanted everyone to be aware of the Russians and to challenge them whenever they were carrying the puck. In the nets, Wilson started Hebert and Constantine went with old reliable, Arturs Irbe.

The game was also the first big one the Sharks had ever played. Two inexperienced teams came out of their locker rooms too high, each picking up stupid roughing penalties in the first seventy seconds of play. During the ensuing four-on-four, Makarov circled with the puck low inside the Anaheim zone and avoided a check from Dollas before jamming one into Hebert. He followed it, and the puck found its way into the net.

The Ducks complained, and the referee called upstairs to the video replay judge. The replay seemed to clearly show Makarov knocking the puck out of Hebert's glove in the crease, but the goal was allowed.

A minute and thirty-four seconds into their biggest game of the year, the Ducks trailed by one. In Chicago, the Kings had fought their way to a tie, which left them four behind the Sharks pending the result of the game in progress. Midway through the period, Ozolinsh passed the puck to Makarov in the Duck zone, received a return pass through Dollas' legs and fired a shot through the five-hole between Guy's pads.

When Todd Ewen received a penalty for boarding late in the period, 17,310 Shark faithful went nuts, celebrating the incipient power play by clapping their hands together like a hungry shark devouring its prey, and the GLM line weaved their magic again. Makarov fed Larionov who found a wide-open Garpenlov rushing the net. Garpenlov scored at 17:00 to make the count San Jose 3, Anaheim 0. The Ducks could not seem to get anything going. On the bench, Wilson and Sims looked more grim than angry. The period ended with the Sharks completely in command. In their most important game, the Sharks had scored three goals in the first period for the first time all year.

Wilson had to do something to shake things up. He couldn't replace his eighteen skaters, although he would have liked to, but he could switch goalies. Hebert hadn't given up any soft goals, but two goals had come off rebounds. A change was needed, and, after all, who better to stop a group of Russians than another Russian. Shtalenkov took his place in the net to start the second period.

The Sharks tested Mike three times in the first few minutes, and Shtalenkov made the saves. The Ducks even had a power play and got a few good chances of their own. As soon as the power play ended, Garpenlov got the puck deep in the Anaheim zone from Larionov and found Ozolinsh streaking in from the point. Ozolinsh beat Shtalenkov before Mike even saw the shot. Ozo's second goal of the night was his twentieth of the season and left him second in the league in goals by a defenseman behind only Al MacInnis. A few minutes later, Norton fed Makarov at center ice and Makarov skated past Houlder and around Lebeau, waited for Shtalenkov to commit, then ripped a shot into the upper left-hand corner of the net. In six games, the GLM line had combined for 10 goals and 18 assists in mesmerizing the Ducks. Near the end of the period, Makarov beat three men but shot the puck into the side of the net. No matter, the scoreboard read DUCKS 0 SHARKS 5 at the end of two.

Between periods, the Shark broadcast team interviewed an ex-Shark, David Williams. Williams thought his Ducks got frustrated when they fell behind so far so early. They'd expected a close, low-scoring game like the first four contests. The prediction had been half-right; the Ducks' offense was low-scoring. The only open issue was Irbe's pursuit of his second shutout of the year against the Ducks. As bad as the Ducks were in the first two periods, they managed to come out even worse in the third. Apparently demoralized, the Ducks stood still and refused to hit anyone, acting as if they just wanted the clock to run out. As the period continued, Grimson, Ewen and Corkum started to take the body, but no offense could be found. Late in the period, Todd Elik beat Shtalenkov with a great move on an uncontested rush. Irbe turned back the Ducks' final chances to preserve the shutout. When they return to the San Jose Arena next season, the Mighty Ducks will be trying to break a two-game scoreless streak in that building. Joe Sacco summed up everyone's feelings in the locker room when he said, "that was probably our worst game of the year."

The Ducks now trailed the Sharks by five points with seventeen games left in their season. They had more than enough time to make up that ground, but they would get no more head-to-head chances to beat the Sharks. The next shot at points would be in Phoenix against the Blackhawks. The neutral-site game, the fourth of the year in Phoenix, might have been considered a home game for the Ducks. Hardly. The decent-sized crowd at the America West arena seemed to be entirely made up of Chicago snowbirds that had migrated south and west to keep track of their beloved Cubbies during spring training.

In an attempt to bounce back from the disappointing performance in San Jose, Wilson started Shtalenkov in the nets. A big game, and the Russian was still looking for his first NHL win, but Hebert had done little to please Wilson since the Tugnutt trade. Eddie Belfour was in the nets for the Blackhawks. When Chicago plays Anaheim, it's almost like watching an intra-squad scrimmage. Both teams play dump-and-chase hockey, take the body all over the ice, and defend their own blue line ferociously. The main difference is that Roenick, Chelios and Belfour wear Chicago sweaters. Some nights, that makes all the difference.

Frustrated by the effort against San Jose, Wilson shook up his lines. Lebeau centered Loney and Sacco. Van Allen teamed with Valk and Yake, and Sweeney and Douris played with Corkum, while the fourth line saw very little action. On an early power play, Troy Loney had a chance in front of the net but deflected Dollas' shot into the crowd. After ten minutes of action along the boards, the teams were scoreless and the shots were even at two. Then Sweeney tripped a Blackhawk and Valk drew a high-sticking call moments later. Forty seconds into the five-on-three, Christian Ruutu sliced open the Duck penalty-killers with a diagonal pass to Murphy who roofed the puck high into the net. In the last five minutes of the period, Joe Sacco had three tremendous scoring opportunities, but Belfour stoned him cold. With the puck loose some thirty feet away from his net at the close of the period, Shtalenkov did something most unRussian, venturing out there to beat Joe Murphy to the puck and poke-check it away and keep the game close.

Early in the second period, Sacco got loose on a short-handed breakaway. With a Blackhawk defenseman trying to pull him down from behind, Sacco rushed the shot and Belfour made the save. A few minutes later, Murphy also had another chance. All alone in front of the net, he faked a shot, getting Mike to go down but the Russian lifted his left pad to stop Murphy's quick shot. When Sean Hill lost the puck to Michel Goulet, Shtalenkov made another huge save. At the other end, Van Allen controlled a rebound right in front but shot the puck wide. Back in the Anaheim zone, Chelios and Roenick both put tough shots on Shtalenkov, but the Russian handled them with ease. Sacco had another short-handed breakaway and Belfour came two full strides out of his net to cut down Sacco's angle and make the save. Despite a lot of good offensive chances, the score remained 1-0, Blackhawks, after two periods of play.

Sacco had yet another chance as the third period opened, but Belfour would not relent. Shtalenkov finally cracked when Goulet roofed a backhander with the goalie scrambling on the ice to cover a rebound off a shot by Roenick during a four-on-four situation. While the Ducks were losing, the out-of-town scoreboard showed the Sharks leading Buffalo by two goals in the second period at San Jose. The Ducks' chances in the third period were becoming rarer and rarer as Belfour continued to shine. The crowd saluted his effort by chanting "ED-DIE" after each save. As time started to run short, the Ducks got hurt by a couple of questionable minor penalties. Late in the period, Frantisek Kucera drew a Chicago penalty. Soon, Wilson pulled his goalie to create a six-on-four advantage. Roenick won the initial face-off from Corkum and knocked a wraparound pass off the boards to Murphy, who had somehow slipped behind the Anaheim defense. Murphy controlled the puck and skated in for an easy empty-net goal that sealed the game. Belfour held on to his shutout as the Ducks failed to score during an abbreviated road trip.

Wilson was philosophical after the loss. "What can you do? Eddie Belfour made some big saves when he needed to, and we had some bad luck when we had opportunities with the net open. We just couldn't score. Mikhail was solid. I don't have anything negative to say. We tried hard, we were physical, and we were even with them, chance for chance. I liked what I saw with those new lines. We skated well and we defended well. Unfortunately, they have a lot more skill. We bounced back real well from the San Jose game. You just can't measure everything in wins and losses, particularly in the first year."

With the team looking for an offensive boost, Wilson had no idea when Semenov would return full-strength from his elbow injury. Ironically, Kariya, the kid with the magic touch, was about to renounce his NCAA eligibility, which meant talks could heat up between Ferreira and Baizley. Power outage or no, Ferreira made it clear that the Ducks would not suddenly open their wallets. According to Jack, Kariya would not get the Daigle contract in the $2 million per year range that Baizley was seeking.

The Ducks returned home the next night to face Buffalo and the league's top goaltender, Dominik Hasek. Six points behind the Sharks, they needed to right themselves immediately. Both teams were playing the second in back-to-back games, with the Sabres coming from behind the night before to tie the Sharks.

Hebert was back in the nets, but Don McSween would be out because of chicken-pox he'd caught during the road trip. Grimson was a late scratch as Wilson tried to put more offense on the ice in the return of Jarrod Skalde. Each team had a few good chances in the opening period, but Hebert and Hasek appeared sharp and neither team scored. The Ducks had now gone 147 minutes since their last goal.

The Ducks started the second period by wasting a power play without getting any shots on the net. Eight and a half minutes into the period, Bob Corkum and his linemates made an ill-advised line change right as the Sabres gained control of the puck at center ice. In an instant, the Sabres had three men skating in on two lonely defenseman, Hill and Ladouceur. Dave May got the puck uncontested on the right wing, darted in front of Hebert and scored.

That goal proved to be all the Sabres would need. Late in the period, Valk and Skalde got loose on a two-on-one. Skalde shot the puck into Hasek's body and the Czech left a rebound. With Hasek sprawling on the ice, Valk rushed his follow-up shot and pushed it into the goalie's pads. As the team continued to struggle to put the puck in the net, Wilson started to mix up his lines again. Early in the third period, Sacco and Yake both had good chances as the pace of the game picked up dramatically. The Sabres counterattacked. Deep in the Ducks' zone, the Sabres won a face-off back to Donald Audette at the point. Audette made a great cross-ice pass to May, who flipped a one-timer into the net at 7:13 of the third period.

A minute later, the Ducks were back on the power play. They got three more chances and continued to fail to convert. The home crowd even started to boo a little, only finding joy when they were informed that the Kings were losing to Chicago across town. With seven minutes left to go, Ferner got tagged with a hooking penalty. A minute later, Ladouceur battled Khymlev for the puck in the corner. The play looked clean, but Laddie got hit with a holding penalty. For the second night in a row, any chance the Ducks had to come back was being eliminated by a bad late call. It had been happening all season long, but with the team fighting to stay in the playoff race it became more noticeable. First-year teams don't get any breaks from the refs. Down two men, the Ducks could not stop another great pass by Audette to Mogilny, who scored into an open net to end any remaining suspense. All year long, the coaches and front office had expected the offense to go through a bad stretch. The nightmare hit them at just the wrong time. When they needed to get hot for a playoff run, they could not put the puck in the net. The time since the last goal had now reached 187 minutes and counting. No other NHL team had suffered through three consecutive shutouts in five years. Not the Panthers, not the Lightning, not the Sharks and not even the woeful Senators.

Wilson refused to panic. "We had more chances than they did and we outshot them, but we just can't score right now. It is very frustrating. In three games we haven't seen a goalie make a mistake. Then you've got to really be able to earn your goals and we don't seem to be capable of doing that. Sometimes you wonder where perspective is. We're a first-year team and we're having trouble scoring goals. We said early in the season that that would be a weakness. The other teams are really starting to crack down. We'll regroup."

Wilson wanted his players to get some rest and get back to the basics. "I just told them to relax and stop thinking about scoring. Just put shots on goal. A lot of guys are trying to do too much, they need to go back to basics. Right now, we're not shooting it. I think we're a little bit leg-weary, we're just not getting to the net."

While he was satisfied with the effort of his own team, he was frustrated by the calls late in the game. "A five-on-three with five minutes to go generally isn't called. I guess we're gonna get a lot of young referees the rest of the way. We'll be the victims of whatever mistakes they make; it's just something we have to deal with."

Joe Sacco, who was getting more chances than anyone else, searched for explanations, especially for an excellent opportunity early in the third period. "I didn't get that shot off the way I wanted. I wanted to go up high, but I didn't get time. Maybe we're pressing a little too much. It's frustrating, but we can't get down on ourselves."

By this point in the season, the veterans of past playoff races had become the team leaders. The former Canadien and Blue,

Todd Ewen, was as close to the heart of the team as anyone. "We can't just flick a switch and start scoring. This is where you build character. We still have high expectations of ourselves. Our final goal's to make the playoffs, but all we can do is win our next game, our next period, our next shift. Baby steps all the way."

Ewen refused to give an alibi. "Sure, we've got key members out of the lineup and calls not going our way, but those are scapegoats. We need to look to ourselves. You can't just forget about a loss. You've got to learn from it and look at what happened and look in the mirror to see what you can do to make our performance better. We're gonna see who pulls us through."

Trying to release the pressure, Wilson gave the team a day off to go play some golf and forget about the drought. By the time the Ducks returned to the rink for their next game, they had to face two facts. The Sharks now led by eight points, having beaten the Isles the night before behind another two-goal night by Ozolinsh. More importantly, Eddie Belfour, coming off back-to-back shutouts of the Ducks and Kings, would be in the opposition nets. Having played well against Buffalo, Hebert got the call again against Chicago.

Three of the team's best players, Semenov, Kasatonov and McSween, remained on the sidelines with a variety of ailments. Before the game, trainer Blynn DeNiro, who had been begging to sing the Star Spangled Banner, finally got his chance. He delivered a rendition of the national anthem that was singular. DeNiro's off-key singing left everyone hoping he would stick to his day job. Their ears still ringing, the Ducks flew at the Blackhawks from every direction. The first ten minutes represented the best hockey the Ducks had played in weeks. The forwards put ten shots on Belfour during the sustained flurry. Unfortunately, Belfour was on his game again, and the only goal during the Ducks' domination came at the other end of the ice. Joe Murphy stole the puck from Peter Douris and carried it deep into the corner where he saw Michel Goulet cut behind Patrick

Carnback. Murphy fed Goulet, who jammed the puck through Guy's legs from five feet away.

Things looked even worse when the Blackhawks went on the power play after Garry Valk was whistled for holding. The scoreless streak had reached the two hundred minute mark. After the initial face-off, the Ducks immediately cleared the zone and Bob Corkum found himself all alone on a shorthanded breakaway. Before the game, Douris had told Corkum just how to handle this situation. "Peter said if you have lots of time, fake your shot, drop your shoulder, and go around him," Corkum said after the game. Bob did just that, deking and pulling the puck back onto his forehand to send Belfour sprawling. Corkum flipped the puck into the open net easily. The drought had ended, and fans and teammates leapt to their feet to celebrate. The box score would read Corkum unassisted at 12:03 of the first period, but Douris deserves a nod, too.

Just forty seconds later, Joe Sacco got loose on another shorthanded breakaway, his fifth of the week, and made a brilliant move, but as he pulled the puck across, it skipped and he could not put his shot on the net. Four minutes later, Chicago, which had raised its game, scored again on a deflection off a hard slapshot by Chelios. The period ended with Chicago out in front, 2-1.

Chicago came out strong to start the second period. Again, the counter-attacking team was rewarded first. At 7:55, Douris made a great play to secure the puck and then made a brilliant pass to Corkum, who scored on a one-timer. The Ducks had tied the game, and this time Douris' assist would be recorded. As the period continued, Corkum had another good chance and David Williams hit a cross-bar, but the game continued even with frequent end-to-end rushes, a more wide-open game than the one three nights earlier in Phoenix. Late in the period, the Blackhawks scored again when Roenick fired a shot that a screened Hebert never saw.

Roenick showed another dimension of his game early in the third period when a lead pass by Sacco led Troy Loney right into Jeremy's neighborhood. The all-star flattened Loney with a clean check that had to be the hardest delivered all season at the Pond. Clean, physical play made the smaller players on the ice invisible. As big a game as Corkum had, Stephan Lebeau struggled mightily. The bigger Blackhawks gave him special attention, hitting him all over the ice. On most nights in the NHL, size competes, and speed kills, but Lebeau could not use his speed with any impact against Chicago. Lebeau played gamely, working along the boards all night, but observers now understood why Lebeau often was scratched when the Canadiens went into Boston Garden or Chicago Stadium. His game needed more room than those teams would allow him. The Ducks failed to put much pressure on Belfour during the period, and the game ended 3-2, Chicago. They had scored, but they hadn't won.

Wilson accepted the defeat calmly. "We worked real hard once again. We scored a couple of goals and hit two posts on the one power play," he said just afterwards. "Joe Sacco might have missed the turning point of the game. If we'd have had two short-handed goals on one shift, that might have opened the flood gates. I'm optimistic that we can still make a run at it. We don't have superstars who can turn the game with a magical moment. Jeremy Roenick rose above everyone else tonight with some big hits and a beautiful goal that was the difference in the game. If we had a player like that, which we will in a couple of years, we could turn things around. Right now, we're a little tired and there's not a lot of confidence in the room. We just have to work with what we have."

Wilson was asked whether it was a relief to finally see his team score. "We still lost the game, but the monkey's off our back. Also Blynn's off our back," Wilson joked. "If we had won or scored six or seven, then he'd be like Kate Smith. He'd be out there every night. And I don't know if I want to hear that every night or if the fans should be subjected to that."

Wilson believed that his players were wearing down because most of them had never had so much ice time in their careers. "You need to build up a good conditioning base over the summer or you'll wear down. Our players are starting to find that. But it's also my job to regulate their batteries a little, and I pushed a lot of players in a lot of games when the games were on the line. We won some of those and now we're paying a little bit of the price for that. So we've backed off a little bit in practice. When you're losing, it's easy to get tired. What weighs on you is losing and then not scoring and then on top of that you're in a playoff race. A number of factors affect a player's perception of pressure. As a coaching staff, we haven't put a lot of pressure on the players. Management and the fans haven't either. The pressure comes from within the players and they have to cope with it."

Corkum, the slump-breaker, acknowledged that pressure. "It was very important to finally score. Everyone's been telling us to relax, and the day off yesterday really helped, but no one likes to lose. It's human nature to press a little."

The losing in Anaheim hadn't stopped, but the Sharks lost at Calgary a day later and had four days off. The Ducks still trailed by eight points, but two quick wins would put them just two games back before San Jose hit the ice again. The next opponent was Ottawa, a team still trapped in expansion hell that trailed all teams in goals scored and goals allowed. If ever a game looked easy, it was this one.

Wilson went back to Shtalenkov in the nets. Hebert had been solid against Chicago, but the Russian had played well so far and was still searching for his first NHL win. Five minutes into the game, no one had scored, but the outcome was clear. Semenov, Kasatonov and McSween were still out, weakening the Ducks, but Ottawa could not execute a pass or even clear their zone.

On the first Anaheim power play, Lebeau, free from harassment, set up Loney, who scored easily. Two minutes later, Ewen bombed a shot from the point that hit Ottawa goalie Craig Billington's glove. Billington didn't close his glove, the puck flew up in the air, dropped on the ice in the crease and trickled across the red line. This Ottawa team was the league's worst joke, playing at a level of incompetence that the Mighty Ducks had never approached. Late in the period, Corkum and Sweeney set up Hill in front for another goal.

The rest was just statistics; the game was over. In the middle of the second period, Ewen crunched a Senator and received a double minor. During four minutes on the power play, the Senators managed just two weak shots. There had been other games where Anaheim had outplayed their opponents, but never before had they toyed with someone. Wilson spent the game fretting that his players would develop bad habits during the increasingly loose play. Valk scored late in the second period. Early in the third period, Douris set up Corkum with a brilliant pass for the second time in two games and Corky fired a wrist shot past the second most unlucky man in the arena, backup Senator goalie, Mark LaForest. Midway through the last period, Dennis Vial broke up Shtalenkov's shutout. The final score was 5-1, Anaheim.

Wilson was still concerned about the level of his team's play. His efforts were a big reason the Ducks had never shown any signs of deteriorating into another Ottawa. "You get a 3-0 lead halfway through the first period, and it's hard to focus for sixty minutes against them. It was disappointing to play like that defensively, but I sort of expect that. Our forecheck and our defense are the best part of our game. If we try to get fancy in the neutral zone, then we're not an effective team. Tonight was a tough game for a coach to watch because it's hard to get your points across when you have a three goal lead. I suppose you'd rather win ugly than lose pretty."

Three short weeks after the Tugnutt trade, the goaltending situation was back in the air again, at least according to Wilson. "Mikhail did a great job. He made some really nice stops. I've had confidence in him all the time. Basically, Guy's the guy who's gotta do it as the number one. At the moment, if Mikhail's gonna be as hot and solid as he is, we'll go with him for awhile. He hasn't made any mistakes and I like what I see. He's aggressive. When the goalie's aggressive, that probably makes everyone else a little more aggressive."

Shtalenkov was very pleased with his performance. "I'm just happy today because it's my first NHL win," he said after the game. "I was surprised when they traded Ron. I thought I'd spend the rest of the year in San Diego. I rented a place for the year down there. A shutout would have been great, but it's not very important. If we win is more important."

The Ducks had two days off before a game back at the Pond against the Kings, a team they'd failed to beat in four previous games that featured bad calls, brilliant play by Kelly Hrudey, and a five-point game by Gretzky during the war of words between him and Tavares. Minutes after the game ended, all anyone could talk about was the Kings.

Corkum readied himself for another night of chasing the Great One, who was within one big night of catching Howe. "Anytime you can hold Wayne to a couple of points, that's great," said Corkum, who also believed he would be able to contribute offensively. "Obviously, our job will be to hold him down, but they play that up-and-down style and our chances will come through their turnovers."

Terry Yake was confident and believed the key would be limiting the Kings' power play chances. "We've outplayed them in a number of games, but we've made mistakes," Yake said. "We've got to work harder against them. We can't afford to be in the box against them, but we're still gonna have to play a physical game."

One man who would miss the game was Don McSween. Catching the chicken-pox for the first time as an adult is awful for anyone, but it was torture for McSween. He had it on the bottom of his feet, in his ears and throat, and underneath his tongue. Worst of all was the feeling that the team was being hurt. "The timing's really poor now," McSween said. "I mean, I played down in the minors for seven years, and I couldn't get them then."

The Kings had something worse than McSween's chicken-pox, but few had made a good diagnosis, so any attempt at cure seemed unlikely. The defending conference champions had won just four of their last twenty-five games. They had reacquired Marty McSorley from the Penguins, but it had cost them Tomas Sandstrom. The loss of Sandstrom, Paul Coffey, Corey Millen and Bob Kudelski had caused the Kings to become no more than a decent offensive team. Barry Melrose had asked for most of these trades, but when they started to look bad, he shifted responsibility to the front office.

A game against Ottawa promised the chance for the Kings to get healthy before they came to the Pond, but instead it deteriorated into something ugly. A report in the *New York Post* indicated that Melrose was about to be fired. Acting as if a win over Ottawa would save his job, Melrose brought in Tony Robbins for a two-hour session of positive thinking and chants that left many Kings rolling their eyes and shaking their heads when they emerged from the locker room. Between periods of an easy win over the Senators, Melrose came on the cable broadcast to assure his relatives in Canada, who were pulling the game in on a satellite dish, that he was fine. Despite the win, rumors continued to fly, and the ugliest rumor of all was that Melrose himself had spread word that his job was in jeopardy. The theory was that Melrose had two goals: fire up his slumping players and force management to choose sides in the power struggle between Melrose and Kings general manager Nick Beverley.

No matter that the Kings had the game's greatest player, because Wayne had the flu. To add to the Kings' burdens, the Ducks' coaching staff indicated that the Kings believed the Sharks were their only serious competition. Wilson asked his players to question why the Kings were not paying any mind to them. "L.A. has forgotten we're part of the formula here," said Wilson. "You can't just talk about San Jose when the Mighty Ducks are ahead of you."

In a game that mattered as much as the game in San Jose, Wilson started Shtalenkov in the nets for the second straight game. He also put a new face in the lineup. Winger John Lilley, fresh from the U.S. Olympic team, would skate on Corkum's line in his NHL debut, shadowing Gretz and Kurri all night. The Gretzky watch had reached full-alert status, with over two hundred media from across North America on hand in case Wayne netted three goals. A juiced crowd booed the introduction of the Kings, and then, with the release of the Mighty Ducks sequel less than two weeks away, Emilio Estevez, the actor who plays the team's coach in the movie, dropped the puck in an honorary face-off between team captains Gretzky and Loney.

It was the last time Wayne would see Loney all night. Every shift he took Corkum was so close he could read the letters JFC inscribed on Gretz' helmet. Wayne wore the initials on his headgear to honor the memory of his close friend and business partner, the great comic actor John Candy, who had died of a heart attack a few days earlier.

Three minutes into the game, Stu and Marty brawled as both benches pounded their sticks against the boards and the crowd roared with approval. Everybody in the Pond felt an adrenaline rush; a full-scale rivalry had arrived. A minute later, Terry Yake drew a holding penalty, but the Ducks killed it off without allowing a shot. A subsequent Anaheim power play proved equally quiet. Midway through the period, Ewen and Rychel fought for at least the third time during the season. The new kid,

Lilley, was playing a physical game also, sending his wiry, little body at everyone.

While the game was hard-hitting, everybody had room to skate. Lebeau took full advantage, making a beautiful cross-ice pass that caught Sacco in full stride racing past McSorley. With a forehand shot over Hrudey's left shoulder, Joey finally converted a breakaway after two weeks of near-misses. Little more than a minute later, the Kings tried to convert a five-on-three with Gretzky running the point for a full minute. Corkum held his position, blocked shots and refused to go for any fakes as the Ducks killed yet another penalty.

Rychel, still angry about his pummeling at the hands of Ewen, picked a fight with the smaller, less aggressive Dollas. Bobby just held Rychel until the linesmen jumped in to break it up, but the two men were sent off. Late in the period, LA's Robert Lang caught the puck along the boards behind the net, worked himself in front, and scored. Corkum, who'd easily played half the period, had backed away from Lang to defend the pass, and now the game was tied after one despite the Ducks' clear superiority. Was the script of the earlier losses being replayed?

Wilson, who had worn glasses instead of contact lens for the first time all season to try and break the California jinx, was not worried. Between periods, he told his players to be a little more disciplined. "I said we played a great period. When you consider we were eight minutes shorthanded to two minutes for them, I thought we dominated territorially," Wilson recalled just after the game. "I was very pleased. I just reminded our team that we can't spend all night in the box because that gives that team momentum. Although we may kill the penalty off, if they get three or four good scoring chances, they've got us back on our heels."

The Ducks got their own power play early in the second period. Yake made a great play, faking a wrist shot from deep on the left wing that caused Hrudey and his defenseman to commit. As Yake deked, David Williams pinched in from the point. Yake fed Williams the puck and David roofed a wrist shot past Hrudey at 3:22 to put Anaheim back in front. Lebeau set up a few more near-misses and then Todd Ewen drew a penalty on Zhitnik by rushing the net. During the ensuing power play, Houlder fired a puck into a mess of bodies in front of the net, Sacco took a whack at the puck, which bounced off Hrudey and sat at the left edge of the crease. Lebeau slipped in and jammed it home. At 11:36 of the second period, the Ducks had their first two-goal lead of the year against their rivals. As the period continued, the Ducks got another power play as ref Kerry Fraser made calls that the Ducks hadn't seen in months. The period ended with Anaheim leading 3-1, after peppering Hrudey with twenty shots during the period.

The power play carried over into the third period, and when Tim Sweeney converted a backhander off a long rebound of a Sean Hill shot, the game was effectively over. A combination of flu and Bob Corkum's work had Wayne Gretzky taking oxygen on the bench as the game progressed. Nine minutes after his first goal, Sweeney was credited with another when a rebound of a Houlder bomb bounced in off his skate. Hrudey argued furiously, and the replays showed he was probably right, but the refs let the goal stand.

A four goal deficit was too much for the once-proud Kings to take, and Zhitnik started a fight with Lilley, and Tony Granato jumped in to help Zhitnik. As third man in, Granato received a game misconduct from Fraser. A few minutes later, Lang made his second great play of the night, setting up Mike Donnelly for a power play goal to wrap up the scoring.

The win left a sweet taste in Wilson's mouth because his team now had five days off before its biggest road trip of the season. Sitting on a loss, a fifth straight loss to the Kings and an 0-11 record against their two California rivals, would have been awful for the team. "This is one of the best games we've played.

This is gonna be special because we finally beat our arch-rival, but, biggest of all, we beat a team that we're battling for a playoff spot with and we came through in the clutch in a big game against, on paper, a very good team," Wilson said. "We shut them down. They looked tired. They played a game last night and we were able to jump all over them."

A beaming Terry Yake reveled in the moment. "Of course, it's special. A lot of fans were still cheering for LA tonight and we want to convert them to Duck fans. We're getting ourselves back in the race. We didn't want to get too fired up. Without fail, it seems like when we get too fired up, we make mental mistakes. We were a little calmer, talked about discipline. Some of those first-period penalties was just emotions running high."

Tim Sweeney couldn't help smiling as he talked to reporters. "I'm just happy for our team right now. We've finally got that monkey off our back. We've finally beat a team from California. In the past, we got caught up in their style. We can't do that because they have so much talent. We read their defense pretty well. We were able to score on a couple of three-on-twos and two-on-ones. It's only one year, but I think it's a pretty good rivalry."

Wilson singled out the performances of Lebeau and Lilley. "I knew it would be Stephan's best game," Wilson explained. "L.A. plays a much more wide-open style which suits Stephan fine. There's not a lot of checking, there's some open ice and he was able to take good advantage of it tonight. Lilley was excellent. I'd never really seen him play before, but Jack liked what he saw and knew he was available. We lack the small, aggressive speedy guy who's able to jump in there and give the odd hit. He really fired up our bench tonight. I really liked what I saw. He's got a future with us. Now we've got some guys who can skate with the Kings. Joe Sacco, Tim Sweeney, Terry Yake, Stephan, now Lilley, and, when he's healthy, Tony can skate with them."

Lilley, the twenty-one-year-old out of Boston University, had a night to remember. "I felt good. The guys and the coaching staff welcomed me. I felt that I held my own. I was a little nervous, but it's been such a long year for me: playing in the Olympics, then going to San Diego and coming here," Lilley said in the locker room after the win. "There wasn't as much pressure as the Olympics, but I'd prepared for that all year. Here I just jumped in so I think here I was a little more nervous. Your first NHL game is something you've been waiting for your whole life.

Lilley believed his role was simple. "I just have to go out and just use my speed and try and get in there and forecheck and do the little things well. Bob Corkum talked to me a few times on the bench and really helped me defensively. He told me where I should be when I was out of position a few times."

If Lilley embodied something new, the goaltending situation had reverted to its status three months earlier. "We're back to 1A and 1B again, which is fine with me," Wilson said. "Shtalenkov's been very solid since he's been up. The other guys hadn't beaten a team in California so Mikhail deserved a chance."

Shtalenkov's calm response to questions after the game perfectly mirrored his ease on the ice. "It's exciting to play against Gretzky. The whole team played very well, and we didn't give them many good chances to score tonight," Mike said. "Playing back-to-back games is no big deal for me. It's coach's decision. I have to work. This is my job. I'm very quiet in life. In goal, I am the same guy. I adjust to what's going on on the ice. I have to learn to move out a little more. In Russia, for a goalie, you stay back in the net. It's more a reading game."

Wilson let his thoughts drift back to the playoff race where the Ducks now trailed the Sharks by only four points, only one more than before they'd gone into San Jose. The Sharks had a game the next night against the pathetic Senators and then a two-game series with the Kings. "We need help. We need Los

Angeles to help us out," Wilson admitted. "They've gotta help themselves; they're not out of it yet. I'm not saying I like our chances, but at least we have a chance and we're the relaxed team. You know San Jose's putting pressure on themselves to make the playoffs. With Los Angeles, obviously a lot of people are under pressure there."

Scoreboard watching was all the Ducks could do for the next five days, but Wilson intended to enjoy the victory over the Kings. "We've got tomorrow off. We've got a pretty light schedule the next few days," Wilson said, smiling. "I'm gonna hit a golf ball and drive down the highway with the Eagles blaring on my stereo."

When Ottawa dumped the Sharks in San Jose the following night, Wilson surely cranked up that stereo a little louder. And when the Kings beat the Sharks at the Forum and then tied them in San Jose, Wilson's smile must have been contagious. Three weeks left to go in the season, and the Mighty Ducks, his team, still had a chance to reach the playoffs.

16

A Homecoming of Sorts

I can say that that was the first time this season that I was really disappointed with the effort of some people, particularly the hometown guys. They just didn't want to compete. When that happens, you're gonna get run right out of the building.
—Ron Wilson

At the beginning of the Ducks' last long road trip, Ferreira had traded Ron Tugnutt, a goalie many had seen as the team's best choice when he was picked in the expansion draft. That same night, Alexei Kasatonov, a player many considered the team's best defenseman, had suffered a broken foot that would sideline him for six weeks. With Kasa and Tugger absent, the defense expected a struggle. Except for the embarrassing game in San Jose, the blue-liners had remained totally solid, even weathering the absence of Don McSween for a few weeks. Mark Ferner and David Williams had stepped in and performed more than adequately.

Suddenly, Ferreira had a stockpile of decent defensemen. With the team opening its last extended road trip in Dallas, Jack worked the phones as the trade deadline neared. St. Louis showed interest. The Blues felt they needed help shoring up their defense corps before the playoffs, especially after the Petr

Nedved signing cost them Jeff Brown and Brett Hedican. The Blues came after Kasatonov, and Ferreira asked for a kid the Blues had picked in the second round of the 1993 entry draft, Maxim Betz. Betz, a winger from Moscow, had torn up the Western Hockey League as an eighteen-year-old. Scouts believed Maxim was at most two years away and could be a star. With Kasa out at least another week, he wouldn't be able to make much difference in the final playoff run. Bobby Dollas had become the team's best defenseman. The loss could be survived, especially if Scott Chartier was ready by the start of next season as everyone expected.

While the announcement of the trade did not create the same awkwardness at practice as the Tugnutt/Lebeau deal had, the shock waves in the locker room may have been greater. Here the team thought they were in the midst of a playoff race, five points out with twelve games to go. Apparently, the front office was playing for next year, trading a vet who could help now for a kid who might help someday. A quiet sense of betrayal was felt by many of the players, a sense that they were fighting their hardest with limited resources and their legs were being cut out from under them. San Jose had traded two of their defensemen, Mike Lalor and Doug Zmolek, for veteran scorer, Ulf Dahlen, to give their offense a kick-start. The Sharks clearly were trying to win now, but the Ducks didn't know what their front-office was doing.

What they were doing was looking at the longer picture. A playoff appearance would be nice, but how far could they realistically expect to go? Nobody believed they could win a Cup this season, but everyone believed they would have a chance at the big prize in about three years. Who would help more then: Kasatonov or Betz? Kasa would be in his upper thirties and likely out of the league. Betz might not develop as expected, but if he did, he would be entering his prime.

Ferreira explained his decision-making process later. "My

philosophy on a trade is whatever you're giving up, you have to be able to replace. You're either replacing it in the trade you're making or somewhere within your system. If you can make a trade with that philosophy, then what you're getting is a bonus. We're trading Kasa, but we had Chartier and Nikolai Tsulygin coming along."

Tavares wanted fans and media to appreciate that the front office couldn't just improve the team overnight. "What people don't understand is this is a business where you can't just will yourself better players. You either got to trade for them or you gotta draft them. Nobody is out there just letting you pick their pocket. You've got to give value for value, for the most part. People say you don't have much offense, why don't you go out and buy some offense? You don't buy hockey players, you trade for hockey players or you draft them. The Gretzky situation has only happened once in the history of the league."

Tavares also believed that the Ducks had brought a more detached, rational process to evaluating their own players. "Look at each player: his age, his physical condition, his injury history and how that's gonna affect his longevity. And you project it out. Do you go in and make trades for a guy that's gonna help you for a maximum of two years? I don't think so. That doesn't do anything for us. That's why we haven't made a ton of trades. We take a longer view of things. We have made a determination that we're gonna approach this sport much more in a business fashion than I think a lot of other teams do. Just as there is a planning process that happens for a business, we have a rolling five-year plan for our players. This sounds cold, but players are assets. Players have an estimated useful life, not as a person, but as a hockey player. When you have a hockey player as your asset, you've got to plan on that player becoming obsolete over a period of time. We sat back and said we'd look at our players and decide how many of our players are "keepers" and where do we have to upgrade. Are we gonna trade a 32-

year-old guy for another 32-year-old guy? No, it doesn't fit into our five-year plan. Any time that we can upgrade ourselves, we will."

For the front office, the trade for Betz represented a clear upgrade. The Mighty Duck players wanted help now, and the coaches felt that pressure as well. What the brain trust believed was you only sacrifice your future when you have a clear need and a great chance at the Cup. Detroit was a perfect example. Their skaters were probably the best in the NHL, but they were weak in the nets. When Buffalo offered Grant Fuhr, reduced to a backup role by Dominik Hasek's brilliance, for the Red Wings' young stud, Keith Primeau, it was a trade that Tavares personally believed had to be made. But Detroit backed off and settled for Bob Essensa in a deal that didn't cost them Primeau.

The road effort in Dallas left little to be desired, but the Stars were just too strong. Mike Modano scored twice as Shtalenkov suffered the loss. Dallas led by two goals most of the game. Carnback scored in the final seconds to make the contest seem closer than it had really been. "We played well, but we kinda broke down in some key moments," Todd Ewen said later. "It hurt us when they scored right away. They're known really well for having a quick start. If you give up four goals, it's tough to win. We just have to get back to basics and focus on our defensive play because these points are so vital now. Teams have better scoring ability than we do, but a good nucleus defensively can take you a long way."

The game's highlight had been Stu Grimson's first goal of the season. Grimson had been struggling for weeks with injuries to his hands that limited his shooting and fighting ability. Late in the second period, Grimson and Carnback had entered the Dallas zone together. Carnback threaded a pass through traffic to Grimson, who snapped off a one-timer that momentarily cut the Dallas lead to one. Stu's teammates hugged their friend and defender as hard as they could. The celebration was Stu's first since New Year's Eve, 1992, and not even the loss could mute everyone's happiness for Grimson. Halfway across the country, the Sharks had scraped together a tie in Pittsburgh to push the Ducks six points back.

One night later, Wayne Gretzky finally secured The Record. He beat Vancouver goalie Kirk McLean to set off a tremendous celebration. The Howes were nowhere to be seen, but at least Wayne's family was on hand to share his moment. The season remained bittersweet for the Greatest One as his Kings lost the game at the Forum.

After Dallas, the Ducks went on to Boston. A visit to the Duck locker room often sounds like a trip back to Beantown, the air rich with the accents of Bob Corkum, Joe Sacco and Tim Sweeney. Now John Lilley had been added to the mix, and Peter Douris, who had played his college hockey in New Hampshire and put on a Bruins' sweater for four years, had a touch of New England in his timbre as well. Army, the young assistant, still sounded like he'd be more at home on the Cape than in Anaheim Hills. Wilson's voice had nary a hint of the Back Bay after his many travels, but Wilson's years in New England showed in the mess of friends and relatives that gathered at the Garden to see him work.

Any games at Boston Garden, the most intimate venue in the NHL, are special, but the strong local connection of so many players and coaches made it one of the most anticipated games of the year for the Ducks. The Bruins had not won in two weeks and were faced with the absence of two injured stars, Cam Neely and Raymond Bourque. As they dressed in the tiny, beat-up dressing room ten yards off the ice, the Ducks prepared for a low-scoring, hard-hitting game on the small ice surface.

Wilson, still wearing his lucky glasses, started Hebert and scratched McSween, who had skated well in practice but was still a little weak, and Van Allen. Lebeau, who often watched his fellow Canadiens from the Garden press box, opened the scoring by picking a loose puck out of a pile of bodies in front of the Boston net and beating a prone Jon Casey at 4:25. From that point on, the Bruins became the aggressors. Tim Sweeney, who seemed to be pressing a little before the home folks, hooked a Bruin defenseman at the thirteen-minute mark. Garry Valk worked his tail off to create some pressure shorthanded and drew a hook on new Bruin Al Iafrate, acquired from Washington for Joe Juneau. Adam Oates set up a few more opportunities before the period ended, but the Ducks were still on top. The Bruins had more chances, but Hebert had stopped every one. Another Duck, Lilley, the kid from Boston, looked great, darting and stinging his larger opponents like a mosquito.

Between periods, the scoreboard watching heated up. San Jose trailed Toronto in the first period and faced a back-to-back game in Winnipeg the next night. If the Ducks could hold on, the race might get tight over the next forty-eight hours. Three minutes into the second period, Bruin defenseman Glen Wesley launched a long shot between Ladouceur's legs that hit Hebert in the side and trickled over the red line. A soft goal, but the game was still even. The Bruins continued to buzz the Anaheim net. One shot hit a post and another just missed the upper right-hand corner. With Van Allen, their normal center, sidelined, Yake and Valk skated with Carnback. During a brief respite from Bruin pressure, the threesome worked the puck along the boards in the Boston end. Valk got the puck in front and shot it into Casey. Yake jammed the rebound home at 5:46 to put the Ducks back in front.

The next ten minutes must have seemed like ten days to Wilson. Twenty-nine seconds after Yake's goal, Oates sprung Ted Donato on a breakaway. Donato beat Guy with a forehand on his blocker side. Ten seconds after that, a hard check broke a pane of glass behind the Duck net, stopping action while a replacement was installed. On the out-of-town scoreboard, the Sharks continued to trail in Toronto. On the ice, Hebert downed some water and tried to regain his balance under the Bruin onslaught.

A new window in place, the Bruins continued their assault. A minute and a half later, Donato half-fanned on a shot in front. The slow-moving puck froze David Williams for an instant as he decided whether to go after the puck or the nearest body. The owner of that body, Glen Murray, his back to the net, was first to the puck and fired a turnaround shot that beat Hebert at 8:08. Twenty seconds later, Murray had another chance and Oates was everywhere as the Ducks were completely besieged.

At 9:07 of the second period, Wilson called timeout to see if he could rouse his players. Right after the game, Wilson explained his first mid-game timeout of the season. "I told them we weren't competing and that we were just standing around, awestruck by the big, bad Bruins who weren't that big and I don't think they're that bad. We got intimidated by their tradition. That's why I called it and we didn't respond at all at that point. I'm not going to name names, but we had some guys who were shitting their pants out there. Plain and simple, that's probably why we have them."

Wilson was angrier than he'd been all season. They were embarrassing him and themselves in front of friends and family. Nothing Wilson said made any difference. Twenty-four seconds later, the Bruins scored again on the kind of long pass play that had been impossible against the Ducks on almost any other night of the year. A few minutes later, Stu started a fight with Jamie Huscroft that left one hand so messed up that minor surgery was performed between periods to excise the built-up scar tissue. Even the fight did nothing to spark the Ducks as Oates and Iafrate continued to shoot freely. Shots for the period had reached 14-2, Boston, and almost every Bruin shot came from in close. At 13:55, another point shot by Wesley was tipped in by Daniel Marois. In just over ten minutes, the Bruins had found the Anaheim net five times.

As the period closed, Anaheim got a few good chances. Hill caught a post and Casey gloved a shot by Yake after it was three-quarters over the line. The frustration showed as Sacco and Loney scrapped with a pair of Bruins after the horn sounded. More bad news arrived from Toronto where San Jose had scored two quick goals to take the lead in the third period. In Boston, the third period promised little more than a break between tirades for the Duck players. The Bruins continued to dominate the action, but Guy refused to yield any more goals. With about five minutes left in the game, Valk made a powerful move to the net and set up Sean Hill, who drilled a shot past Casey. That goal ended the scoring with the Bruins on top, 5-3.

The score was less revealing than the absence of color in Wilson's face when he talked to reporters outside the visitors' locker room. "We competed in the first period, but we stopped competing in the second. They just basically outworked us. First period, we were fine. They're gonna be in your zone a lot. They like to forecheck but we defended well. They weren't getting many opportunities but we just started making one mistake after the other. We seemed to give up easily. We just knuckled under to the pressure of the Bruins. We've got to play harder than that, especially at this point in the season. This is crunch time. Maybe the paint's come off and the real leopard spots are starting to show."

During the post-game interviews, Wilson was drained, still angry but exhausted and impatient with having to analyze the game. "Some guys didn't seem like they wanted to be on the ice so let them sit on the bench for a while. It's one of those games where you tear up what happened and get back to work. We've got to find a way to put this behind us and bounce back against Hartford and Philadelphia." Wilson was asked about Adam Oates' brilliant game, highlighted by four assists. "I didn't even watch their team," he said hastily, before leaving to see his relatives. "I was concentrating on our team."

Stephan Lebeau had seen a performance unlike those his Montreal team had produced in crunch time over the past few years. "In the second period, they were more angry than us. We were waiting for them," Lebeau said. "They put a lot of pressure on us. We stopped skating, and we stopped hitting. We stopped forechecking, too. They were all over us in the second period and we didn't react. It's not the kind of game you want to have at this time of the season. We're still alive. It's pretty tough. We need to take care of ourselves. Tonight's a lesson that we can't stop playing for twenty minutes."

One of the homeboys, Tim Sweeney, didn't seem all that upset with the effort. "I don't look on it as a disappointment. I just look at it as Boston really played a good game. They hadn't won in seven games. They came out really hungry in the second period and we didn't respond the way we wanted to."

The man who'd faced the barrage of shots had had a strange night, maintaining his optimism despite the disarray in front of him. "I had good concentration," Hebert said after the game. "We had a pretty good first period. It was one of those nights when I felt so good that I thought I could be the difference in sneaking away with a win. Casey was kinda napping at times. It's a tough game down there when you don't face many shots. Even after Sean Hill's goal, I still thought we had a chance to get another quick one and pull the goalie."

While the Ducks tried to explain their awful performance, San Jose held on to win in Toronto. The following night, the Kings won in Edmonton and the Sharks easily beat Winnipeg. The situation had quickly turned desperate. Now ten points behind the Sharks with ten games left in the season, the Ducks had even slipped two points back of the Kings. Every game was now a must-win game.

The first challenge would be the Hartford Whalers, a recent source of embarrassment to the league. A number of coaches and players, including the underage defenseman Chris Pronger, had gotten involved two days earlier in an early-morning incident at a bar owned by quarterback Jim Kelly in Buffalo. And their GM had had his own alcohol-related incident. To top it all off, the Whalers had been eliminated from the playoffs in Buffalo just before the Ducks arrived in town.

The problems in Hartford served as a reminder about how lucky Disney had been so far in their association with the NHL. They had drafted character guys, but no one could stop players from drinking after games. Aggressive young men, alcohol, and early-morning hours can be a recipe for disaster, but the character that the Ducks displayed on the ice seemed to carry over off the ice.

After the dismal effort in Boston, Wilson shook things up, getting Van Allen and McSween back in the lineup. Hebert, who was blameless, took his place in the nets again. The Ducks came out in an exceptionally defensive frame of mind. The night off in Boston left Van Allen more determined than ever to show his worth to the team. He got two great chances early in the period but failed to convert. Third time lucky. Short-handed, Van Allen blocked a shot from the point, controlled the puck, skated by the immobile defenseman and down the ice where he fired a shot over Jeff Reese's left shoulder to put the Ducks up by a goal at the end of one.

Early in the second period, the video replay official awarded Hartford the equalizer on a backhander by Andrew Cassels. Guy trapped the puck on the ice, but was it across the red line? The replays were inconclusive because the puck was hidden under Guy's glove which rested atop the line, but the scoreboard showed a tie game. Six minutes later, Sweeney, united with his regular center, created a turnover at center ice and skated in with Van Allen on a two-on-one. At the last second, Sweens got the puck to Van Allen, who made a great shot from an impossible angle to put Anaheim out in front.

A minute later, Douris put a tough shot on Reese and the

rebound just sat there. Ewen overpowered the Whaler hanging on his jersey and jammed the puck home to make it 3-1, Ducks. The Whalers looked like a team that had closed up shop for the season. Troy Loney, who'd missed the beginning of the trip to stay in Anaheim with his wife during the birth of their third son, Clint, got involved in some physical play along the boards and drew a penalty late in the period. Moments after the penalty ended, Duck defenseman Mark Ferner and Sean Hill got caught out of position, and the Whalers converted.

The Ducks held just a one-goal lead despite outplaying the Whalers. If Hartford applied any pressure, the third period would be tense, but the Whalers weren't up to it. Pronger, the teen Hartford had wanted to suspend for his involvement in the incident, might have been better left in his street clothes tonight. His big shot remained wild and off-target, denying Hartford any good chances even late in the game after the Whalers pulled their goalie. With the 3-2 win, the Ducks added the Whalers to the Jets and Rangers on the list of teams they'd swept in their inaugural season.

After the game, down in the basement of the Hartford Civic Center, Wilson looked a lot healthier. The color had returned to his cheeks. "We wanted to get back to the little things we were doing. With the air going out of the playoff balloon, we just wanted to regroup and keep it interesting for ourselves. A lot of our players are not just playing for this year, they're playing for next year, for their careers, their futures. I wanted to make sure they didn't lose their focus. In Boston, we got very tentative as the pressure increased. We seemed to protect ourselves as individuals and not think about the team. We played with a little more desperation tonight. In the Boston game, we ran like turtles into our shells. Tonight, we were able to regroup during the TV timeouts when we slipped back into those tendencies."

Wilson was especially pleased that Hebert was back on his game. "The three games that Guy watched did him a lot of good.

He pouted a little bit about it the first week or so and didn't work hard in practice. Then he saw he better start respecting Mikhail as a solid goaltender and a competitor. After that, he really worked hard in practice and came back with two solid games. I thought he was excellent in Boston and I thought he was the difference tonight."

As far as Wilson was concerned, the Boston fiasco was behind the team now. He had no regrets. "If San Jose keeps winning, no matter what we did in Boston, we're not gonna make it. We just have to finish strong. If we're lucky enough to make the playoffs, then we do. I'm not gonna lose any sleep over it. We played better when we weren't thinking about it."

Van Allen reflected on how he'd benefited from the night off in Boston. "I sat up there and reevaluated. I had a little bit of jump in my legs tonight. I never really feel that confident about my shot," Van Allen admitted after having had numerous chances to get his first NHL hat trick. "For years, I've been a passer and I've played with goal scorers, but Tim Army's trying to get me to shoot a little more"

The Ducks had lost five of seven with Don McSween on the sidelines, and he was happy to be able to contribute to righting the team. "A couple of times I was out there longer than I wanted to be, but Simmsie used me pretty well. He shuffled me in and out and then Fernsy pulled his groin. He was out and we had to go to five D. More or less, it's getting used to the pace of the game. You start moving your feet, you get hit a few times and you hit a few guys. It felt fine."

Hebert rushed through his post-game interview so he could see his mom for the first time in seven months. Hebert disagreed with Wilson's assessment of his response to Shtalenkov's increased playing time. "I don't think it's pouting. That's pretty unprofessional. If you don't appear to be disappointed, I think there's something the matter. Any coaching staff should be happy that a player's not ecstatic that he's not in the net," Hebert admitted. "I'm sure there's some validity. I felt I should be in there. I felt it was up to me to lead the team into the playoffs. I thought I became the number one and only a disaster would unseat me. I don't think that ever happened, but since we're so close to the playoffs, losing a couple of games was enough for him to make a change to see what would happen."

The next night in Philadelphia, Hebert would finally get a chance to play in games on consecutive days, an opportunity he'd asked for all season long. The Flyers were caught up in a race with the Islanders and Panthers for the final playoff spot. They'd underperformed all season long, including a bad loss at the Pond, and Flyer fans wanted head coach Terry Simpson to be fired. Earlier in the day, the Kings lost a day game in Vancouver, which left their hopes in jeopardy. At the Spectrum, the Ducks came out focusing on the defensive end yet again. After one period, the Flyers had outshot Anaheim, 9-2, but the game remained scoreless. Fifteen hundred miles to the west, the Blues jumped out to an early lead over the Sharks.

By the time the scoreboard read STL 3–SJ 1–2ND, the Ducks had gone seventeen minutes between shots on net. Yake, Van Allen and Sweeney slowly brought Anaheim back to life. Todd Ewen even blew by Eric Lindros with a burst of speed. Just when things started to look better, the Flyers got a great chance. All of a sudden, the Flyers had a three-on-zero with Mark Recchi carrying the puck up the middle and Lindros and Mikael Renberg on his wings.

Guy Hebert had the best view of the play. Here's how he saw it. "Fortunately, they gave it to the wrong guy, Recchi, who's really a shooter. He was coming in the middle with both guys trailing him so I think they were just gonna let him walk in on a breakaway and look for any rebounds. That's the way I was gonna play it. All of a sudden, I saw this cranberry-eggplant-colored guy come sliding through. He never gave up; figured he could get a stick on the play and he did. That's as good a defensive play as I've seen this year."

That cranberry-eggplant-colored guy was Bobby Dollas, and it was easily the defensive play of the year. "We had a four-on-three and we ended up turning it over. I guess one of their guys came out of the box. I'm looking back and I say to myself, 'my partner ain't there.' And I see Lindros, Recchi and Renberg and I'm going, 'Jeez, I gotta get back.' What happened was once they crossed the blue line—fortunately for me Recchi is a left-handed shot—he stopped for a second, maybe to make a pass or shoot. On that hesitation I hit the stick at the same time and pulled it and slid it behind the net. I lunged for it. I'll get it maybe one time in ten. I was pretty happy I got it. For them, it might have been a little demoralizing."

The Flyers' attack weakened a little as the game became more physical. Again, Lilley was hitting people all over the ice. At the end of the period, he flattened Rob Brind'amour, a tough Flyer who had at least fifty pounds on the gritty little winger. The game remained scoreless, but across the country the Sharks had gotten two quick goals to even the score in St. Louis.

Between periods, Mark Ferner talked about the Ducks' slow starts. Their strategy was to try and play the whole game at an even pace, which meant that every night they would have to survive a juiced opponent's early onslaught. He felt that perhaps the players had a tendency to overemphasize their defensive responsibility and stay back a little too much. Sometimes, those tendencies would snowball and last an entire period.

Early in the third period, the Flyers caught the Ducks in the middle of a line change and made them pay on a goal by Allan Conroy, who caught Hill out of position again. The Flyers held a 1-0 lead for less than five minutes. Six minutes into the period, Ewen checked the puck free for Carnback. Carnback fed Douris, whose extra shifts replaced Grimson on the fourth line, and Peter hit a half-speed shot along the ice that slid by goalie Dominic Roussel.

Two minutes later, Corkum found Valk open thirty feet from the net. Valk's shot was hardly a rocket, but Roussel never reacted to it. As the Ducks celebrated their 2-1 lead, the Flyers fans booed Roussel mercilessly for his second soft goal in two minutes. Amazingly enough, Simpson pulled him. Just a handful of seconds earlier, Roussel had completed more than three-quarters of his second shutout of the season. Now he was gone, replaced by rookie Frederic Chabot. Across the country, Sergei Makarov had done it again, putting the Sharks ahead late in the third period. The Ducks couldn't afford to leave the Spectrum with anything but a win.

Their playoff dreams fizzling, the Flyers fought hard for the equalizer with Lindros out on the ice every other shift. With four and a half minutes left to go in the game, Valk and Garry Galley tangled in the corner. Galley took a dive, but Kerry Fraser called Valk for holding. During the first shift of the ensuing power play, the Ducks suffered an awful setback. Bob Corkum was trying to clear a Flyer out of the slot and the Flyer's skate got up and grazed the front of Corkum's right skate. It looked like the most innocent play in the world. When trainer Blynn DeNiro tried to treat the injury on the bench, a big pulse of blood spurted out, and DeNiro immediately got Corkum off the bench where he could be treated. Unfortunately, Corkum wears the tongues of his skates down. What might have been a scratch was in fact a ruptured tendon across the front of his right ankle.

Instead of being able to enjoy his best NHL season to date, Corkum would spend the off-season first in a cast and then in rehabilitation. It didn't seem like a just reward for a great year, but hockey's not always fair. For what it's worth, as soon as the game ended, Wilson asserted that "Corkum had to be proud of the season he just had." The summer might be a little easier because Ferreira had promised to renegotiate Corkum's contract to reward him for his efforts.

Back on the ice, Van Allen killed most of the rest of the power play by stealing the puck and playing keepaway. When the Flyers finally froze the puck, a large number of fans started giving coach Simpson a hard time with a "Terry Must Go" chant. Terry called a timeout to get his first line a blow and then sent them back out. After the Flyers won the ensuing faceoff, Galley got the puck to Recchi, who wound up and nearly fanned. His nick sent the puck slowly forward where Renberg quickly swatted it past a screened Hebert to tie the game at 17:12. As the clock wound down in Philadelphia, San Jose's lead in St. Louis became a victory after being posted as a final.

Time ran out, and the Ducks entered the overtime period with an abysmal 1-4-5 record in their first ten overtime contests. If anything, the Flyers had been worse, blowing ten games either in the last two minutes or overtime. Simpson sent out Lindros' line against Wilson's combination of Van Allen, Lilley and Valk. Seconds after the opening face-off, Lilley fired a turnaround shot at Chabot, who allowed a long rebound. Valk scooped it up and fired the puck past Chabot. Before he even knew he'd scored, his teammates swarmed all over him along the boards furthest from the bench. Valk's second goal of the night had salvaged the first road overtime win in the franchise's history.

On the bench, Wilson screamed in ecstasy. A few minutes later, he still looked overjoyed. "It was a great way to gut out a win. When you go back-to-back at the end of a road trip, you're not exactly sure what to expect. We gutted it out. Our club's been confident on the road all year. We've won in some tough buildings: New York, Chicago, Toronto, Vancouver, Calgary. We persevered even when they could have looked up at the scoreboard and quit. We've decided to put making the playoffs on the back-burner and just finish with a bang. It's good for the franchise, and it's important for the players. We want to finish ahead of our rival, L.A."

Wilson had nothing but praise for the Sharks. "You've gotta

give them credit. They go on the road for five games when a lot of people thought they would fold and they took nine points. So what are you gonna do? Their coaches have done a good job, and the Russians have played really well down the stretch."

Wilson especially wanted to praise the two men who combined on the overtime goal, Valk and Lilley. "It's great for Garry. He's struggled a little bit scoring the last couple of weeks. He got rewarded tonight. And I'm glad that John Lilley was able to pick up the assist. He forechecks, and he doesn't care how much bigger the other guy is. He does play like he's got a chip on his shoulder. He's right in everyone's face. That's what we need at this point in the season. We're a little leg-weary right now and he was able to give us that shot in the arm."

For Valk, the overtime goal was almost routine. "John Lilley made a good play putting it on net. I was going to the net like I usually do. I don't know if it was a missed assignment for one of their players. I ended up walking in all alone and the puck is laying there and I managed to put it upstairs. I thought it hit the crossbar. I didn't even really realize it went in until everyone jumped on the ice. Guy Hebert was the story tonight. He was last night as well."

Hebert was pleased the way he bounced back. "Last night was a tough game but I didn't really feel that fatigued today. We had a good full day of rest instead of an afternoon game. I think that helped out a lot. It's one of those games when I'm seeing the puck pretty well. I didn't want to say anything to jinx myself but I was thinking a shutout might be possible. Also, I had a good view of the out-of-town scoreboard. As far as I know, CuJo's never lost to San Jose and I thought he'd do me a favor. He's gonna hear it from me. I looked up at it one time and saw St. Louis with a 3-1 lead and it looked OK. Then I saw the final score before our overtime—but I shouldn't have even looked."

Douris, who scored the Ducks' first goal, felt he got lucky. "That one just baffled him. The puck was moving along the ice and it hit his stick. It didn't have a lot of sock on it. That was my knuckle puck," Douris said, smiling at his reference to the Mighty Ducks' movie. "We played a good game. Lilley's a little freight train out there. It makes a big difference, it's a blow to your ego when a smaller man hits you, and they looked like they got frustrated when things didn't go their way. It's tough, the fourth game in six nights, but we kept it close. Coming back after that game in Boston shows our character."

Despite injuries and a possible crisis in confidence after a bad loss, the Ducks had gritted out two tough wins. Add the Flyers to the list of teams the Ducks owned in year one. As they headed back to Southern California, the playoffs looked unlikely, but they again had reason to be proud.

17

The E Word

Whereas the [Kansas City] A's organization was rather a grimy, dirty machine, grotesquely inefficient and with a personality nobody liked, the Royals tended to the other extreme; they seemed antiseptic, colorless, mechanically efficient and with not much personality to like or dislike. This was a very welcome change. We had moved from the slums to the suburbs.
—Bill James, *The Bill James Baseball Abstract*, 1986

Uttering the E-word—expansion—was forbidden for players and staff of the Mighty Ducks of Anaheim. Violators were fined, and the two-figure punishment escalated as the number of people who heard the slip-up increased. By calling themselves an expansion team, the theory was that the Ducks would create an expectation of failure. Night after night, Wilson would stop just as he was about to speak the magic word and would gather himself to say "first-year team."

First-year team or expansion team, by the time they returned home from Philly, the Ducks were essentially finished in the playoff race. The Ducks lagged ten points behind the Sharks, thanks to another San Jose win that pushed the Shark unbeaten streak to six and counting. Two primary goals remained: getting more wins than the other first-year team, the Florida Panthers, and finishing ahead of their cross-town rivals, the Kings.

The first game back in Southern California, a visit to the Forum, would go a long way towards answering the second question. The Ducks beat the Kings easily as Lebeau, McSween and Sacco had big games. The 5-2 win was Hebert's first over the Kings. The Ducks had closed the season series with their neighbors on a high note, winning the final two games convincingly.

The next night, Edmonton beat the Ducks at the Pond in overtime, 3-2. Whatever suspense remained was drained out of the race as the Sharks continued to win. Just one year removed from a battle with Ottawa to stay out of the cellar (or perhaps in, so as to draft Alexander Daigle), San Jose had set a record for the biggest one-season turnaround in NHL history. The Ducks stayed statistically alive a few more days by beating Toronto, 3-1, behind another fine effort by Hebert. The game-winning goal by John Lilley was the young man's first NHL goal, but the Ducks were still one loss or one San Jose win away from elimination.

After the Toronto game, the Ducks headed out on the road for one last time. They were back in Western Canada, site of their best trip of the season, and their first game would be in Calgary. The night before, the team gathered in a sports bar to watch the Sharks play the Kings. The Kings had been eliminated a week earlier and put together another sub-par performance. The Sharks won and celebrated their first playoff berth.

In Calgary, the hopes of his team finally dashed, Wilson searched for other ways to find meaning in the final five games. Before the King game, the coaches had watched a broadcast of a Panther game during which the Floridians displayed a number of lists of top performances by first-year teams without including the Ducks.

With Florida still in contention for the final Eastern Conference playoff spot, Anaheim's players and coaches felt their accomplishments might be overlooked. Fifteen players—

Carnback, Corkum, Dollas, Douris, Ewen, Ferner, Grimson, Hill, Houlder, McSween, Sacco, Skalde, Sweeney, Valk, and Van Allen—reached new career highs for points in a single season. Even so, no player would score fifty-five points or twenty-five goals. Anaheim, like almost all recent expansion teams, failed to average even three goals a game. As a team, the Ducks would not be able to total more points than Florida, but they could still win more games.

Their first effort in Calgary revealed a team still depressed by its playoff elimination. Although Garry Valk scored in the first minute of the game, Calgary, needing a win to clinch the division title, put Anaheim through twenty minutes of hell. Hebert handled seventeen of nineteen shots to keep the Ducks, credited with just one shot during the first period, within range.

Anaheim's second shot of the game got by Vernon early in the second period to tie the score at two. The Flames reclaimed the lead a short while later. Twenty-six minutes into the game, after five goals had been scored, Vernon finally recorded his first save. A quiet crowd on hand to celebrate a win that would clinch the division title clapped derisively. The Flames outshot the Ducks by more than thirty shots, but the final outcome remained in doubt until Al MacInnis scored an empty-netter that did nothing to spark Flame supporters. When Hebert was announced as the number-one star for his heroic efforts, the fans seemed more appreciative than they'd been all night.

After the game, Hebert talked about what might motivate the team. "We still have a chance to tie Florida or get ahead of them. We've set some new goals for ourselves, and hopefully the next four games will be better than this one. We'd like to finish ahead of L.A. I thought maybe we had an off first period, but we've done that recently so I wasn't too concerned. We were still in good shape after the first. I don't think we ever got on track. We had a lot of tired bodies, but I don't think we had our minds in it because we were officially eliminated."

Wilson had not talked to reporters after the game, but Hebert had seen his displeasure. "Ron didn't come in and start kicking garbage cans or throwing things, but I don't think he was real pleased with the effort. He expected more out of us. The crazy thing was we were still in the game. No matter how bad we played, we still had a chance at the end to tie it when he pulled me."

With Corkum already out and Val Allen home with his expectant wife and Ewen sidelined by a shoulder sprain, Wilson was running out of forwards. Maxim Betz, acquired in the Kasatonov trade, would get his first start in Edmonton while Sweeney would play center for the first time in a decade. The Oilers scored an early goal, but Carnback got it back for Anaheim late in the second period before a feisty Oiler crowd. For the second straight game, Hebert was getting shelled, but he was even better than he had been in the Saddledome despite being bowled over by an Oiler rushing the net. Hebert had remained prone on the ice for a few minutes before shaking it off.

Hebert wasn't the only one getting hit; the Oilers and Ducks were playing Anaheim's chippiest game of the year. Lebeau and Yake were both knocked out of the game. Even so, the Ducks took charge in the third period on goals by Valk, his third of the trip, and Sweeney. One more time, the Ducks had bounced back from a poor game by fighting through a tough night and finding a way to win. The victory was their thirty-second of the season, which tied Florida and surpassed the prior record.

Wilson had expected his team to lose after the first period. "Tonight, the game looked not much different from the other night in Calgary. I thought we'd gotten all the juice out of the orange, but the guys really came to play in the second and third period and we took it away. I certainly didn't expect to beat thirty-one wins. That was done in '67 when they played predominantly against expansion teams. They got thirty-one wins with sixty games against expansion teams. We've got thirty wins against established teams. I'm just glad we didn't play sixty games against expansion teams because our record would have been brutal. We'd have gotten smoked; we might have won only three games this year."

Anaheim had won just two of twelve against their expansion brethren, but the win over the Oilers loosened Wilson's demeanor considerably. "It got chippy because we didn't show up physically in the first period and they took some liberties. The turning point was the hit Stu put on Stephan Lebeau. That was the hardest hit of the season. Steph got up with a bloody lip, and Stu went into the penalty box. Otherwise, Stephan might have punched him on the bench. That's not the first time this season Stu's got the wrong man."

After laughing, Wilson became more serious. His team's health was falling apart. "What we needed was Stuey to hit people. He went four periods without throwing one body-check. Even with his hand taped up, he's gotta hit because they took liberties. So we end up with some guys hurt because we came out and played a very passive first period. If we had come out and played hard in the first five minutes, they'd have said, 'OK, we'll just play a regular hockey game, we won't bother with this baloney.' They run our goalie and we help their guy up and we're not even worrying about Guy. That can't happen. So we talked about it between periods and the players responded."

Hebert had made the difference again, according to Wilson. "Guy was really outstanding. He found that he's gotta be a focused, intense person to be successful as a goalie. He's got twenty wins on an expansion team. That's a great accomplishment for him."

The final road game of the year came in Vancouver. The Ducks had opened their road schedule with an impossible win over the Rangers six months earlier. If anything, tonight's contest looked even more difficult. With Yake and Lebeau joining the list of players sidelined by injuries, the Ducks had just one healthy center left and would have to play minor-leaguers whose names Wilson couldn't even remember. Paul Kariya, who was now working out at home in Vancouver, trying to become ambidextrous like Gordie Howe, had talked to Wilson before the game. Wilson had made the youngster an offer. "I talked to Paul for about an hour. We passed the hat tonight among the players, hoping that seventy-five bucks would convince him to get in there and play."

For one more game, an opponent came hard at the Ducks early. On this afternoon, Shtalenkov weathered most of the storm, allowing just one goal. Late in the period, Sacco set up Sweeney for the equalizer. With young forwards on the ice in need of guidance, Loney, the captain, led the way with superior defensive effort, taking over in the corner where Corkum had previously done the dirty work. Lilley, the little freight train, bugged Bure, the superstar, just enough to cause the Russian to retaliate with a slash that was caught by the referee late in the third period. On the ensuing power play, Carnback, who'd been double-shifted all night, scored his second goal in two days. Bure drew a penalty of his own a few minutes later, but Valk and Semenov double-shifted to kill off the power play. As the clock wound down, the Canucks pulled McLean and Sweeney immediately found Sacco who scored his second empty-net goal of the year to clinch the victory.

Wilson had one more win over his former boss. "This was unbelievable with what we had to work with tonight. We were down to one regular center. We didn't want to be quite as aggressive forechecking because we were a little tired and we had guys playing out of position. I was getting frustrated at the liberties Pavel was taking, but this is exactly what we wanted to do, we wanted to frustrate them. They're worried about hitting us and they forgot about scoring. And we won on the scoreboard. They might have beat us up a little bit physically but the bottom line is we won."

Winning twice in Vancouver was especially sweet for Wilson, who'd been stung by criticism in the local press when he was an assistant. One of his responsibilities in Vancouver had been the power play, which often struggled mightily. Wilson continued to draw the ire of a few Vancouver scribes, who wondered how he could possibly have been as successful as he had been with the Mighty Ducks.

In fact, Anaheim's power play productivity was among the bottom three in the NHL. Anaheim ended the season as the only team in the league without a player in double figures in power play goals. The area was again Wilson's responsibility, but this time the blame lay squarely on the shoulders of a cast of players lacking in firepower. Wilson and Ferreira agreed that one clear area of need was a defenseman who could quarterback the power play more effectively than Houlder and Hill had during the season.

While those moves were still months away, the victory over Vancouver secured a better record for the Ducks than the Kings. "Finishing ahead of the Kings is a great feeling," Wilson said. "We want to set the record for wins by a new team. We wanted to break the record for road wins by an expansion team with Florida. Florida finishes with 18 and we've got 19, so there's a little record to celebrate."

Wilson could not get over the win. "I'm thoroughly amazed. The first ten minutes I was thinking, boy, it's going to be tough to keep this one in single digits. Just when I think we're dead, it's like Lazarus arises and away we go. We just refuse to give up. That's not me or the coaching staff, that's the character of our players. They don't want to be known as an expansion team, there I said it." Wilson laughed, knowing that he would draw a fine for that little slip.

The money would be well worth it. Both game and trip had gone so much better than anyone had expected. The Little Expansion Team That Could just kept on chugging. Florida would equal but not surpass the Mighty Ducks' victory total. With Kariya and company on the way, the new E word in October 1994 would be expectations.

18

Pond of Dreams

I told them I was proud of them. What we had this year was special. Some teams never get that kind of camaraderie and chemistry and they've been in the league for fifty years. We somehow got lucky enough to pick all the right guys in the draft.
—Ron Wilson, after the final game of the season

The Ducks returned home from Vancouver for their final two games of the season. Sad news followed the team back. Frank Griffiths, long-time chairman of the Canucks, had passed away. Wilson would fly up to Vancouver to pay his respect to his former boss between games. He would be accompanied on his return from Vancouver by Paul Kariya. The Ducks wanted the kid to get to know his teammates and see the facilities for the first time.

In the next-to-last game of the season, the wheels finally came off. Calgary came in and easily handled an Anaheim team that was at two-thirds strength. The final score was 3-0, and the Ducks had almost no scoring chances. Despite the loss, the players and coaches did not seem upset at all, choosing to focus on what had already been accomplished or what was to come.

"We've got nothing to be ashamed of. Look at who's injured. Our three top scorers are out. Unfortunately, we don't have a lot of depth. We're asking guys to do things that just aren't possible," Wilson said. "Calgary's very patient and waits for opportunities for counter-attacks."

After seeing Calgary handle his team twice in less than a week, Wilson was convinced that the Flames would be the team to beat in the Western Conference and expected them to meet the Penguins in the Cup finals. One thing he was having a hard time getting people to believe was that the Sharks would beat the Red Wings because of Irbe and the defense in front of him. No one could argue when he credited Shtalenkov after another excellent effort. "Mikhail's played great. We knew he would, and that's why we made the change because we felt that he was just as good, if not better than, Ron Tugnutt," Wilson said. "And I think he's proven that in the games he's played. He's been solid."

Bobby Dollas was already worried about how ready the team would be in six months. "I hate to say it, but next year could be a sophomore jinx. We'll have to get a quick jump and have a better October."

Wilson and Ferreira were already making plans to avoid next year's bump in the road. "Next year, you go into the season with the teams shooting for you. Hartford, Philly, the Rangers, Winnipeg, the teams that we swept, are gonna be looking to play us. Teams won't take us lightly," Ferreira believed, even as he considered whether the team would need to start looking at some of its younger talent at the NHL level. "We're not gonna bring in kids just to bring in kids, but sometimes you have to take a step back to take two steps forward. We're looking to get better long-term. Our goaltending and our defense were really good. As a first-year team, we tried to establish an identity. With the size of our team, that was easy."

Wilson worried more about work ethic than anything else. He could count more than a dozen games that had been won primarily through wearing down a more talented opponent.

Most of his players had set new career highs in key categories. Perhaps they would not believe they had any more to give; after all, maybe they didn't. Wilson wanted more talented young bodies on the roster. A competitive environment at training camp in September would ensure no one slipped into complacency.

One of those young bodies sat next to Wilson on the flight back from Vancouver after the Griffiths funeral. For Paul Kariya, it was his second trip ever to Southern California. Kariya had been to Anaheim once before a few years earlier to see Disneyland. He'd also done just enough surfing to know that he was best suited for frozen water. During the three-hour flight, one of the brightest young coaches in the game talked hockey with one of the most intelligent rising stars.

"Ron and I have similar ideas about where the game of hockey is headed and how the game of hockey should be played. We were talking about ways to get around the neutral-zone trap. One way is taking away the center-ice line. If you can make one rule change to take away the neutral zone trap, that's it. They don't have it in college, and it makes the game more exciting," said Kariya, who'd watched the Ducks from afar and respected Wilson's efforts. "He's just done a great job for this team. He's a key to their success. It's been a dream season."

Paul's biggest moment since the Olympics had come as a fan sitting in front of his TV set at home. He would always remember where he was when Wayne scored goal number 802. "I was sitting with my family watching the game. It was such a tremendous accomplishment that I got the chills down my spine."

Now Paul wanted to provide some thrills for those who enjoyed watching him play. "In Canada, you grow up watching Hockey Night in Canada every Saturday night. It's like a religion. I'd certainly love to play on Hockey Night in Canada. The biggest thing is to have Don Cherry talk about me. I don't know what he'd say about me, but it'd be nice to be on his show."

That moment will probably come a lot sooner than Paul imagined a few hours before the Ducks' final game. While Kariya was dreaming about an appearance on the "Grapevine," everyone was preparing to thank each other for a season of dreams. The whole organization wanted to thank the fans in a very public display. In a more private way, Wilson and his assistants wanted to thank his players for their efforts.

Army put together a video of season highlights that included nice plays by everyone in the locker room. He cut the video together over music from the movie "Field of Dreams" and a song by Canadian rocker Bryan Adams from the mid-80s entitled "The Summer of '69." The chorus of that song featured the line, "those were the best days of our lives." After everybody watched the video, Wilson addressed the team. "For us as coaches," Wilson said, "this has been the best year of our lives and we hope it has been for you."

"You can always take what you did this year with you. You will always be remembered. When we started, everybody made fun of the team name, the jersey, the movie and now they're looking at us differently. You put a pride in wearing that Mighty Duck jersey. A few years from now, when this team wins the Stanley Cup, people will look back at this team. You established the road to that first Cup and that will live with this organization forever."

The fans were rewarded with the best pre-game show since opening night. The William Tell overture boomed from the Pond's sound system as fireworks were set off. For the first time all season, two mascots worked together, twin Wild Wings, to help spell out a sign made of fireworks that read "Duck Fans Are #1." Applause continued to roll down from the rafters as smoke filled the arena and the players took the ice for one last time.

The opponent, the Vancouver Canucks, were readying themselves for a first-round playoff encounter with the Flames. Pat Quinn started back-up goalie Kay Whitmore to keep him sharp before Kirk McLean's anticipated run of games in the playoffs. The first period was all Ducks. Patrick Carnback, the Swedish center who'd finally been freed from playing with the two bruisers, set up opportunities for Sacco and Yake. Even so, the period remained scoreless. In the second period, the Canucks finally awakened when Bure scored on a breakaway. Tim Hunter added a second goal later in the period.

As the game moved into the third period, the Ducks struggled to avoid a shutout on their final night. The twenty-fifth consecutive sellout crowd cheered every rush. Carnback set up Sacco a few more times, but Whitmore had Joe's number. The only man to play every game during the first season, Sacco put five shots on net during the game to add to his team-leading total of 206, but he could not break through for what would have been his twentieth goal.

At 7:16 of the third period, Terry Yake turned a seemingly harmless pass from Troy Loney into something dangerous with his next move. He flicked the puck across the ice to David Williams, who buried the final Duck goal of the year behind Whitmore. Williams, who'd been quietly effective along the blue-line ever since returning from San Diego, had been a plus-13 over the last half of the season. The assist by Yake was his fifty-second point and broke a tie between Terry and Corkum for team scoring leader.

Down a goal, Wilson pulled Hebert at the end of the game in an effort to tie the game. Ron sent out Carnback, Lilley, Valk, Sacco, McSween and Houlder for what looked to be the last shift. The Ducks lost the faceoff and the Canucks sent the puck down the ice. McSween outraced Geoff Courtnall to touch up the puck and draw the final icing call. Wilson sent out Van Allen for the season's last faceoff. Van Allen pulled the puck back to Houlder, but Houlder's shot missed the net. The Canucks got the puck up ice and had a chance to score an empty-netter. In yet another demonstration of the competitive fires that burned inside this team all year long, Van Allen went down to block the final shot as the horn sounded.

The Ducks were not headed to the playoffs and had not even won their final game, but their fans did not want them to leave. After the Canucks perfunctorily celebrated their season-ending victory, seventeen thousand fans jumped to their feet and clapped their hands together. The players skated around the ice for a few seconds and then disappeared into their dressing room.

Wilson made one last speech to the assembled group of players. It was a bittersweet moment. "Enjoy tonight because for a lot of us, it'll be the last time we'll be together. Just examine your team pictures because yearly there's seven or eight guys that change, even from a championship team."

Even if there had been a few tough nights, the season held great joy for Wilson because of the relationships that had been formed. "You never know what guys' personalities will be, but here they're tight. The guys had a real togetherness. They really liked one another and sacrificed for one another. That's something we as coaches can't take credit for. When a coach says 'you guys have to like one another', it doesn't happen. Being a coach is like being a parent. Sometimes, the environment takes control," Wilson said as he looked to next year. "Even for a tight-knit group like us, we didn't make the playoffs so we have to find ways of making improvements. I think we pushed a lot of guys to the best that they can perform. If it's not good enough, you've gotta improve. You tweak here and there. We'll probably have six or seven new guys in our lineup to start the season next year. Who? I don't know. Who'll be gone? I don't know. I hope our guys don't think they won the Stanley Cup because we set a few records for a new team in the league. We still didn't make the playoffs. But you have to make the playoffs to be a success."

Wilson was proud of a number of the team's accomplishments. "We had the best goals-against in the division and kept it under three. We did the job defensively. Now we've gotta score a few more goals. That's why you see Paul Kariya around here today. We'll be a little more exciting offensively next year. If you work hard, you reap the dividends and that's what we did. We convinced our players at the beginning of training camp we would have success. It was simple, hard work by everyone in our organization from the drafters to the people who got the building ready to the people who sold season-tickets. Everybody worked their rear ends off, putting in a lot of long nights. Our players did the same thing."

Wilson refused to single out any player's performance. "They all surprised me. They all played better than I thought they would. Coming from a team with a lot of talent to a team of guys who were all third and fourth liners or even in the minors, I wondered if I had any talent. I discovered that hard work almost makes up for talent, but you do need skilled people in your lineup. Across the hall, the Canucks had a disappointing year, but they still got in because of the talent on that roster. That's the only way you can make the playoffs."

"If everyone's patient, we'll have Kariya, Karpov, Tsulygin and this year's picks. If we can build upon this tradition of hard work and solid defense, a couple of years from now, we'll have a strong contender. Every friend I know in hockey was telling me I was crazy to take the job because it could be the last coaching job I would take, but I was confident it wouldn't be, and I don't think..." Wilson's voice trailed off as he had a sudden realization. "Maybe it will be my last coaching job. I hope that I am still here in ten years."

Perhaps the itinerant wanderer would stick around for a while. In a league where even successful coaches rarely last than more than a few years with the same team, one couldn't help but feel that Wilson and the Mighty Ducks were only at the beginning of a beautiful relationship.

After the final game, Hebert wanted to talk about the whole season. "Our success puts pressure on the coaching staff, as well as the players, but it's a great thing to build on. I just figured it was gonna be a great experience. Winning takes the pressure off. No matter how this ended, getting to play was gonna be better than past years for a lot of guys." Guy believed he was playing as well as he had all season. "After the trade with Ronnie, I was feeling a little tired and had to play through that to get my second wind. I feel pretty good right now."

Writers often grow frustrated when they don't get useful quotes after a game. There's no question that a part of the players' fame and big salaries is produced by media attention, and writers expect players to understand the value of the transaction. Even so, explaining failure time and again gets tiresome awfully fast. After three losses that stung, even Wilson skipped post-game press conferences because he just wasn't up to it.

The players who deserved credit for facing the heat after every loss were whoever was playing goal, and Terry Yake. The few times when other players treated even the writers they liked as if they were diseased, the goalies and Yake would patiently answer questions that ranged from tough to silly.

After the final loss, the team's leading point scorer reflected on the year just ended. "Tonight kind of epitomizes our season," said Yake. "We worked our butts off and lost close games. As the season got tougher, we managed to play with everybody. Next year, hopefully we'll win more of our one-goal games. We've got two great goalies. I can't say enough about how they played this year. Whether we played good defense in front of them or bad defense, they stood on their head all year."

"Being the leading scorer's nice, but I'm gonna look at my actual numbers. The total was definitely low. I bought a lot of editing equipment to look at things that I can try to improve. I want to get eighty or a hundred points. I'd definitely like a little more ice time, and I'll figure out what I have to do to get that," Yake continued as he looked to the future. "You want to make improvements every year. If somebody comes in, they're gonna have to beat somebody else out to make the hockey club. If they get the job, we've made an improvement. That will make training camp intense."

The first day of that training camp was some hundred and fifty days away, but for half the roster, the hockey season wasn't quite over. The World Championships in Italy would start in just a few weeks. As the Ducks gathered for celebrations and a few final rounds of golf, the NHL playoffs got underway. Next year, they expected to be more than spectators.

19

Kariya, Tverdovsky, Cup?

I played against Bobby Orr, and this kid is Bobby Orr. Vancouver had the Russian Rocket. Well, this kid is the Russian Skyrocket.
—John Ferguson, Ottawa director of player personnel, describing Oleg Tverdovsky

With the Ducks' inaugural season over, the players hung around Anaheim to get in a few rounds of golf. The league turned its attention to the playoffs where San Jose performed just as Wilson had expected. Once they got a toehold in the series with Detroit, the Sharks refused to go away, finally beating the Red Wings in a dramatic Game Seven in Joe Louis Arena. Two months earlier, Tavares had noted that if he had been in Detroit GM Bryan Murray's shoes, he would have traded Primeau for Grant Fuhr. The failure to improve their goaltending—if anything, Chevaldae performed better for Winnipeg than Essensa did for Detroit—cost Detroit. Bowman benched Essensa and the rookie netminder Osgood struggled through an inconsistent series. A costly lesson had been learned again: trying to win the Cup without an elite goaltender was suicidal. Murray would be looking for work within a month.

As the Sharks moved on to face Toronto, elsewhere, two ex-Ducks failed to perform up to expectations for their new teams.

The Stars swept Kasatonov's Blues in the first round. While Kasa did not deserve much of the blame, the collapse reflected poorly on St. Louis' late-season front office moves designed to give the Blues a chance for a serious run at the Cup. In the Montreal-Boston series, the Canadiens found themselves dependent on Tugnutt after Patrick Roy's appendicitis. With the heat of a big playoff game finally on him, Tugger had a bad night, and Les Habs eventually lost the series. Tugnutt explained afterwards that he couldn't be expected to perform at his best when he was getting limited playing time. It was one alibi the Ducks would never have to hear.

* * *

Meanwhile, almost half the Duck team gathered in Italy for the World Championships. Carnback joined the Swedes and Shtalenkov was top goalie for the Russians while the still-unsigned Kariya joined Bobby Dollas on the Canadian squad. As for the U.S. team, Wilson was head coach and brought Army along to work on the bench handling the defensive changes. Wilson filled his roster with Lilley, Sweeney, Sacco, Hill, McSween, and Hebert and asked them to execute the same system they'd been playing all year. Once again, Wilson's men played well on the road, winning their first three games in their bracket before being overwhelmed by the Swedes and the Finns. As the Americans slipped back to earth, the Russians held themselves down, tanking their final first-round game against Canada to ensure a quarterfinal match with the United States.

The American team hadn't beaten a team from Russia, the Commonwealth of Independent States or Soviet Union in an important tourney in the fourteen years since the Miracle on Ice at Lake Placid. Wilson used the deliberate Russian loss to motivate his team. Wilson and Army warned the players to expect to face a Russian team that could outskate them like the Swedes and Finns had.

"In Europe, it's a puck-possession game. If you chase them, that's what they want. They call it 65/35; they have the puck 65 percent of the time and North Americans have it 35 percent of the time," said Army. "We said, let them have it. Let's clog the neutral zone, frustrate them entering it, force some turnovers and counterattack at the right time. We decided to play the one-two-two: our first guy would step up inside their zone, our two wings would lock their two wings. We knew they were one-on-one players and they'd turn the puck over. We told our players to get the lead if we can and, sure enough, Craig Janney got a big goal on a four-on-three. They came on in the last half of the game, and Guy was unbelievable. It was a marvelous effort by our guys."

Sweeney got one of the team's second period goals as the Americans built a two-goal lead. As the Russian pressure increased over the last thirty minutes, Hebert, handling a shot a minute, stood on his head for one last time, preserving a 3-1 lead in an impossible, emotional victory. Without any televised coverage, this game could not possibly have the significance of the Miracle on Ice, but for Wilson, it was a sweet win nonetheless. In the semis against Finland, the Americans were swamped again, losing 8-0, and taking penalty after penalty as their frustration grew. Despite some unnecessary roughness, the Americans flourished during two competitive weeks of play.

By the time the final rolled around, Kariya, playing on a line with two young NHL stars, Jason Arnott and Brendan Shanahan, had established himself as the top forward in the tournament by leading Canada to seven straight wins with five goals and six assists. Only the young Finn Saku Koivu, whose rights were retained by the Canadiens, was turning as many heads. Kariya's training time in Vancouver had paid off: Paul was not the same player he'd been just three months earlier in Lillehammer. He looked stronger and faster. Perhaps both sides had been frustrated by the inability to reach agreement but nobody could deny Kariya had gained a tremendous amount of valuable experience, at least the equal of a year in the NHL. "Paul played really well at Worlds," said Army a few weeks later. "He established that he could play at the top level. He showed a lot of passion and he gains confidence each time he plays. He makes everyone around him better."

The final was a taut affair in which Kariya set up Rob Brind'amour's come-from-behind goal that sent the game into overtime. After both teams failed to score in the last few minutes of play, Canadians held their collective breath as their boys entered into a shootout to decide a championship with the nightmare in Lillehammer still burned in Paul's memory. Kariya failed to score again, but Luc Robitaille and Joe Sakic traded goals with Jari Kurri and Mikko Makela in the first round. Robitaille opened the sudden-death round with a goal and Bill Ranford, the goalie of the tournament, made the winning save on Mika Nieminen. The Canadian team flooded the ice, celebrating Canada's first world championship in men's hockey in 33 years. For Kariya, the joy of winning overwhelmed any lingering disappointment of losing the Olympic final. For Dollas, the world championship was the culmination of the best year of his career and completed the jump from the minor leagues to elite defenseman. Perhaps the shootout Eisner wanted would fly with Canadian fans after all.

* * *

Back in North America, Bure and McLean had reached a new level to carry the Canucks easily past Dallas and Toronto, who'd just edged the Sharks. The question was no longer when Bure would become the best player in the game but instead when the world would recognize that it had already happened. As a Russian and a scorer, he seemed likely to suffer an even greater backlash than Gretzky, but his play could no longer be questioned. In the lower forty-eight, Messier delivered a guaranteed game six win for the Rangers by scoring the come-from-behind goals in their semi with New Jersey. Then, in game seven, Richter and Brodeur were magnificent as the rivals battled into two overtimes before the Rangers finally prevailed.

In the Cup finals, despite a brilliant Game One upset led by McLean's 52 saves, Vancouver could not stay on the ice with the Rangers the first four games. Brian Leetch took over, his four goals and five assists in the first four games leading the Rangers to a 3-1 lead. With the 54-year drought about to end, New Yorkers and their media lost their minds. While parade plans became front-page news, the feud between Keenan and Smith heated up again when Keenan refused to deny rumors that he was going to jump to Detroit after the season ended. Amidst the fury surrounding the Rangers, the Canucks regained their sense of balance in the Garden, becoming more physical with Leetch and winning Game Five, 6-3, on the strength of two goals each by Bure and Geoff Courtnall and a bad game by Richter. Back in Vancouver, the Canucks rolled the Rangers again, 4-1, on Courtnall's second consecutive two-goal night. For two games, the Canucks had held Leetch to one assist.

The biggest U.S. TV hockey audience ever and the biggest audience in Canada since the '72 Canada Cup tuned in for Game Seven, the first ultimate game in a decade. Unfortunately, in New York, Bettman had been unable to coax the Rangers' pay-cable outlet, MSG network, to allow ESPN to broadcast the game in the New York metropolitan area. ESPN's announcing teams had ranged from excellent to mediocre, but they'd shown inspiration in their production. The development of a goalie-cam tucked into the back of each net allowed viewers a perspective they'd never seen before, a better view of every goal and each tough save. The drama of the series was captured brilliantly by both cameramen and directors who were mastering the intricacies of the game. Viewers knew how many minutes and shifts Bure and Leetch, the series' stars, had played. Scoring chances were analyzed on telestrators between periods. The game's tactics and individual brilliance were coming to life, and fans couldn't get enough.

As a new wave of viewers became exposed to hockey, the one thing missing was fights. The playoffs prove every year that when the results of the game truly matter, fighting disappears. The games were physical, featuring tremendous checking, especially by the Canucks in the last three games. There were even occasional cheap shots, but no more than in a less-meaningful regular-season game. Both Keenan and Quinn gave their enforcers most nights off during the series as they searched for ways to get other more significant advantages.

The one thing that neither man tinkered with before Game Seven was goaltending. Richter and McLean had each had one weak game, but otherwise, both men had been brilliant. Leetch beat McLean to break out of his scoring slump on a beautiful play by Zubov and Messier to put the Rangers on top early. Adam Graves scored his first goal of the finals a little later in the first period, but the Canucks would not go away.

In this spectacular series, Game Seven was Trevor Linden's night. First, he cut the lead to one on a short-handed goal early in the second period. Messier answered with a power play goal before the period ended. Linden scored again early in the third period. The Canucks came at Richter the rest of the night, hitting two posts in the third period before finally pulling McLean for an extra attacker. Ferreira, a close friend of Ranger GM Neil Smith, had been rooting all series long for New York to win the Cup. Now, watching the final minutes at home on TV with his wife, he found himself wanting the Canucks to even the score. He did not want this incomparable season to end.

The Canucks continued to get the puck deep in the Rangers' end where the defenders would tie it up and depend on Messier to win faceoffs like he had all season. Even Linden couldn't win draws from Messier. The crowd counted down the final seconds. The Rangers were champs. The curse of 1940 had been broken. A fan at the Garden held a sign that read, "Now I can die in peace."

A Russian, Bure, had led the NHL playoffs in scoring for the first time in league history. When Bettman announced the MVP of the playoffs, Brian Leetch became the first American ever to win the Conn Smythe Trophy. One of the greatest seasons in league history was capped off by the best celebration in all of sports. Messier, the Rangers' captain, hoisted the Cup over his head and began the victory laps around the ice. The Cup was passed from player to player, a moment for the team to share its hard-earned glory with its devoted fans.

The quality of the series, along with a New York champ, caught the media's attention, at least for a few moments. Leetch, Messier and Richter kept hitting the national stage, with appearances on *The Today Show, The Late Show with David Letterman*, as well as with Howard Stern's nationally-syndicated radio show. The celebration was capped by a huge parade in Manhattan.

That same week, a slightly more formal NHL celebration occurred in Toronto when the annual awards were dished out. Sergei Fedorov continued the Russian ascendance, becoming the first Russian to grab the Hart Trophy as league MVP while also claiming the Selke for best defensive forward. Buffalo's Dominik Hasek became the first European to win the Vezina as the league's best goaltender. As if his career accomplishments were not enough, Gretzky picked up yet another Ross as scoring champ and his fourth Lady Byng for sportsmanship.

* * *

In Anaheim, the Ducks' front office was busy finding the next Kariya. All the scouts returned a month before the draft to prepare their final draft board. The key man in the room was David McNab, the Director of Player Personnel. McNab, a tall, bespectacled Minnesotan, had played back-up goaltender for Bob Johnson at the University of Wisconsin in the mid-1970s. More importantly, David's father Max and brother Peter had both played in the National Hockey League. "Every meal we spent together, we talked hockey," McNab recalls with a faint Upper Midwestern twang.

When David's skills proved insufficient for even the low minors, he wanted to find a way to stay around the game he so dearly loved. His father, by then GM of the Washington Caps, hired David and turned him loose to scout young talent. At the age of 22, David hit the road with a company car, a company credit card and a few thousand dollars advance money. His first year he worked for nothing but expenses but it might have been the best year of his life. After four years in scouting with the Caps, he went to work for the Whalers where he spent seven years before joining the Rangers' staff in 1989 where he worked with Neil Smith.

McNab and Ferreira had known each other for years, and had attended a game one night in Saskatchewan where the weather was so cold that they kept their car running outside the rink during the game for fear the battery would conk out. To stay warm between periods, the two men sat on the engine of the machine, more tractor than Zamboni, that resurfaced the ice.

When Ferreira was hired by Tavares, he knew he wanted to bring in McNab to be the head scout, but that Smith wouldn't allow it until after the entry and expansion drafts. Ferreira waited and McNab signed on immediately after the draft. "Jack was my idol in scouting. I think Calgary won the Stanley Cup because of Ferreira. He was the best at judging talent. If you're a career scout, you want to work for the best. I would have taken the same job with the Ducks that I had with the Rangers so I could work for Jack."

McNab and Ferreira were part of a group of scouts that included Gauthier and Neil Smith, among others, that broke into the league about the same time . They represented a new generation in scouting. In the past, scouting jobs had been seen as little more than a reward for loyal ex-players. The new class enjoyed discovering kids. They traveled more and received more resources and decision-making authority from their front offices.

McNab knows the Ducks have to gain ground on the league's elite through acquisition of young talent. "Right now, we're thirty-five points behind the Rangers," notes McNab. "If we draft as well as they do over the next five years, you've got to figure we'll still be that far behind. When you look back, the most successful drafters took the big gambles. Every round you've got to shoot for the home run."

"In the second round, you can take a guy who's a lock to be in the NHL but his upside's at best as a third-line player. You're not gonna look stupid if you draft him because he'll show up in an analysis in a few years in *The Hockey News*. Another guy might be behind him but improving faster. If you project four years ahead, that guy'll be a star. Of course, if he stops developing, he won't make the league and you'll look bad. You've got to take that guy every time. Edmonton took those kind of risks with Fuhr, Coffey and Anderson. It made them a powerhouse. You can't worry about failure, either as an organization or as an individual."

Where the Ducks hope to separate themselves from other talent evaluators is in the area of character evaluation. "Most people use a similar on-ice evaluation and all scouts work hard. It's almost impossible to find someone other teams haven't seen. So if you're going to try to do it differently, you have to look at the off-ice, to see who's going to make the best teammate."

"I'll have a two-hour meeting with a player and come away saying 'yes or no.' It's not a moment, more of a feeling I develop. I have no problem eliminating a top player with a character flaw. No kid is too good to pass up. Every year, two or three guys excite the hell out of me to talk to. This year, I talked to 50 or 60 guys and there's one guy that has just blown me away."

A month before the draft, McNab promised to reveal the name of that player after the draft. What was clear was the Ducks had the same four choices at the top of their board as most other teams: Radek Bonk, the huge Czech center who'd torn up the IHL; Ed Jovanovski, the big Canadian defenseman who'd improved immensely over the last year; Oleg Tverdovsky, a Russian defenseman who'd already been compared to Orr by Ottawa GM John Ferguson; and Jamie Storr, potentially a once-in-a-decade goalie.

Each of the players would fit into the strategy that the Ducks had divined from analyzing the Fantastic Four: Oilers, Bruins, Isles and Canadiens. The requisite elements included a 100-point center (hopefully already drafted in Kariya, but Bonk could fit the bill), an outstanding offensive defenseman (either Jovanovski or Tverdovsky—the roster certainly didn't have one), and an elite goaltender (Storr might be that good; of course, Hebert and Shtalenkov hadn't shown any reason to believe they couldn't do the job). The Ducks' decision about the top man on the board was unanimous, if secret.

To make up thirty-five points was going to require tapping untraditional talent sources. A year earlier when McNab came aboard, Ferreira had sent him out to answer two questions: who's the best overage player in Junior? who's the best free agent available in U.S. colleges? McNab and Gauthier had snatched up Scott Chartier in answer to the second question. In Canada, Richard Green saw a big, skilled left winger playing for Brandon and McNab came up to take a look. He was scoring three points every two games and he was tough as well, a prototypical power forward no more than two years away. In the dead of winter when the rest of the league was pointing only towards the entry draft, the Ducks signed Mike Maneluk to a multi-year contract. Two extra prospects was the first step in cutting into the 35-point deficit.

Now it was time for another McNab special. The morning of the day of the first two rounds of the entry draft, the NHL holds a supplemental draft for North American college players who are over 20. Teams that miss the playoffs are each given one pick in the same order as the entry draft. It was traditionally a draft where all the teams took American college players. Nobody seemed to respect Canadian university players. Florida took a defenseman from Harvard with the first pick and the other eight teams that picked took Americans as well, but the Ducks had something up their sleeves again. Steve Rucchin was his name and he'd been buried at the University of Western Ontario. McNab was thrilled to get a huge center who could score and play the physical game.

Other exciting things were going on at the draft as the Ducks tried to address their key needs up front plus put offense on the blue line. Trade talks were underway with four teams. Deals became contingent on completing other deals so that holes would be filled. Meanwhile, McNab met with a skilled Swede named Johan Davidsson. He was the player the Ducks hoped would slide to the second round pick but the Devils—who had a late first-round pick—showed their interest in him by putting him through a private work-out on the morning of the draft.

While the manoeuvring continued, the coaches arrived in town almost as a formality: they hadn't seen the prospects play and they weren't involved in the decision-making. Of course, they provided feedback on the team needs as NHL-level trades were contemplated. Just as he arrived, Army received a fascinating offer. A year after leaving his alma mater to come to the Ducks, his athletic director at Providence offered him the head coaching job. It was a golden opportunity, and he'd always dreamed about becoming a head coach.

For Army, the next 48 hours were agony. As the Ducks' front office whirlwind continued, Army tried to take stock. After a year in the NHL, his long-term goals had solidified. He wanted to stay on track to be in line for a head-coaching job in the NHL somewhere down the line. He was afraid that he would get lost no matter how successful he was at Providence. The Athletic Director tried to convince him that former Providence coach Rick Pitino had gone on to the Knicks and back to college at Kentucky where the NBA still pursued him.

Army wasn't so sure. For one thing, the NBA seemed to be shying away from perhaps the best coach in the college game in Mike Kryziewski because of his lack of pro experience. For another, the NHL, if possible, was even worse than the NBA when it came to their dismissive attitude to those around the college game. Army didn't want to be buried in college. In the end, though, he kept coming back to the feeling he'd had all year.

"Every day I wake up, I'm thrilled to death. Ron and Al have been great. The NHL is the pinnacle of the game. We're putting together a young team that could challenge for the Cup within a couple of years. My wife and I love living in Southern California. I love my job. Why leave that?"

As Army politely declined the Providence offer, the Ducks announced that they had acquired partial ownership of the Central Red Army team that the Pittsburgh Penguins had created an arrangement with a year earlier. The new agreement would allow the Ducks to gain a better toehold in the most difficult area to scout new talent. McNab described his journeys to Moscow as a minefield, with few people he could trust. Beyond creating a network of sources for McNab in Russia like he had in Canada and the States, the purchase allowed another opportunity for the merchandisers to prove their ability. In the heart of what had once been the most virulently anti-communist region of the United States, Disney would sell the jersey of the Central Red Army hockey team, one of the former Soviet Union's proudest cultural resources.

McNab's new contacts would help in the future, but this year's decisions already had been made. All the Ducks could do was wait on the Panthers. Media speculation before the draft had split off Jovanovski and Bonk as clearly being one-two in the minds of all the insiders, but, unlike other years when the first team made their intentions clear far in advance, the Panthers refused to confirm their interest. The Ducks, if possible, said even less.

When the Panthers announced their pick, everyone at the Ducks' draft table held their breath. "The intensity was unbelievable," said McNab a few hours later. "I've never seen a table so committed to one player." The Panthers took Jovanovski, the big Canadian defenseman they believed could become another Scott Stevens. Anybody watching the Ducks could tell they would get their man. McNab was on his feet, laughing, clapping people on the back. He was as excited as he'd been all year. McNab and Gauthier took the stage to announce the pick. The coin flip a year earlier to determine draft order and the Panthers' decision to pass their pick to Anaheim that year had all been irrelevant. In both drafts, each team had gotten the player they would have taken with the higher pick.

"The Anaheim Mighty Ducks select Oleg Tverdovsky," Pierre said, to the shock of those in Hartford. All the experts had believed Bonk was the best player on the board. Now everyone wanted to know if the Ducks had been scared off by the rumored $4 million a year contract wanted by the big Czech.

The implication that Disney had ordered the front office to take the cheaper player rankled Ferreira. They had selected the man they would have taken if they'd had the first pick. Everyone—Ferreira, Gauthier, McNab, all the scouts—agreed that he was the best player on the board. McNab had liked him so much that he'd sent the North American scouts to Europe to see him in a junior tournament, but they were not to talk to any of their peers about him. In fact, the scouts were warned not to put themselves in a position where they might come in contact with Oleg. They would not let anyone know how much they wanted the kid. Everybody who'd seen him had been blown away by his speed, his vision, and his crisp, long passes. Here was the first great Russian defenseman, the Russian Orr. They'd hit a home run, but all people asked about was Bonk.

McNab thought Bonk would be a fine NHL player, but Tverdovsky was a once-in-a-lifetime choice. The Ducks did not expect to be picking this early in the draft anytime in the near future. What clinched the deal was McNab's off-ice judgment. The kid's character had overwhelmed McNab; Tverdovsky was the unnamed guy who had "blown him away," as McNab had said a month before the draft.

What had blown McNab away was an interview he had with Oleg in Moscow in early February. Tverdovsky had grown up in Donetsk, a big city in the Ukraine surrounded by mines that reminded visitors of the worst aspects of Pittsburgh. The son of an engineer, he'd left Donetsk on his own when he was fifteen to play hockey in Moscow. For two years, he'd lived in an awful neighborhood in an unheated apartment so he could learn his craft. As a sixteen-year-old, he was playing in the top league for Krylja Sovetov Moscow.

When McNab talked to Tverdovsky, he was reminded of a talk he'd had with Pat LaFontaine, another player McNab had fallen in love with. "Oleg was funny, personable, and relaxed. He had a unique aura. I knew that was the guy. He would have no problem fitting into the locker room."

One detail stood out for McNab. No matter where he is on the planet, from Tokyo to Toronto, McNab eats at McDonalds. It's how his peers always find him. McNab's dinner with Tverdovsky was in an upscale hotel restaurant, but David promised to take

Oleg to the McDonalds in Moscow the next time he was in town.

At the team party after the draft ended, Oleg came up to McNab and asked him in perfect English, "Do you want to go get a Big Mac?" McNab looked at Oleg quizzically, and the Russian teenager smiled at him. The kid remembered everything, and he was already making jokes in English. He would be just fine.

The only worry for the Ducks now was what to do with Tverdovsky's family. Before investing in Oleg's future, it seemed smart to bring his relatives out to avoid the extortion problems that were haunting other players. Oleg would be making more than enough money to support his family, but would his father, a mining engineer, want to leave his life behind? It would be a lot easier for Oleg to adjust to American society than for his parents. The Ducks could only make everything as easy as possible for Tverdovsky. They could ask him to bring his family out, but they couldn't force him to do it. Everyone would hope for the best.

With their second pick, the Ducks selected the Swedish forward, Johan Davidsson. McNab believed Davidsson, a competitive triathlete, was the best athlete in the draft. In the year of the behemoth, every other team had prioritized size. Ever contrary, the Ducks had pursued speed and skill with their first two picks. The Ducks already had one of the biggest rosters in the NHL. Now they were making up ground in other areas. "If I'm Paul Kariya," said McNab, "I'm happy to see who's selected."

After the first two rounds of picks, trades started to come into focus. With Tverdovsky expected to quarterback the power play over the next decade, the Ducks wanted to bring somebody in to shepherd Oleg. Ferreira decided he wanted the Islanders' Tom Kurvers, a veteran defenseman who moved the puck very well and could run the power play. The Ducks' defense had been solid in its own zone all season long, but they hadn't made good transitional passes. The Islanders had been overpowered by the Rangers in the first round of the playoffs and wanted another power forward. They wanted Troy Loney; nobody wanted to lose the team captain, but the team needed to upgrade its defense. Loney would go.

Acquiring Kurvers made a crowded blue-line situation even worse. The team now had ten NHL-level defensemen on the roster. Ottawa had been looking for a defenseman in Hartford and was offering two picks. Ottawa wanted Sean Hill, the kid that Ferreira had brought from Montreal with him. The Ducks offered another defenseman, but the Senators would only take Hill. The last month of the season, Hill was being scratched more frequently than any other defenseman. He'd slipped in the eyes of the front office, but he was only twenty-four. He might still improve. They didn't want to give up on Hill, but they believed he was no longer among their top six defensemen.

The Ducks had waited a long time before they started trading, but their aggressiveness was breath-taking. Ferreira had seemed reluctant to move players, but, a few weeks before his first vacation in four years, Ferreira had found ways to address what everyone agreed are the team weaknesses. "He's just started," said McNab. "We just wanted to give Jack the talent to start making deals."

Tugnutt, the goalie who had recorded Anaheim's first win; Kasatonov, the Ducks' first all-star; Loney, the team's first captain; and Hill, the skater who had scored the first goal in team history; were all gone. Kariya, Karpov, Tsulygin, Rucchin, Maneluk, and Tverdovsky had yet to arrive, but the Ducks believed they had all the pieces in place for a not-so-distant run for the Cup. They had the goaltending, and the 100-point center and offensive defenseman were on their way.

The Mighty Ducks of Anaheim could not be completely judged for years, but everyone in and around the organization believed more progress had been made than anyone could have imagined. The journey from whipping boy to serious playoff contender in less than a year testified to the intelligence of the front office and the coaching staff.

The predictions from north of the border that the entry of Disney into the NHL would spell the beginning of the end had proved to be absurd. The presence of mascots and cheerleaders and endless promotions did not change the team's commitment to its on-ice goals. The entry of the Mighty Ducks immediately made the NHL a more interesting, more competitive league. Bettman and Eisner were pushing the league slowly in the right direction, and the toughest critics had to be happy with the 1993-94 season. Everyone hoped the sequel would be even better.

Appendix 1

The 1993-94 Anaheim Mighty Ducks

Players	GP	G	A	PTS	+/-	PIM
26 / Robin Bawa Right Wing 6'2", 215 lbs. Born Chemainus, BC, 28 years old. Claimed from Sharks in 1993 Expansion Draft. 2nd season.	12	0	1	1	-3	7
43 / Maxim Bets Left Wing 6', 192 lbs. Born Chelyabinsk, USSR, 20 years old. Acquired 3/21/94 from Blues with sixth-round pick in 1995 Entry Draft in exchange for Alexei Kasatanov. Rookie.	3	0	0	0	-3	0
21 / Patrick Carnback Center 6', 187 lbs. Born Goteborg, Sweden, 26 years old. Acquired 8/10/93 from Montreal with Todd Ewen in exchange for a third-round pick in 1994 Entry Draft. Rookie.	73	12	11	23	-8	54
20 / Bob Corkum Center 6'2", 210 lbs. Born Salisbury, Mass., 26 years old. Claimed from Sabres in 1993 Expansion Draft. 4th season.	76	23	28	51	4	18
2 / Bobby Dollas Defense 6'2", 212 lbs. Born Montreal, Quebec, 29 years old. Claimed from Detroit in 1993 Expansion Draft. 5th season.	77	9	11	20	20	55

16 / **Peter Douris**   Right Wing
6'1", 195 lbs. Born Toronto, Ontario
28 years old. Signed as a free agent
7/22/93. 4th season.   74   12   22   34   -5   21

36 / **Todd Ewen**   Right Wing
6'2", 220 lbs. Born Saskatoon,
Saskatchewan, 28 years old.
Acquired 8/10/93 from Montreal
with Patrick Carnback in
exchange for a third-round pick
in 1994 Entry Draft. 8th year.   76   9   9   18   -7   272

34 / **Anatoli Fedotov**   Defense
5'11", 180 lbs. Born Saratov, USSR,
28 years old. Chosen tenth round
of 1993 Entry Draft. Rookie.   3   0   0   0   -1   0

3 / **Mark Ferner**   Defense
6'0", 195 lbs. Born Regina,
Saskatchewan, 28 years old.
Claimed from Senators in 1993
Expansion Draft. 2nd season.   50   3   5   8   -16   30

32 / **Stu Grimson**   Left Wing
6'5" , 225 lbs. Born Kamloops,
BC, 29 years old. Claimed
from Chicago in 1993 Expansion
Draft. 4th season.   77   1   5   6   -6   199

6 / **Sean Hill**   Defense
6'0", 195 lbs. Born Duluth,
Minn., 24 years old. Claimed
from Montreal in 1993 Expansion
Draft. 2nd season. Traded to Ottawa
after 93-94 season.   68   7   20   27   -12   78

23 / Bill Houlder Defense
6'3", 220 lbs. Born Thunder Bay,
Ontario, 27 years old. Claimed
from Sabres in 1993 Expansion
Draft. 3rd season.

80	14	25	39	-18	40

7 / Alexei Kasatanov Defense
6'1" , 215 lbs. Born Leningrad,
USSR, 34 years old. Claimed from
Devils in 1993 Expansion Draft.
Traded 3/21/94 to Blues in
exchange for Maxim Bets and a
sixth-round pick in 1995 Entry
Draft. 5th season.

55	4	18	22	-8	43

17 / Steven King Right Wing
6'0", 195 lbs. Born East
Greenwich, RI, 25 years old.
Claimed from Rangers in 1993
Expansion Draft. 2nd season.

36	8	3	11	-7	44

29 / Randy Ladouceur Defense
6'2", 220 lbs. Born Brockville,
Ontario, 32 years old. Claimed
from Whalers in 1993 Expansion
Draft. 12th season.

81	1	9	10	7	74

47 / Stephan Lebeau Center
5'10", 173 lbs. Born St. Jerome,
Quebec, 26 years old. Acquired
2/20/94 from Montreal for Ron
Tugnutt. 5th season.

22	6	4	10	-5	14

48 / John Lilley Right Wing
5'9", 170 lbs. Born Wakefield,
Mass., 22 years old. Signed
3/9/94 as a free agent. Rookie.

13	1	6	7	1	8

27 / Lonnie Loach   Left Wing
5'10", 180 lbs. Born New
Liskeard, Ontario, 26 years old.
Claimed from Kings in 1993
Expansion Draft. 2nd season.   3   0   0   0   -2   2

24 / Troy Loney   Left Wing
6'3", 210 lbs. Born Bow Island,
Alberta, 30 years old. Claimed
from Penguins in 1993 Expansion
Draft. 10th season. Traded to NY
Islanders after 93-94 season.   62   13   6   19   -5   88

45 / Scott McKay   Center
5'll", 200 lbs. Born Burlington,
Ontario, 22 years old. Signed
8/2/93 as free agent. Rookie   1   0   0   0   0   0

39 / Don McSween   Defense
5'll", 197 lbs. Born Detroit,
Mich., 30 years old. Signed
1/12/94 as free agent. Rookie.   32   3   9   12   4   39

44 / Myles O'Connor   Defense
5'll", 190 lbs. Born Calgary,
Alberta, 27 years old. Signed
7/22/93 as free agent. 2nd year.   5   0   1   1   0   6

14 / Joe Sacco   Right Wing
6'1", 195 lbs. Born Medford,
Mass., 25 years old. Claimed
from Toronto in 1993 Expansion
Draft. 3rd season.   84   19   18   37   -11 61

19 / Anatoli Semenov   Center
6'2", 190 lbs. Born Moscow,
USSR, 32 years old. Claimed
from Canucks in 1993 Expansion
Draft. 4th season.   49   11   19   30   -4   12

10 / **Jarrod Skalde** Center
6'0", 170 lbs. Born Niagara
Falls, Ontario, 23 years old.
Claimed from Devils in 1993
Expansion Draft. 2nd season.   20   5   4   9   -3   10

8 / **Tim Sweeney** Left Wing
5'11", 185 lbs. Born Boston,
Mass., 27 years old. Claimed
from Boston in 1993 Expansion
Draft. 3rd season.   78   16   27   43   3   49

33 / **Jim Thomson** Right Wing
6'1", 220 lbs. Born Edmonton,
Alberta, 28 years old. Claimed
from Kings in 1993 Expansion
Draft. 3rd season.   6   0   0   0   0   5

18 / **Garry Valk** Left Wing
6'1", 205 lbs. Born Edmonton,
Alberta, 26 years old. Claimed
from Canucks in 1993 NHL Waiver
Draft. 4th season.   78   18   27   45   8   100

22 / **Shaun Van Allen** Center
6'1", 200 lbs. Born Shaunavon,
Saskatchewan, 27 years old.
Signed 7/22/93 as free agent.
2nd season.   80   8   25   33   0   64

4 / **David Williams** Defense
6'2", 195 lbs. Born Plainfield,
New Jersey, 27 years old.
Claimed from Sharks in 1993
Expansion Draft. 3rd season.   56   5   15   20   8   42

25 / Terry Yake   Right Wing
5'11", 190 lbs. Born New
Westminister, BC, 25 years
old. Claimed from Whalers in
1993 Expansion Draft. 4th year.   82   21   31   52   2   44

Goaltenders	W	L	T	GAA	SV%	SO

31 / Guy Hebert
5'11", 185 lbs. Born Troy, NY
27 years old. Claimed from
Blues in 1993 Expansion Draft.
3rd season   20   27   3   2.83 .907   2

35 / Mikhail Shtalenkov
6'3", 180 lbs. Born Moscow, USSR
28 years old. Chosen fifth round of
1993 Entry Draft. Rookie.   3   4   1   2.65 .909   0

1 / Ron Tugnutt
5'11", 160 lbs. Born Scarborough,
Ontario, 26 years old. Claimed from
Oilers in 1993 Expansion Draft.
Traded 2/20/94 to Montreal for
Stephan Lebeau. 6th season.   10   15   1   3.00 .908   1

Appendix 2

1993-94 NHL Final Standings

Western Conference

Pacific Division

	W	L	T	PTS
Calgary	42	29	13	97
Vancouver	41	40	3	85
San Jose	33	35	16	82
Anaheim	**33**	**46**	**5**	**71**
Los Angeles	27	45	12	66
Edmonton	25	45	14	64

Central Division

	W	L	T	PTS
Detroit	46	30	8	100
Toronto	43	29	12	98
Dallas	42	29	13	97
St. Louis	40	33	11	91
Chicago	39	36	9	87
Winnipeg	24	51	9	57

Eastern Conference

Atlantic Division

	W	L	T	PTS
NY Rangers	52	24	8	112
New Jersey	47	25	12	106
Washington	39	35	10	88
NY Islanders	36	36	12	84
Florida	33	34	17	83
Philadelphia	35	39	10	80
Tampa Bay	30	43	11	71

Northeast Division

	W	L	T	PTS
Pittsburgh	44	27	13	101
Boston	42	29	13	101
Montreal	41	29	14	96
Buffalo	43	32	9	95
Quebec	34	42	8	76
Hartford	27	48	9	63
Ottawa	14	61	9	37

Appendix 3

1993-94 Mighty Ducks Statistical Standings

Home Record: 14-26-2   Road Record: 19-20-3
OT Record: 2-5-5   Penalty Minutes: 17.9 (3rd)
Goals For: 229 (23rd)   Goals Against: 251 (T-8th)
Power Play: 14.4% (T-25th)   Penalty Killing: 82.7%
(6th)

Goals By Period	1	2	3	OT	Home Attendance: 696,560
Mighty Ducks	64	89	74	2	16,989 avg/gm
Opponents	84	80	82	5	99% capacity

Hockey Books from Polestar Press

Polestar Press publishes best-selling hockey titles. These books are available in your local bookstore, or directly from Polestar Press. Please send a cheque for the retail price of the book, plus the relevant shipping and handling costs: $4.00 for shipping the first book, and $1.00 for each subsequent book. American customers may pay in U.S. funds.

All-New Allstar Hockey Activity Book • Noah Ross & Julian Ross • $6.95 Can/$5.95 US
A new collection of quizzes, games, radical stats and trivia for young hockey fans.

Allstar Hockey Activity Book • Noah Ross & Julian Ross • $6.95 Can/$5.95 US
Hockey history, Soviet hockey cards, and hours of hands-on fun for young hockey fans.

Basic Hockey And Skating Skills: The Backyard Rink Approach • Jeremy Rose & Murray Smith • $16.95 Can/$14.95 US • A comprehensive, non-competitive method for learning the fundamentals of ice and in-line skating. Includes plans for building a backyard rink.

Behind The Mask: The Ian Young Goaltending Method, Book One • Ian Young & Chris Gudgeon • $18.95 Can/$14.95 US • Drills, practice techniques, equipment considerations and more are part of this unique goaltending guide.

Beyond The Mask: The Ian Young Goaltending Method, Book Two • Ian Young & Chris Gudgeon • $18.95 Can/$14.95 US • Book Two of this effective goaltending series focuses on intermediate goalies and their coaches.

Countdown to the Stanley Cup: An Illustrated History of the Calgary Flames • Bob Mummery $19.95 Can/$16.95 US • Highlights of nine exciting seasons of this successful hockey club.

Country On Ice • Doug Beardsley • $9.95 Can/$8.95 US
The story of Canada's compelling attraction to the game of hockey.

Elston: Back To The Drawing Board • Dave Elston • $12.95 Can/$11.95 US
Sports-cartoonist Elston's comic view of the world of hockey.

Elston's Hat Trick • Dave Elston • $14.95 Can/$12.95 US
The third in this best-selling cartoonist's collection of irreverent, hilarious hockey cartoons.

Hockey's Young Superstars • Eric Dwyer • $16.95 Can/$14.95 US
Profiles and action photos of Bure, Leetch, Lindros, Mogilny, Sakic, Modano and others.

Lords of the Rink • Ian Young & Terry Walker • $18.95 Can/$14.95 US
The ultimate guide to goalies and goaltending from the goalie guru Ian Young.

The Rocket, The Flower, The Hammer and Me: An All-Star Collection of Canadian Hockey Fiction • Doug Beardsley, editor • $9.95 Can/$8.95 US • Exciting stories from writers like W.P. Kinsella, Hugh MacLennan, Brian Fawcett and others.

Taking The Ice: The Mighty Ducks of Anaheim • Dean Chadwin • $7.95 Can/$5.95 US
A young fan's guide to the Pond and to some of the great players on the Mighty Ducks.

Order books from:
Polestar Press Ltd., 1011 Commercial Drive, 2nd Floor
Vancouver, British Columbia
Canada   V5K 3A7